With one quick twist, he shoved her face against the wall.

"Move and you're history," the intruder said, pulling Julianna's hands behind her.

That voice. She knew that voice.

Swiftly, big deft hands patted her down, moving under her arms, sliding around to her breasts, then down between her legs, at which she felt a familiar pull low in her stomach. He clicked on the light and yanked her around.

His eyes went wide. "Jules?"

Five years and he still looked the same. Same cobalt-blue eyes that crinkled around the corners whether he was smiling or not, the same lean, hard features that said he was a man's man – a man with a purpose – and always in control. Qualities she once thought sexy and desirable.

He was so close she felt his heat. His familiar scent made her blood rush. And if the look in his eyes was any indication, he felt the same. But then, lack of desire had never been their problem. In the end, desire hadn't helped the marriage. She hated what they'd done to each other in the year before the divorce.

Things that would stay with them forever.

Available in August 2007 from Mills & Boon Superromance

Husband and Wife Reunion

LINDA STYLE

MILLS & BOON®
SuperROMANCE

*First published in Great Britain 2007
Harlequin Mills & Boon Limited,
Eton House, 18-24 Paradise Road, Richmond, Surrey TW9 1SR*

© Linda Fensand Style 2006

ISBN: 978 0 263 85795 5

38-0807

*Printed and bound in Spain
by Litografia Rosés S.A., Barcelona*

Dear Reader,

I'm delighted to again delve into the inner world of
law enforcement – a world that's always intrigued me.
While career choices took me in another direction, I
did enrol in my city's civilian police academy. Little
did I know that the six-week class would spark the idea
for this story.

Husband and Wife Reunion is about second chances,
and don't we all wish we could do some things over?
But even when given the opportunity we don't always
make the best choices. I believe true character is
revealed by the choices we make when our personal
risks are the greatest. Detective Luke Coltrane is a
man who has hit rock bottom. He's lost his son and
his wife, alienated most of the people he loves, and
it nearly cost him his job. But he's on the mend and
determined to put his life in order, starting with his
relationship with his father. But he never expected to
run into his ex-wife, Julianna, back home in Santa Fe.
That's one fence he knows he can't mend. To do that,
he'd have to take the greatest risk of all…and open his
heart to love.

Luke and Julianna have been through a terrible
tragedy. In order to find love and commitment again,
they must overcome nearly insurmountable odds. I
didn't know until I wrote the end of this book whether
they'd be able to do it or not. I'm happy with the
outcome and hope you enjoy Luke and Julianna's
story.

I always like hearing from readers. You can write to
me at PO Box 2292, Mesa, AZ 85214, USA or e-mail
me at LindaStyle@cox.net.

For upcoming books and other fun stuff, visit my
website at www.LindaStyle.com and
www.superauthors.com.

May all your dreams come true,

Linda Style

For Courtney and Connor,
You are the stars that light up my life.
I love you both.

My sincere thanks and appreciation to all the people who contributed to the research for this book – the professionals with the Los Angeles Police Department, the city of Los Angeles Chamber of Commerce and the Orange County RWA members who so generously shared their expertise about the City of Angels.

Many thanks to my editor, Victoria Curran, for her guidance and uncanny ability to see the essence of a story. Since this is a work of fiction, I've taken some liberties with facts where needed. Any errors are solely mine.

CHAPTER ONE

"YOU CROSSED THE LINE. You're going to regret it."

Julianna Chevalair listened to the distorted digitalized voice, heard a click and then the dial tone droned in her ear.

She swallowed around the tightness in her throat, closed her eyes and waited for the next message. The recorder had indicated there were three.

"If you don't stop, I'm going to stop you."

Her heart raced. She'd ignored the caller's earlier e-mails warning her to stop writing the story, and the second installment was about to run in the magazine's next issue.

A moment later, the next call started. As she listened, the hairs on the back of her neck stood on end. A chill ran up her spine. Hands shaking, she clicked off in the middle of the message.

How had he gotten her number?

The Achilles' Heel received dozens of crank

calls, letters and even more e-mail messages from readers who didn't like some of its stories. But this was new. She'd never received a phone call at home before. And the two e-mails she'd gotten prior to leaving San Francisco had definite threatening undertones.

It creeped her out and she'd jumped at Abe's kind invitation to stay at his ranch outside Santa Fe. Now the decision seemed even more right. No one knew where she was, not even her editor. Her ex-father-in-law's ranch was the last place anyone would expect her to go.

She heaved a sigh, fell into Abe's recliner, its leather soft and cracked with age, and switched on her laptop. When she finished the piece she was working on right now, she'd be done with the series about a little girl's abduction and murder in Southern California.

It was only one of many she'd written about missing children who'd met the same fate. And someone wanted her to stop. She bristled at the thought. If anything, he'd made her even more determined to complete the series. She'd never give in to a coward who made anonymous threats. She'd finish the story even if she had to go somewhere else to do it. But she *would* finish.

She pulled up Word on her laptop, went to the last page of the story and typed in, "If you recognize anything about the individual profiled in this article—if you know *anything* about this case, call the LAPD, your local FBI office or 1-800-CRIME TV. Help us take this killer off the streets before he harms anoth—"

A noise outside made her sit up straight as a soldier. She stopped typing. She was used to city sounds, but here in the desert, in the stillness of the night, every small noise seemed magnified.

Listening, she heard nothing more. Okay, she was jumpy because of the messages, but that really was silly; the calls had gone to her condo in San Francisco two thousand miles away.

Abe had complained about a family of javelina disturbing his chickens; maybe that's what she'd heard. He'd had trouble with coyotes, too. It certainly wouldn't be a visitor at two in the morning—Abe didn't have visitors any time.

She smiled, thinking of the old man sleeping in the back wing of the sprawling adobe ranch house. Besides being her ex-father-in-law, he was a friend, a surrogate father who'd taken her in, no questions asked. Abe might be cranky and more stubborn than a donkey, but she loved him dearly.

Except for the soft light of an old faux oil lamp across the room and the glow from the laptop screen, the rest of the house was dark. No lights were on outside either since Abe insisted on conserving energy. He called himself thrifty. Others called him cheap.

A coyote bayed in the distance, its lonely howl a faint echo in the vastness of the high desert, reminding her how far they were from Sante Fe. Yet, here, she felt a peace she never enjoyed at home. The air was so pure that sounds traveled for miles, the sky so clear, she could see the Milky Way, like a road of sparkling light against a velvet black backdrop. She hadn't seen the stars like that since she was a kid and had taken a trip with her mother in their VW bus to Arizona.

Julianna hauled in a deep breath and kept on typing, the keys clicking loudly in the quiet.

Another sound…from the kitchen. Her fingers stilled as the doorknob rattled and her heartbeat quickened. Was someone trying to get in? She heard a crash and the doorknob clattered again.

She pulled her cell phone from her briefcase. They were so far out in the boonies, it would take forever for anyone to get there, but she punched in 911 anyway.

Nothing but static. Then somewhere between the crackles, she heard a voice. She rattled off her name, Abe's address, her cell phone number and that she thought someone was breaking in, hoping whoever was on the other end had heard her.

She should wake Abe. But shouting for him wouldn't do any good because the old man took out his hearing aid at night and he was deaf as a post without it.

Her heart pumped like a piston in her chest. Her gaze went to Abe's rifle in the gun rack against the far wall. She crossed the room, found the key to the case and took out one of the rifles. The wood on the butt felt smooth under her fingers, but she'd never handled a gun in her life. She'd probably shoot herself.

What the hell. It was protection. She opened the drawer and scooped out some rifle shells. All she had to do was put them in and pull the trigger. She'd seen Abe do it before.

She pocketed two shells, then, gun against her chest, edged down the hallway toward Abe's room to wake him. He knew how to shoot. Besides, what was she going to do? Force a burglar to leave at gunpoint? Tie him up for the police? How long would it be before they arrived? *If* they arrived?

With each step, she tightened her grip on the weapon. She couldn't imagine who would break into an old man's house in the middle of the night when he had nothing worth stealing. It could still be an animal searching for food. In California she'd heard of bears and bobcats wandering into homesteads. She was going to feel pretty silly if that's what it was.

But animals didn't rattle doorknobs. She heard a dull thud and before she could react, the door to the hallway creaked open. A large male form appeared, shadowed in the opening.

Oh, God! Adrenaline coursed through her. She raised the gun, butt end up, and mustering all her strength, smashed the man on the head.

He grunted…but he didn't keel over.

Oh my God! She dropped the gun and turned to run. Fingers dug into her shoulder and in one quick movement, he shoved her face against the wall and pulled both her hands behind her.

"Move and you're history," the intruder said, his voice low and raspy.

That voice. She knew that voice.

Swiftly, big deft hands patted her down, moving under her arms, sliding around to her breasts, then down between her legs, at which she felt a familiar pull low in her stomach. He clicked on the light and yanked her around.

His eyes went wide. "Jules?"

Words stuck in her throat. Abe had assured her there wasn't a chance in hell she'd run into her ex. Frowning, she flung off his hands and rubbed her arms where he'd manhandled her. Then she saw him reach for his head. He was bleeding. Scowling and bleeding.

"You coulda killed me."

She stiffened. "That was the intent. I thought you were a burglar. Most normal people don't come in through a window, y'know."

Blood trickled down his forehead and she realized how hard she'd hit him. "Geez, I'm sorry, Luke. Here, let me get something for that."

As she turned to go, he grabbed her by the arm. "What are you doing here?"

"What am *I* doing here? I think I should be the one asking you that question."

"This is my father's house."

"Well, I'm here by invitation. Abe told me you hadn't been here for a year."

A puzzled look crossed his face. "It couldn't be that long."

She shrugged. "That's what he said." She could tell Luke felt guilty about it. Luke was never good at hiding his reactions. If he was irritated you knew it. If he was happy, you knew that, too. Angry, you *really* knew it. But he kept his thoughts, his reasons behind the emotions locked inside.

"Yeah, well, if it's been that long, then he'll be pleased to see me."

"Not with you dripping blood all over his floor." He seemed to have forgotten about his head and was staring at her instead. She gave him a shove, urging him down the hall to the bathroom. "Let's do something about that cut." Once inside the tiny room, she pulled a washcloth from the linen closet and moistened it under the faucet. "Here, this will help."

He took the cloth and, looking in the small mirror above the old cast-iron sink, applied it to his forehead.

Five years and he still looked the same. Same cobalt eyes that crinkled around the corners whether he was smiling or not, the same lean, hard features that said he was a man's man—a man with a purpose—and always in control. Qualities she'd once thought sexy and desirable.

"Your hair is different," he said, still looking in the mirror, but gazing at her.

"Different than what?"

"Than before. No ponytail." His eyes narrowed. "What *are* you doing here?"

"Is that important?"

"Still good at answering questions with a question, aren't you?"

"And you're still good at thinking everything is your business when it's not."

A tight smile lifted his lips. "Touché."

With that one small concession, an uncomfortable silence fell between them, a silence laden with recriminations and guilt. Their divorce had been inevitable, filled with heartache and pain. The hurt was so great, she couldn't be around him and vice-versa. She'd even moved from L.A. to San Francisco to lessen the chances of running into him.

In the confines of the small bathroom, he shifted his stance and lifted one foot to the edge of the tub, effectively imprisoning her between his leg and the sink.

He was so close she felt his heat. His familiar scent made her blood rush. And if the look in his eyes was any indication, he felt the same. But then, lack of desire had never been their problem.

In the end, desire hadn't helped the marriage either. She hated what they'd done to each other in the year before the divorce. Things that would stay with them forever.

"Okay, here's a question you can answer. How's my father?"

She shrugged. "You know Abe, he wouldn't admit to anything even if he were inches from death's door. Personally, I think he'd be a lot healthier if he stopped smoking."

"Fat chance of that."

"I know."

"So let's quit the sparring and you tell me what's up with the visit."

She sighed in resignation. He wasn't going to give up. "Your father invited me for a vacation. I needed one." She crossed her arms. "Now it's your turn."

"I'm taking a couple weeks off. And since I hadn't seen Pops for a while, I thought I'd check how the old rooster was doing."

"*You're* taking time off?" He never took time off.

Just then she heard a loud banging at the door. "Oh Geez. I called the police. That's probably them."

They went into the living room. Spotlights flashed through the window, rotating red and blue, lighting up the room like a nightclub. Another percussion of knocking rattled the house. "Sheriff's department. Open up."

She crossed the room and threw wide the door. A tall man in a black hat stood in front of her. His badge said he was indeed the sheriff.

He peered inside. "I'm Sheriff Ben Yuma. I received a call."

Julianna flipped on a light switch next to the door. "I'm sorry, Officer. I called because I thought someone was breaking into the house, but I was wrong."

The sheriff glanced at Luke. His dark eyes narrowed.

"Luke Coltrane, LAPD," he said, pulling out his shield. "I came to see my father, forgot my key and decided to use a window."

The sheriff brushed a hand across his smooth chin, assessing both of them. "With bad results, I see."

"I was protecting myself," Julianna countered. "Well, I thought I was anyway."

"What the hell is going on here?" Abe's gravelly voice resounded.

Julianna turned. "Abe, what are you doing up?"

Luke gave her a pointed stare, a slow smile tipping his mouth at the corners. "Question with a question," he said under his breath, as if proving his earlier point.

She wanted to laugh, but held it back. He knew exactly how to get to her. Make her laugh and she'd forget everything. But not anymore.

Ignoring him, she glanced at Abe. Though Luke loved his father, there'd always been tension between them. In five years of marriage to Luke, she'd never figured out exactly why. Luke had always passed it off as his father being too hard on him, making him feel he couldn't do anything right. She'd always thought there was more to it.

When Abe saw Luke, he looked surprised at first, but then his mouth turned down, his expression dour. He acknowledged the sheriff and then turned back to Julianna. "I'm up because someone's making so much racket it's impossible to sleep. And that's saying a lot since I can't hear worth spit."

Julianna crossed to Abe and placed a hand on his arm. "There's nothing to worry about. I thought there was a burglar and called the sheriff. But it was only Luke, so everything's okay and you can go back to bed. We'll talk in the morning."

"We will not." Abe made his way to the couch and eased onto the sagging cushion. "Sheriff, you want to arrest someone?"

"Someone?" The sheriff glanced at the only other people in the room. Luke and Julianna.

"I invited one person to stay here. The other is a stranger to me. And apparently he broke into my house."

Luke's nerves bunched. Okay, that was his dad's way of getting back at him for staying away so long. He had to admit it had been awhile, so he probably deserved whatever lambasting he got. Still…his dad was irritating the hell out of him. "Fine. I'll leave right now."

For a fraction of a second, Luke thought his father seemed a little crestfallen. But the reaction quickly passed.

"If that's what you want, then go," Abe said gruffly.

What Luke wanted was a soft bed. After driving six hours from L.A. to Phoenix and another six to Santa Fe, he was dog-tired. But his old man wouldn't be satisfied until he had it all.

Abe wanted Luke to grovel *and* apologize. "I came to see you, why would I *want* to go? Why don't we let the sheriff get on with his business and we can talk about everything in the morning."

The sheriff shifted his feet, crossed his arms. "You got a problem with that, Abe?"

"I got a big problem standing right in front of me."

The sheriff frowned. "So do you want me to arrest him?"

Luke groaned. *Another nutcase.* "For what reason?" he asked incredulously.

"Whatever reason I want." The sheriff shrugged and smiled, his teeth bright white against bronzed skin. "We do things differently out here than in the big city."

Great, just what he needed. His father's wrath and a rogue sheriff who didn't give a rat's ass about procedure. And then there was Julianna. Dear Jules. He cleared his throat. "Fine. Arrest me if you want. Otherwise, I'm outta here." He turned to leave.

"Suit yourself," Abe spat out. "Never could stick anything out."

Luke edged toward the door, primed for a

comeback, but then, for the first time since his father entered the room, Luke noticed how frail he seemed. He'd lost weight, and his face looked gray and haggard, the lines deeper, more like canyons instead of crevices. "Okay then," Luke said, "if it's up to me, I need a good night's sleep. I'll leave in the morning."

Abe scoffed and with great effort tried to rise from his seat on the couch. Julianna hurried over, but Abe waved her off, then took hold of the armrests and laboriously lifted himself to his feet. "I'm going to bed."

The sheriff tipped his hat. "Seems everything's okay here, so I'll be on my way, too."

That left Luke alone with Julianna. The woman he'd once thought was the center of his life. The woman whose very presence pounded in another sharp reminder that he'd lost everything that had made life worth living. A reminder that he'd failed her and their marriage.

"I'm turning in, too," Julianna said, her voice oddly quiet. "I'm in the back bedroom, so you'll have to take the smaller one."

"Fine with me." Only he knew there wasn't a chance in hell he'd get any sleep with her in the next room.

CHAPTER TWO

THOUGHTS OF JULIANNA had kept him awake for a while, but it was the nightmares about the kidnapping that woke him a mere three hours after he'd gone to bed.

He rolled over, sweat pouring from his body, sheets drenched.

As Julianna's face loomed in his mind, muscles cramped in his chest. The death of their son had created a chasm between them and destroyed their marriage. Seeing Julianna brought it all back in spades.

He had to go. No matter how much he wanted to mend the rift with his father, he didn't know if he was strong enough to stay in the same house with Julianna. It had taken him too long to get back on track. He couldn't jeopardize everything he'd accomplished.

For nearly four years, he'd gone through the motions of living. He went to his job, he went home and went to sleep, but not before consuming copious amounts of alcohol to speed up the process. He'd alienated his father, put his friends at a distance and had been within a hair's breath of losing his job.

Life might not be everything he wanted, but at least he was among the living again. His job and his friends were all he had.

The sharp ring of his cell phone surprised him. He was used to calls at any hour when he was in L.A., but he hadn't expected to get them here. "Coltrane."

"I need some information," Captain Jeff Carlyle's rough voice blared. The captain had seen him through some tough times. Luke owed him a lot.

"Sure. What's up?" Luke had been working on two high-profile cases before he left L.A. The missing congressional aide, Michelle Renfield, who they suspected was dead, and the latest Studio Killer case, a serial murderer who specialized in killing porno flick stars near the location where their latest movie had been shot.

"It's Thorpe."

"Figures." Congressman Thorpe was the prime suspect in his aide's disappearance three years ago. Thorpe was suspected of having an affair with her and though they'd found no conclusive evidence of his involvement in her disappearance, Luke hadn't let up on his investigation. But Thorpe didn't like anyone messing with his life and he'd let Luke know it. "What's his problem now?"

"His attorney's threatening a lawsuit. Says you have a vendetta, that you've prejudiced the public with your investigation and that it's detrimental to his upcoming election."

"I thought my taking a vacation was supposed to help, get me out of sight for a while. Besides, Thorpe should've thought about that when he seduced a sixteen-year-old and forgot he had a wife."

"She was twenty."

"She wasn't when he met her. He's a predator." Luke's grip on the phone tightened.

"Okay, I know how you feel about it. But the reason I called is to make sure there's no question on procedure if Thorpe's attorney goes ahead with the suit."

"None whatsoever." He might be aggressive in his investigations and quick to jump on things, but he was thorough.

"I also wanted to tell you I'm putting St. James and Santini on the case."

Luke's nerves tensed. He'd worked his guts out on this case and now because some politician threatened to sue, he had to give it up?

"It's not permanent," Carlyle said. "And they've both got full loads right now."

That meant the assignment was only for looks. No one was really going to work on it. "I'm on it again when I get back, right?"

After a long pause the captain said, "Sure." Then he asked, "How's your father?"

"He looks terrible."

"Well, you've got two weeks, or longer if you need it. I just wanted you to know." Carlyle clicked off.

Luke felt satisfied. The captain knew Luke would be pissed if he came back and found the Renfield case had been pulled out from under him. It didn't matter if Jordan and Rico actually worked the case or not.

That Thorpe's attorney had the gall to file a lawsuit burned Luke's ass. Thorpe had the kind of connections that might help him if he was ever arrested and brought to trial—only the congressman wasn't about to let it go that far. He wanted to be vindicated now and a lawsuit would probably guarantee it if no other evidence turned up.

Yeah, well, Luke didn't give a damn about anyone's connections. With every fiber of his being he believed Thorpe was responsible for the disappearance of the young aide. If the evidence showed he was right, the congressman was going to jail.

Whether he was reelected or not. As far as his having a vendetta—if seeking justice for murder victims was a vendetta, then yeah, he did have one. And the sooner he got back to L.A., the better.

Only in this case, justice would have to wait. He had to first assess his father's health and see what he could do to help him while he was here. Maybe find him a hired hand—someone who could stay at the ranch. And when his father discovered that plan, all hell would break loose.

"GOOD MORNING," Julianna greeted Luke when he came in from outside. "Out doing chores?" She busied herself making coffee, trying not to look at him.

"Funny," he said, letting the kitchen door slap shut with a bang.

"Well, you know there's plenty of work to do around here. Too much for your father." She scooped some coffee into the basket.

"I noticed. Everything seems to have fallen apart since I was here last."

"He could use some help."

"He could easily afford to hire someone."

"You mean if he wasn't so stubborn and didn't think he could do everything himself."

He paused for a moment, as if considering what she'd said. "Yeah. While I'm here, I'm going to see what we can do about getting him help."

"Good idea." But she hoped that didn't mean he intended to stay for long.

Luke sat at the old oak table, wearing only a white T-shirt and faded jeans, his sandy sun-bleached hair still wet from the shower. He smelled of fresh soap and shampoo, and just looking at him made her breath hitch. Still. After all these years.

"Weren't you cold out there without a jacket?"

"I'm tough," he said, smiling.

She turned and retrieved a pan from the maple cabinet next to the harvest-gold stove that had one door half hanging from its hinges. Even though she had her back to Luke, she felt his gaze boring into her.

"You never did answer me last night," he said. "What brings you here?"

She turned, leaned against the counter. "I answered you. I said I was invited and I came."

He arched his brows without commenting. It was obvious he didn't believe her and his smug know-it-all attitude annoyed her. "I don't need a reason to visit someone I care about."

Luke had been gone most of the time they were married so she doubted he had any idea she'd developed such a close relationship with his father, or that they'd become even closer after the divorce.

"I could ask you the same thing. What's the *real* reason you're here?"

He shrugged. "I don't need a reason to see my father."

"And when did that become important?" The second the words left her mouth Julianna regretted them. Abe didn't get along well with people in general. She also knew the distance in Abe's relationship with Luke hurt Luke a lot—but just like his father, he was too stubborn to admit it.

"I'm sorry. I shouldn't have said that." She turned away. "But…can you at least tell me how long you're staying?"

He shrugged. "It depends."

She heaved a sigh. If he wasn't going to leave, then she would have to. Just talking with Luke made her anxious. Made her remember too much. And her only defense seemed to be anger. She wasn't proud of that, but there it was. "Well, don't let my presence be a factor in your decision. I'll be leaving soon."

"You're not going anywhere," Abe's voice boomed as he came in and joined them in the kitchen. "What kind of nonsense is that?"

The scent of hazelnut coffee wafted through the room and she noticed the pot had stopped burbling. She reached for the old chipped mugs, brought them to the table and poured them each a cup. "I've been thinking it might be…easier if I go. Besides, I have more investigative work to do on the next series and—"

"Well, you just stop that kind of thinking, young lady."

Julianna had to smile. She didn't want to hurt Abe's feelings, but if Luke stayed, she had no choice.

Luke leaned back in his chair, raised his arms and clasped his fingers behind his head. "You can both stop worrying. I've got to get back to L.A. Something has come up."

She raised her chin. Of course. The job. The job that was more important than just about anything. But she'd swallow her tongue before she'd say it. If it meant he'd leave, she was grateful.

Abe coughed. "I'm going to work on the fence out on the line."

"What's wrong with the fence?" Luke asked.

Julianna glanced at Abe.

"Someone keeps tearing it down."

"Really. Why would anyone do that?"

"Duke Hancock wanted that piece of land for years, but I told him I wasn't going to sell. Now they want it again."

"Duke died twenty years ago, Dad. And who are *they?*"

Ignoring his son's question, Abe went on. "The fence is destroyed. The cattle can run right through."

"You haven't had more than a few head of cattle for years, and that's not even where they pasture." Luke gave him a look of exasperation.

Abe scoffed. "It needs to be fixed."

"Okay. I'll go out with you to help on the fence," Luke said, then caught Julianna's gaze.

For a moment, she couldn't look away. His eyes were still bluer than Paul Newman's. Intense. Sexy.

"Okay with you, Jules?" He smiled.

A wide white smile. Her heart stalled…in the same way it had when she'd first met him at that environmental rally where they'd been on opposite sides.

And apparently her recent lack of male companionship was making her hormones shift into overdrive. "I'm scrambling eggs. Anyone else want some?"

Luke looked surprised. "You learned how to cook?"

Dammit. She wasn't going to acknowledge Luke's gibes. That's another way he got to her. He knew it and she knew it.

"No one needs to wait on me," Abe sputtered. "I can make my own breakfast. Been doin' it for years."

"I know you can, Abe. But since I'm making eggs for myself, it's no big deal to toss in a couple extra. I'd appreciate it though if I could have the kitchen to myself for about fifteen minutes."

Both men rose. Abe went down the hall toward the bathroom and Luke headed for the living room.

As she watched Luke walk away, an unexpected sadness washed over her. She swallowed back a sudden lump in her throat. After getting the eggs from the fridge, she leaned wearily against the door. What was the matter with her?

Was it being together again with Luke and Abe, like the old days? Was it remembering the love she and Luke once shared? The love. The heartache. The loss.

After three years of grief therapy and finally learning to live in the present, she'd thought she could handle just about anything. But now she felt as if she'd tumbled backward in time as all the memories, all the emotions she'd tried so hard to forget, roared to life once again. She thought she'd resolved all that. Had she only been fooling herself?

Maybe. But she couldn't slide back into the abyss that had been her life. She'd worked too hard to make herself into a whole person again—even though a piece of her would never mend.

She strengthened her resolve and went to the stove.

Seeing Luke again had thrown her off balance. That was all. She'd get over it. She'd carved out a comfortable niche for herself at the magazine. She had a great loft condo in the heart of San Francisco. Her life was good. She cracked an egg into the bowl with so much force it splattered everywhere. Her life was good, dammit.

Except for the loneliness. And right now, she felt more lonely than ever.

But going back home wasn't an option.

LUKE FINGERED THROUGH the magazines piled in the corner of the living room. He didn't remember his father being much of a reader. It was probably why Luke wasn't. That and the fact that he never had time. When he was off duty the last thing he wanted was to read about more crime and world problems.

Most of Abe's magazines were about ranching, except for one called *The Achilles' Heel.* Recognizing the name of the national magazine, Luke was surprised that Abe even had a copy. Hell, he had a whole stack of them. Luke picked one up and flipped a page. Most of the titles had a liberal slant, taking jabs at anything and everything that might be fair game.

Odd, because Abe was the biggest redneck around. Flipping another page, he saw Julianna listed on the masthead as a regular columnist. Ah, now it made sense.

He'd heard Julianna was doing well, but since she'd moved to San Francisco after the divorce, that's all he knew. Reading her brief bio, he felt a moment of pride over her success.

And then sadness. He missed what they'd had before everything went haywire. He missed having a family to come home to.

He dropped the magazine back in the pile.

What they'd had was long gone. She'd made that crystal-clear the day she walked out on him, saying the only way she could find herself was to start a new life.

Instead of staying to work things out, she'd run away. He'd been willing, but she hadn't.

It'd stuck in his craw ever since. No, he didn't need reminders, and as soon as he got his father straightened up, he was outta there.

"Better come and get it if you want to eat," his father said as he passed Luke on his way to the kitchen.

Luke followed Abe, watching the uneven gait in his step, saw the gray in his thinning hair. When had his father gotten so old, so frail? "When was the last time you saw a doctor, Pops?"

"Don't need no doctor. I'm not sick."

They walked into the kitchen together. The aroma of sizzling bacon and fresh coffee made his mouth water. Julianna had set the table and was dishing up the eggs.

"Everyone needs a checkup at least once a year. Especially someone with high blood pressure."

"I go when I'm sick. And it's nobody's business when I go and when I don't."

Luke walked over to the counter, refilled

his coffee cup, then raised the pot to the others. Julianna said, "Yes, please," and his father grunted his response. When Luke finished pouring, he put the pot on the table on a trivet and sat.

The tension in the air was so thick you couldn't cut it with a sharp fillet knife. He felt more uncomfortable sitting here with his father and Julianna than he did scoping out a crime scene.

But his discomfort didn't keep him from noticing how little Julianna had changed in the last five years. She was still slim and toned, and her flawless skin looked even more perfect framed by long, wavy chestnut hair. Silky hair that always fell in his face when she was on top. "You still jog?"

She nodded. "Abe, Luke's right. You really should get a checkup. Everyone needs to do that once in a while."

Luke smiled at his dad with satisfaction, glad that Julianna had supported him.

Ignoring both of them, Abe mumbled around a mouthful of eggs, "If you're going to fix the fence with me you better eat and quit talking."

Luke nearly dropped his fork. It sounded almost as if his father was asking for Luke's help, something he had never done before. Whenever Luke had offered in the past, he got shot down. Maybe there was hope for them yet. "Sure. I'm only going to be here until tomorrow, so we should get as much done today as we can."

Abe's head jerked up. "If that's all the time you got, then we might as well forget it. It's a two-day job at best."

Luke fought another smile. His old man sure knew the art of manipulation. "I'll stay until it's done. If it's done today, I'll leave in the morning. If it takes another day, I'll go home after that."

But he was going to do everything he could to finish in one day. Besides needing to get back to L.A., he wanted to focus on the life he had, not the one he'd lost.

"Fine. Getting the fence fixed is all I care about."

Julianna gently touched Abe's arm. "Luke will help and it'll get done," she said, always the calm one. With her mediating skills, she should've been a diplomat.

She turned to Luke. "Got a big case to get back to?"

He chewed some toast and finished with a sip of coffee. "Always."

"I heard more on the news about congress-man Thorpe's aides, and Thorpe didn't seem happy about it. Is he a person of interest?"

"He's more than interesting to me. The guy's a weasel who thinks he can use his political influence to derail the investigation."

"That's why you're going back?"

"That and a serial killer on the loose."

Julianna's face went white.

Oh, man. Insert foot into mouth. Again. Though he'd long ago separated his personal life from his job, Julianna didn't know how to dissociate. He should've remembered that. "What about *your* career?" he said, changing the subject.

"Uh…it's good." She pushed back the hair from her eyes and tucked it behind one ear. "I'm a regular contributor for a magazine. *The Achilles' Heel.* I like it and it pays well."

He knew it was more than that to her. Writing was a part of her, something she *had* to do. And the liberal magazine was the perfect venue.

"How is Starr?"

She looked surprised that he'd asked. "My mother's fine. Still the same. Stumping for one cause or another. The environment,

PETA, stem-cell research." She smiled. "All good causes."

"Still a hippie at heart, huh?"

"That she is. She thinks it's the seventies, and that she's still twenty, and actually, she doesn't look much older."

"And your sister?"

"Lindsay's married, has two children and lives in London. As far away from Mother as possible."

Luke nodded. "I can understand that." He remembered the strife between Julianna's sister, the yuppie, and her mother. Julianna on the other hand, had been Starr's protégée.

Jules's mother and her ability to suck her daughter into her causes had been another sticking point in Luke and Julianna's relationship.

"Unfortunately, my sister's far away from me, as well. I rarely see Ally and Devon, my niece and nephew."

Julianna would miss that. She'd always loved children. They both did, and he'd been deeply disappointed when she refused to have another child after Michael. He was surprised that she hadn't married again. He wanted to ask her about it but didn't want to open old wounds for either of them.

"Kinda the way Luke thinks, too," Abe said. "Wants to be as far away as possible."

Luke shoved his plate away and leaned back in the chair. "I moved because I was given an opportunity. You didn't want Grandpa's house, remember? That's why he gave it to me." Even though the house on one of the much desired canals in Venice Beach was worth double what the ranch was at the time, his father had turned it down, refused to move to California. Luke suspected Abe didn't want to be beholden to his father-in-law in any way. That and the fact Gramps never thought Abe was good enough for his only child and wasn't afraid to say so.

"You can come out and stay with me any time you want."

"And who would take care of things here?"

"Hire someone. You need help anyway. Then you can come and go as you please."

Abe shoved his chair back and rose to his feet. "I'm not going anywhere and no stranger is going to come in here and take over. Now let's get to work."

Julianna stood and began clearing the dishes. "So, get out of here, you two. I've got to write."

That figured. She was just as intense about her work as he was, only she'd never seen it that way. "What kind of a story are you working on?"

Her brown eyes expanded. "Uh, just a series. I do an installment once a month."

Gazing at her, he barely heard a word. He'd forgotten how pretty her eyes were. Big brandy-colored pools that drew him in, made him want to get closer.

But her evasiveness put things in perspective. In the past, when he'd asked about what she was writing, she'd couldn't wait to share her ideas. Now, it was obvious she didn't want him to know.

Why should she? She hadn't wanted to share *anything* in her life for five years. Maybe she was sharing those things with someone else now? For all he knew, she could have a live-in lover.

"What's the series about?"

She looked at Abe.

"We need to get cracking," Abe said. "We're wastin' sunlight. You can chitchat later."

The lines around Julianna's mouth softened, apparently relieved that Abe had ended the conversation.

And that made him even more curious. Okay. He'd play along. For a while. "I'm with you, Pops. Just let me grab a shirt and a hat."

In the hallway on the way to his room, Luke's cell phone rang. He recognized his partner's number. "Yeah."

"Luke, it's Jordan."

"Hey, bud. What's going down?"

"I wondered if you heard from the boss?"

Luke shifted the phone to the other ear while he pulled on a faded denim shirt. "I did."

"Did he tell you it's the chief who's pushing to take you off the Thorpe case? I heard Carlyle told him to stuff it, in so many words, but—"

"I talked to him. It's no big deal. I can't leave here yet anyway. My father isn't well and I've got to get him some help."

"Bring him here. California has some of the best physicians in the world."

"Great idea, but he's dug in. He'll never leave. And… he has a guest."

"A guest?"

Luke hesitated. "Julianna."

Jordan let out a long blow of air. "Whoa. That's a surprise."

"You telling me."

"What's she doing there?"

"I don't know, but I'm going to find out before I come back."

"When's that?"

"Tomorrow or the next day for sure." Luke started walking back to the kitchen to catch up with his dad.

"Okay. Let me know." Jordan was one of Luke's best friends, and also one of the finest detectives in the Robbery Homicide Division. While Luke often operated without a partner, he'd worked with Jordan on several cases recently.

"I'll call you when I get back."

"Good."

"How's the better half?" Luke asked.

"Laura's great. Today she hired someone to stay nights at the shelter for her so she and Caitlin can move into my place after the wedding. Don't forget, you've got a job next month."

Luke smiled. Jordan could've picked any one of their friends to be best man, Rico or even Tex. But he'd asked Luke. "Not for a second."

As he reached the kitchen doorway, Luke said goodbye and clicked off. Julianna stood only inches away and gave him a knowing look. The one that said he couldn't leave his job for more than five minutes. "That was Jordan. Remember him?"

Julianna's eyes lit up. "Of course. How is he?"

"He's getting married next month."

Mouth open, Jules put a hand to her chest in surprise. "Really! I never thought that would happen." She smiled, showing an expanse of even, white teeth and very kissable lips.

"I'm the best man." Jules had always liked Jordan and for a time they'd all been really close.

"I'd be surprised if you weren't."

The pleased look in her eyes switched to wistfulness. Was she thinking of their wedding? She'd once said it was the happiest day of her life.

"Please give Jordan my best," she said, and then hurried away.

She left him standing there, feeling as if one small moment from the past had somehow brought them closer. But then he could just as easily be misreading things. He did that a lot with Jules. Whenever he'd been sure he knew what she thought or wanted, she'd been on another wavelength altogether.

But there was no denying that something

had passed between them. He just didn't know what the hell it was.

He headed out the back door, glanced around for Abe, who was nowhere to be seen. The old reprobate had probably taken off without him. Luke strode to the barn. As he went inside, the familiar scents of hay and manure took him back to a time when he couldn't have imagined ever leaving the ranch.

The mare was gone, but Balboa stood in his stall and nickered softly at Luke. When Abe had downsized, he'd kept two horses and five head of cattle, just enough to stay busy, but not too much to handle.

Luke talked softly to Balboa before saddling him up. "Hey, big guy. It's been a while." The golden palomino nuzzled him, apparently remembering they'd been inseparable once upon a time. He wished other parts of his life were that easy to resurrect.

He mounted the stallion and headed for the line, not having a clue where the fence was broken. He figured it was at Stella Hancock's property line, otherwise Abe would have no reason to complain about her long-dead husband.

He sat straight in the saddle and took a quick breath of fresh mountain air, a nice change from the smog and gasoline fumes of downtown L.A. Even the salty ocean breezes at his home in Venice were a respite from the pollution that hung like an ochre cloud over the rest of the city.

Out here, he could breathe. The scent of piñon pine teased his senses, reminding him of a time when life was simple and uncomplicated, a time when the only thing he'd cared about was what he was going to do that day.

His mother's sudden death when he was thirteen changed all that. She'd been the peacemaker, she'd held the family together. Clearly something he and his father had no desire to do once she was gone.

Back then his father always blamed Luke's bad behavior on adolescence, but it was more than that. Something he'd long since put out of his mind. He'd never approached his father about it, but he'd always thought Abe knew that Luke knew—and neither wanted to open that door.

One thing was certain, his mother's death had changed his life forever.

He nudged Balboa to a canter. He hadn't thought about that in years. He preferred physical activity over thinking. But being here, seeing Jules again, had him thinking

more than ever. Love complicated everything—and losing everything you loved
made life intolerable.

When they'd lost Michael he'd soldiered
on for Julianna's sake. But when she left…
there wasn't any point to anything. He'd hit
bottom.

The anger he thought he'd buried a long
time ago burned in his veins. Bitterness rose
like bile in his throat. Never again would he
let himself feel so much. If he didn't feel, he
couldn't hurt.

JULIANNA WENT INTO the den to do some
research for her next story. *If* she could concentrate. Luke had said he'd be there only a
day or two. God, she hoped so. He was too
intense. Too probing. She was on tenterhooks
every time he entered the room.

One day she could handle. Couldn't she?
All she had to do was maintain her distance,
keep her mind in the present and stay focused
on the end result. Luke going back to L.A.

She'd made a quick decision not to tell Luke
about the story because she knew the subject
would upset him. She knew that as well as she
knew her deadlines. It would simply make the
time he was here even more strained. He

already suspected she hadn't just come simply because Abe asked her to. As intuitive as Luke was, if she told him about the story, he might connect the two. And if he knew she was being threatened, the cop in him wouldn't let it go. He'd have to take action.

There was no way she could tell Luke. But she had to tell Abe about the phone calls.

CHAPTER THREE

BY THE TIME Luke reached his father, Abe had already taken out the new roll of barbed wire and was trying to fasten it to the fence by himself. "Couldn't wait a few more minutes?" Luke dismounted and strode over.

"Can't wait forever. I'm not getting any younger."

"Not getting any easier to get along with either."

"One of the few good things about getting old. You can say what you want and the hell with what anyone thinks."

Luke couldn't remember a time when his father didn't say what he wanted or ever cared what anyone thought. But he wasn't going to stay that long and he needed his father's cooperation if he was going to hire someone to help out. Getting Abe to accept that help was going to be the tough part.

"We need to shore up the posts first," Luke

said and walked over to one that was tilted at forty-five degrees.

"It'll straighten out with the wire on it," Abe countered.

Luke let out an exasperated breath. He knew he should just agree with his dad and then get out of there. "C'mon, let's do it together."

That seemed to agree with Abe and they both started working on getting the post upright. And while they were somewhat sympatico, Luke said, "I know Jules isn't here just because you asked her to come."

His father turned and looked at him. "Is it such a hard thing to believe, that someone would actually want to be here with me?"

"No, Dad. Of course not. You have company all the time, don't you." No matter how hard he tried to be nice, his father made it impossible and Luke couldn't seem to hold back his sarcasm. But then it wasn't likely he'd hurt the old man's feelings anyway. Nothing fazed his father. And he usually gave out more than he got.

"People never did take to me, like they did your mother," Abe said. "And when she died, it was hard to be nice to anyone."

Including me. But this time, Luke bit back the words. He'd come here to make amends with his father and dammit, he was going to. "I know you missed her. I did, too."

"I still do."

The softness in his dad's voice might've made Luke think he actually meant it. "So why are *you* here?" Abe said. "I know you didn't come to keep an old man company."

Luke smiled, hoping to ease the tension. "But you're wrong. That's exactly why I came. I had two weeks vacation and I thought it a good opportunity for us to... to reconnect."

Abe snorted, then as if he hadn't heard a word, walked to the next post and started righting it.

Yeah. Luke sighed. Had he hoped for a different reaction? What Luke wanted didn't mean squat when it came to his father. Never had. "So, getting back to Jules. I know she likes you and all that, but what's the other reason she's here?"

"Ask her, not me."

"I did. She won't tell me."

"Shoot. If you'd kept in touch with her, you'd know why she was here."

Keep in touch? Where had his father been all this time? Julianna didn't want anything to do with him. It was her decision and he'd respected it.

"And if you hadn't bailed on the marriage, she probably wouldn't be here at all."

Picking up the roll of wire, Luke gritted his teeth. Tension crackled in the air between them. Luke started attaching the end of the wire to the first post. "Dad, that was five years ago. Long enough for you to quit harping on something that's over and done with."

"She was the best thing that ever happened to you," his father grumbled.

Yeah. He'd thought so, too. "Like Mom was the best thing that ever happened to you?" Sarcasm laced his words.

Slowly Abe turned, his eyes narrowing to slits. "Yes, like your mother."

He'd hit a nerve. He'd spent a lifetime wanting to say that and trying not to. And now that he had, he didn't feel any better. "Julianna may have been the best thing for me, but I wasn't the best for her. I doubt she'd agree that there'd been anything good between us."

Abe spat on the ground and grumbled, "People don't always say what they mean, you know."

Yeah, he knew. He saw it in his job all the time. People lied to save their butts. But

Julianna wasn't a liar. She'd meant every last hurtful word. Every time he thought about it… Hell, dealing with both Jules and his father, his head felt about to explode.

"Things happen," Abe said. "Good stuff, crappy stuff. It's called life. If love is there, it's there. People go on."

"Dammit. It's a dead subject, Dad. Now why don't you just tell me why she's here and be done with it."

Abe grabbed the roll of wire Luke held and yanked it away. "I told you. It's not my place. Ask her yourself."

Luke released his grip before the wire cut his hand. Then suddenly Abe spat out a string of cuss words. His face went ghost-white, his lips blue. He staggered back, grabbed his chest and sank to his knees.

Shit. Luke dropped the roll.

"IT'S OKAY, MARK. I'm finishing the story and that's that. I'm in the safest place I could be, under the circumstances."

"But you can't stay there forever."

She sighed. "I know. Once the story is done—"

"What makes you think this lowlife will stop bothering you when you're finished?"

"That's what his threats are about. He doesn't want me to finish, so if I do, he's lost."

"I think you're wrong. It could make him even more incensed that you didn't listen."

That was true. So far it had. "Look, Mark, I'm not going to live my life in fear because of some jackass. No one is going to tell me what I can and can't do when it comes to my writing." Her temper flared at the thought.

"Well, I can."

She stifled a laugh. "Right." Mark was such a cupcake. He'd given her free rein after only a month on the job. And she was careful not to abuse the confidence he had in her. "You'll see. It'll be business as usual after the last installment."

"Damn, I hope you're right. Because otherwise I'm going to feel responsible."

"So, what else is new, *Dad?*" Mark wasn't much older than her own thirty-two years, but he acted as if he was sixty sometimes.

He chuckled. Finally.

"I'll be in touch." As she hung up, Julianna heard something bang outside. She glanced at her watch. Luke and Abe had only left a half hour ago, it couldn't be them.

Just as she went into the kitchen, Abe burst through the back door, Luke right behind him. "What's wrong?"

"Nothing a little good sense won't fix," Luke said.

Abe waved him off with a hand covered with a blood-soaked cloth.

"Oh, you're hurt!"

"Just a little cut. I've had worse. No big deal."

"When did you last have a tetanus shot?" Luke asked.

Abe shrugged.

"That's what I thought."

"That's enough, you two. What we need right now is a first-aid kit. Do you have one, Abe?"

"Under the sink in the bathroom," he grumbled, then quickly added, "But I'm not going to get any shots."

"Can you get it, Luke?" Julianna asked as she lifted Abe's hand to see the damage. "What were you doing?"

"Nothin' I don't do all the time. I just got distracted."

As Abe answered, Luke returned with the kit and handed it to Julianna. She went to work, cleaning the wound, a gash about two inches long. "You really should see a doctor. It might need stitches."

No response.

"While you're taking care of that, I'm going back out to finish what we started." Luke motioned with a tip of his head that Julianna should follow him outside.

"Hold the pressure on it, and I'll be right back, Abe."

Outside on the porch, Luke stood with his feet apart, arms crossed over his chest. "He wasn't distracted," Luke said, keeping his voice low. "He looked unsteady on his feet, as if he was dizzy or something. Then he fell. But he wouldn't tell me what was wrong. Maybe while I'm gone you can find out. I think he needs to see a doctor... whether he wants to go or not."

Julianna saw the concern in Luke's eyes. For a tough cop, he felt things intensely, though it wasn't always easy to tell.

"I'll see what I can do." Before she could go back inside, Luke placed a hand on her shoulder.

"You're going to have to tell me why you're here, because we both know it's not just a visit. I don't have any desire to pry into your personal life... I mean if it's something like you've had a fight with your boy-friend or whatever, just say so and I'll butt out. But if it's something else and it involves my father, then I need to know." He stared at her, determined. "Besides, you know I'll find out one way or another."

The skin on her arms prickled. "And what does that mean?"

He shrugged, but didn't let her go. "I'm a detective."

Annoyed, but knowing he meant what he said, she pulled away. "Okay…it's personal, so butt out." She stalked back inside. It wasn't exactly a lie. It *was* personal…and if telling a tiny untruth meant he'd leave her alone, so be it.

After she finished cleaning Abe's wound and bandaged it as best she could, she said, "So, how about that tetanus shot? I'll be happy to drive you."

"Nearest doc is in a little clinic outside Pecos."

"Fine. Let's go." Before he could protest, she said, "Oh, one other thing."

He glanced at her.

"I received a couple of voice-mail messages on my home phone. Threatening messages."

"The bastard," Abe spat out. "It's a good thing you're here then."

"I was thinking of going somewhere else."

"Nonsense."

She sat on a chair next to him and clasped his good hand. "It's not nonsense. If there's any chance I'm in danger, then my being here puts you in danger, too."

Abe squinted. "Why do you think you'd be any safer someplace else? No one's going to find you here. And if they can't find you, that keeps us both safe. Right?"

She shrugged. "I don't know. I took precautions, but I can't be sure it was enough. I couldn't bear it if—"

He held up a hand. "I won't hear of it," he sputtered. "You leave, you'll have the same problem. This is the best place and that's the end of it."

Julianna smiled, then gave Abe a long hug.

"So, let's quit jawing and get that shot."

"I'll leave a note for Luke."

She started to help Abe get up, but he protested.

"Tell him we're going to the grocery store. He doesn't need to know we went to the clinic."

"I'll write the note however you want it." Luke would know where they'd gone. He was a smart guy. Someone who could unravel puzzles in a flash, who understood people at a glance. And he hadn't believed for a second she was there on vacation. But what difference did it make to him why she was there?

If he'd just finish the fence, hire someone to help Abe and then go home, she'd be fine. But from the determined look she'd seen in his eyes, she had an awful feeling that wasn't going to happen. Luke would hound her until he found out what he wanted to know.

THAT NIGHT during a very late dinner, Luke told Julianna and Abe about his progress with the fence. "But there's still more to do," he said.

Luke didn't ask why Abe's hand was bandaged differently and Abe didn't offer that they'd gone to the clinic. Julianna talked about the weather, of all things, simply because she wanted to get through the meal without any further references to why she was there.

So far, so good, she thought as she brought dessert to the table, a pie that she'd picked up at the grocery store after Abe had his hand stitched and had grudgingly submitted to a tetanus shot.

"Good pie," Luke said.

"Thanks to Sara Lee."

"Pot roast was good, too." Luke forked another piece of pie and brought it to his lips.

Her eyes fastened there, on his mouth, the little indentation in the middle of his top lip.

"I don't remember you cooking much before."

Maybe that was because he was never home at dinnertime. She and Mikey had eaten alone most nights. "I learned a thing or two when I had an exchange student living with me for a while. Actually the student was doing an internship at the magazine and somehow I ended up with her at my house."

"You have a house?" Luke looked surprised.

"A loft condo. No upkeep, and someone else does all the fixing."

He nodded. "Not a bad idea. At my place there's always something going wrong." His bluer-than-blue gaze caught hers. "But then, you know that."

Her pulse quickened. Was he still living in his grandfather's house? The house they'd shared?

"That's why I didn't want that place," Abe grumbled. "Too much fixin'."

Both she and Luke turned to Abe. Then Luke said, "And there isn't here?"

"It's different," Abe said gruffly. "There's memories here."

Julianna sighed. There *were* memories— both here and at the house in Venice Beach. She couldn't believe Luke was still living there.

"The ranch has memories of all kinds," Luke said. "Some good, some not so good."

Abe's chair scraped on the tiles as he abruptly rose to his feet. "I need to feed the horses, and then it's time for me to turn in."

When Abe was gone, she carried some dishes to the sink. "The doctor gave your father a tetanus shot and put five stitches in the cut." Luke was right behind her with the dessert plates. Close. She moved to the side to put the dishes in the dishwasher.

"Good." Luke scraped off a plate and handed it to her.

"He said Abe should come in for a checkup."

Luke gave a dry laugh. "I don't have to guess what the old coot's response to that was, do I?"

"Right. But I think someone really needs to make sure he goes. He hasn't seemed like himself since I got here."

Luke leaned on the counter, watching as

she finished up. She felt sweaty all of a sudden, unnerved to have him so close. It seemed odd that they were talking about Abe as if they were still married.

"If you could work some of your magic to get him to agree, I'd be indebted," he said.

The soft plea in his eyes touched her. She put the last cup into the dishwasher, added soap, pushed the button and started the machine. "I'll see what I can do. But right now, I've got work to do."

Luke's gaze followed as Jules walked away. She'd seemed nervous—as if she couldn't wait to get away from him. If he didn't know better, he might think… But hell, she was probably worried that he was going to ask again why she was there. And truth was, if she hadn't left, he would've.

Repeatedly asking the same question was one way to wear someone down. He did it with suspects all the time when he thought they weren't being truthful. While Jules might not be lying, something was definitely wrong. She jumped out of her skin every time the phone rang.

Walking into the living room, he heard the kitchen door slap shut. His dad coming back inside. Abe had said he was going to bed, and though it seemed early for that, his father'd had a busy day what with the fence and the doctor and all. Luke felt tired, too, but he knew it was more mental exhaustion than physical.

As he reached the worn-out couch, its worst parts covered with a red-and-blue Southwestern serape blanket, he inhaled the familiar scent, a mixture of cigarettes, Old Spice and old man. He glanced around. Nothing had changed. Nothing in the house and nothing with Abe.

Though he'd come here with the idea of smoothing out his relationship with his dad, he could see now it was a bad idea. Abe was too set in his ways. More importantly, his dad didn't care about mending anything between them. And now, in addition to finding hired help, he had to get Abe in for a physical.

He couldn't leave until he had those two things under his belt. He hoped Jules would help. She was good at getting people to do things without them realizing it.

An image of Jules immediately popped into his head. An image of how she looked today, not the one he'd carried for the past five years. She looked more mature, more comfortable in her own skin, and she was every bit as beautiful as he remembered. Just watching her had made his blood run hot…made him remember what it was like to feel something.

Something other than duty and responsibility.

And Jules was the last person he should be thinking about like that. He reached for a magazine. *The Achilles' Heel*. What the hell. Reading might get his mind on something else. He flipped it open. The title of the article practically leaped off the page. "Missing."

He read a couple paragraphs. Turned the page. What the—the story was about a little girl who'd been abducted fifteen years ago in Los Angeles. Renata Willis. He tossed the magazine on the pile and picked up another. Another story with the same theme, but a different child.

Anger rose from the dark well inside him, the place where he'd buried his feelings. How long had she been doing this? A sharp, heart-stabbing pain drove into his chest.

How could she!

CHAPTER FOUR

SOMETHING WAS WRONG. Luke had kept his distance all day, barely grunting when Julianna or his father asked a question. Would he like coffee? Grunt. Aren't you going to have breakfast? At least that one had gotten a grumble that she thought was a "No thanks. Gotta get to work."

He'd left immediately and, since he'd been gone all day, Julianna suspected he'd long since finished the fence. "He can't still be working, can he?" she asked Abe as they finished up dinner. "It's getting dark."

"Luke can take care of himself."

"I know he can, Abe. But for him to be gone so long, something could've happened. Aren't you worried just a little? Curious maybe?"

"Nope. I learned a long time ago that Luke doesn't need anyone to worry about him." He glanced at her from under his brows. "And I think you seem more worried than necessary."

Julianna stared at him in surprise. Abe never talked about anything personal. Never once had he mentioned the divorce. "I don't know what you mean."

As he smiled, the crevices in his face deepened and she saw a glint in his faded blue eyes. Eyes that reminded her vaguely of Luke's. "You know what I mean." He rose from the chair and then raised his hands in the air. "But then I'm an old man and you probably think I don't know what it's like to be in love."

She did a double take. "I…I'm not…there's nothing—"

"It's okay. No need to explain."

Sheesh! What did Abe think? That she'd been pining away for Luke for five years?

JUST AS LUKE WAS finishing up the fence, he heard a noise behind him and turned to see Stella Hancock astride a pinto that looked as old as she was.

"Hello, Luke."

He tipped his Stetson. "Mrs. Hancock."

"How are you? It's been a long time."

Luke drew a breath, then shifted his

stance, feet apart, arms crossed. "I'm fine." He didn't ask how she was and instead said, "I'm surprised to see you out here. You ride out very often?"

She smiled and the fine wrinkles around her eyes fanned out. For a woman who'd spent most of her life on a ranch, she'd aged gracefully. Most ranch women were well weathered by the time they were forty.

"No, I came because I heard you were fixing the fence and I wanted to know how Abraham is doing?"

When he didn't answer right away, she added, "I saw your wi—Julianna at the grocery store yesterday. She told me your father had hurt his hand."

Luke looked away. Jules had met the Hancock woman once when they'd come to visit when they were first married, and she'd been impressed that Stella had run her own ranch after her husband passed away. Luke didn't think it was a big deal, not when you had her money. She might run the place, but other people did the work.

Coughing, Luke grated out, "He had a couple stitches, that's all."

"The last time I saw him in town he didn't look well."

Annoyed that he was even talking to this woman about his father, this woman who'd— Luke stared at her, willing her to get the drift and go away. "I'll take care of whatever is bothering my father."

He saw her wince a little, but she quickly recovered, then said, "That's good to hear. He needs someone right now." Then she pulled on the reins, made a clicking sound and rode away.

What did she mean by that? And how did she know what his father did or didn't need? As far as Luke knew, she and his father hadn't had any contact for years. Maybe he was wrong?

Climbing onto Balboa again, he took a minute to survey the land, a vast span of nature at its best. Just east of the Sangre de Cristo Mountains, the landscape was made up of rolling hills and piñon pine. Mountains and streams surrounded the valley and as a kid, Luke had always thought he lived in a magical place, a utopian paradise. What did he know?

His mother had loved it here and he remembered riding with her often, to picnic or fish or just to soak up the scenery. The land reminded Luke of her. Beautiful in its simplicity, yet strong enough to withstand the elements.

In the end, cancer had taken his mother at

too young an age. But she'd seemed at peace with herself. Unlike him, her faith had held her in good stead. He'd gone the other way, damning whatever forces had taken her from him so soon. And then later, took Michael. And Julianna. If there was a God, he wasn't doing his job.

No, he didn't have the kind of faith his mother had. Why should he?

He touched Balboa's side with his heel, but the stallion wasn't in any hurry to return. The horse probably didn't get enough exercise with only Abe to take care of things, so Luke took the long way back to give the stallion a workout and on the way, he stopped at a shallow creek to let Balboa drink. He dismounted. Except for the burbling sounds of crisp clean water over the smooth rocks, it was so quiet he could hear himself breathe.

Balboa suddenly rose up and whinnied. "What? What's wrong, boy?" The horse snorted and jerked away, spooked. "It's okay," Luke soothed, stroking the animal's neck and scanning the area to see what had scared him. "It's okay, big guy."

As he took in the property on the other side of the creek, on the hill he spotted an animal on the ground. Very still. "It's okay,"

Luke reassured his mount and stroked him again. He tethered the horse to a tree and made his way across the creek, rock by rock.

It was a calf. But what was it doing out here alone? Was it sick? A few more steps and he knew the animal was dead. He didn't want to get too close, but he had to know what had happened. As he moved closer, he saw a pool of blood under the animal's head. The calf's throat had been cut.

On instinct, he reached for his weapon and swung around. Only he wasn't carrying and felt like an idiot. He was standing in the middle of a pasture with a dead calf and he'd reacted like he'd been ambushed by the Mob.

Maybe the captain was right, his nerves were shot and he needed the vacation more than he realized. Even though he'd covered numerous crime scenes, the coppery odor of blood, the scent of death, made him cover his mouth with his hand. He never got used to that. People who thought police were immune to gruesome scenes were either mis-informed or stupid.

He rode Balboa back to the ranch at a gallop and twenty minutes later, after unsad-dling the stallion and brushing him down, he walked into the kitchen. It was quiet, so he headed down the hall and tapped on Abe's door. "It's Luke, Dad. I need to talk to you." Without waiting for an answer Luke opened the door.

"What's wrong?" Abe was sitting in his favorite chair. On the table next to him was a photo of Luke's mother. The room reeked of stale tobacco, even though Julianna had persuaded Abe long ago to quit smoking in the house. She hadn't wanted Michael exposed to secondhand smoke.

Luke pulled an old oak chair up next to his father's and turned on the lamp. "Sitting in the dark for a reason?"

"You get the fence fixed?" his father asked.

"Yep. I did. But I came across a dead calf on the way home. Down by the creek."

"Dead?"

"As a doornail."

"One of mine?"

Luke nodded. "Had your brand. And…it looked like its throat had been slit."

Abe drew back, his face turning red as he glowered at Luke.

"Any ideas?" Luke asked.

"Yeah. Get me my gun."

"No, I mean any ideas who might've done this?"

His father shifted in the chair. "Someone who doesn't like me, I guess."

Well, that took in half of San Miguel County. "Anyone in particular?"

Abe shook his head. "Could be kids. Teen-agers thinking it's fun to wreck people's property."

"This isn't just property, Dad. That calf was a living animal, part of your stock. It's more than vandalism. It's animal cruelty."

Abe took a moment, then said, "I'll take care of it."

Luke crossed his arms. "How?"

When Abe clammed up, Luke bolted to his feet. "I'm going to call the sheriff," he said, turning to leave.

Before Luke got out the door, Abe said, "I said I'd take care of it. I don't want you calling anyone."

His father could be so damned bullheaded sometimes. But maybe it was kids out raising hell. Instead of doping up on meth or heroin as some teens did in L.A., the youngsters here found their fun in other ways.

When he'd lived here, there wasn't anything like this going on. A little vandalism maybe, but nothing so sick. No, whoever had done this had a twisted mind…and no respect for life.

Luke strode into the living room and looked up the sheriff's number. He didn't care if Abe wanted him to call or not. The dispatcher answered, then said the sheriff was out, but he'd be there as soon as he could. Two hours later, Ben Yuma was at the door.

"Twice in one week," Yuma said. "Nothing serious I hope."

"I think it is, but if you ask my dad, you'll get a different answer." Luke went back to tell Abe the sheriff had arrived, but his dad was asleep in front of the TV. Odd. Luke turned off the TV, then filled in the sheriff on what had happened.

"So," Luke said. "You know the area, the locals and their crimes, do you have any idea what's going on here?"

"None yet. I'll have to take a trip out there. There have been similar incidents on other properties. Some ranchers think they're connected to the corporation that's trying to buy up the land around here to build a spa resort."

Abe hadn't mentioned anything about that.

"Others say it's kids. Rich kids with nothing better to do."

"Rich kids? When I went to school here, most ranch kids had to scrape by."

"There's been a big real estate boom in

the past few years, spreading out from Albuquerque and Santa Fe. Condos, planned communities, people with money."

"Whoever did this, rich or poor, they've got some real problems."

"True," Yuma agreed. "I'll be back tomorrow morning to take a look."

When the sheriff left, Luke headed for Julianna's room.

THE KNOCK on her door made Julianna jump. She checked her watch. 10:00 p.m. It wouldn't be Abe, and that left only one other person. "Hold on," she said, "I'll be there in a minute." She saved the story on her laptop, closed the cover and went to the door, opening it a few inches. Luke stood with one arm resting on the door frame.

"We need to talk," he said.

Her heart thumped. "What about?"

"Abe."

She expelled a silent sigh of relief. "Okay. Just give me a minute."

"Sure. I'll be on the patio."

He'd always liked the outdoors, the fresh air, at the beach or wherever. Closing the door, she quickly threw on the pink zip sweatshirt that matched her sweatpants, and then slipped on her flip-flops. She took a quick peek in the mirror. Plain. She'd always been plain. Nothing like her classy sister. She ran a comb through her hair, then dabbed on a bit of lip gloss before realizing the futility. What did she think? That the gloss would somehow transform her into something she wasn't. Dammit, she'd come to grips with her self-image a long time ago. So why were the old insecurities resurfacing now? What the hell, she dabbed on some blush, too, and then headed down the hall.

At the back door she saw Luke sitting outside on a bench. She stopped to look at him. So handsome, so… masculine. Instantly, she remembered how she'd felt being the other half of the couple people whispered about and said, "What is he doing with *her?*" She'd always wanted to feel his equal, like they belonged together. She'd tried hard, but it never quite came together for her.

But when she and Luke were alone, he always made her feel beautiful, as if he saw something in her that others didn't. Something even *she* didn't see. She realized later it had been easy to forgive a lot in their marriage because of those stupid insecurities.

The door creaked as she went out. "Hey."

"Hey," he said, then indicated the place next to him on the bench. He wore jeans and a black sweatshirt and was sitting near the beehive-shaped chiminea in the corner. A crackling fire radiated warmth and the pungent scent of cedar, instantly conjuring memories of better times. The first time she'd met Luke's dad. The Christmas they'd spent here when she was pregnant. Memories she didn't have time for anymore. Luke wanted to talk and that's what she was going to do.

But as she lowered herself to sit next to him, she sensed something was wrong. "What's up with Abe?"

"That's what I want to know. Has he said anything to you about problems on the ranch?"

She shook her head. "No, but he did say he thinks Mrs. Hancock wants him to sell his property."

Luke shifted uncomfortably, as if she'd hit a nerve. "Sheriff Yuma was here a little while ago and mentioned something about a corporation trying to buy up land for a spa resort."

"Do you think someone approached Abe about it? And maybe Mrs. Hancock, too?"

"Could be."

"If she comes by again, I'll ask her."

"No need. Pops wouldn't sell to anyone for any amount of money."

"So, why was the sheriff here again?"

"I called him because when I was out on the line, I found a dead calf."

"Oh, that's awful. But why call the sheriff?"

"The calf's throat was slit."

"Oh, my." Goose bumps rose on her arms. Had the caller found her and was this a warning? "What did the sheriff say about it?" There's no way anyone could possibly know where she was. With help from Patrick, the private investigator she used as a resource, she'd effectively disappeared. Except for calling her editor once a week, she had no contact with anyone else.

"The sheriff said there's been some vandalism at other ranches and they suspect some high school kids may be involved."

She breathed a sigh of relief. That made more sense. "But killing a helpless animal? That's sick."

"I know. Sociopaths are sick. And they start young. Usually with small animals."

The thought made her shiver. She rubbed her arms. "Does Abe know?"

"I talked to him before calling the sheriff."

"How's he feeling?"

Luke shrugged. "With him, you never know."

"I do. I can tell when something bothers him. It's subtle, but noticeable. I see it every time he talks to you."

"Yeah. Well, I've been bothering him since I was thirteen. That's nothing new."

"What I mean is that I can see it bothers him that you two don't get along."

He gave her a sideways glance. "You take up psychiatry somewhere along the line?"

She smiled. "I have learned a few things in that area, but no, my knowledge of your father is based on years of watching how he reacts when you say something that hurts him."

"I don't say things to hurt him."

"Not intentionally, but some of the things you say, do hurt him."

"Well, I'm not going to debate your sixth sense when it comes to my dad. And I'm not going to monitor my words either. He and I have never understood each other and we probably never will."

"So, why are you staying? I thought you were leaving as soon as you could."

Wearily, he leaned against the post behind him so he was facing her. "Things changed."

"Like?"

"One…my dad seems…not himself. Two, I need to find him some hired help, and three, the dead calf. I wouldn't feel right about leaving until those things are resolved." His gaze narrowed as he turned to look at her. "I'd also like to know why you're really here," he said softly. Teasingly.

There it was again. The question that wouldn't go away. She cleared her throat. "When I spoke with your father before I decided to come, he sounded a little flat, depressed almost. I thought maybe my visit would cheer him up." That part was true. She had felt Abe needed someone, if even just another person in the house. He was alone too much.

"Getting help for your father would be wonderful. And it would give him someone to talk to. It has to be hard being alone all the time."

"You'd think. But that's the life he's chosen. He doesn't like too many people." Luke grinned, then touched the sleeve of her shirt. "Except for you."

Julianna's heart warmed at the comment. "He's been the father I never had. Even though I haven't seen him too often, we've stayed in touch."

Leaning back on one elbow, Luke rubbed a hand over the stubble on his face. By the end of the day he always had more than a five o'clock shadow. "I didn't know that," he said, his voice still low, reflective almost.

She shrugged. "No reason you would."

"Well, like I said, there are things I have to do before I go."

"I don't think there's anything you can do about the calf other than let the sheriff handle it. If it is vandals, he'll do something about it."

"But there have been other incidents, so I'd like to know what he's doing about it before I go."

She looked down. "So, when *are* you leaving?"

His eyes sparkled with mischief. "Can't wait to get rid of me, eh."

She laughed, feeling her cheeks flush. "You found me out."

Luke's expression softened. "I always liked the way you laugh."

He'd never told her that before. Hearing it now made her more self-conscious than anything. Sitting here with Luke was a dangerous place to be. She looked away. "I didn't do that very often during the last part of our marriage, did I?" Their last couple of years together had been so bitter, so filled with pain.

"No. But you had good reason." He reached out for her.

Even though his touch was tender, she felt her muscles tense and launched to her feet. "I…I need to go in. I still have work to do."

He stood almost at the same time, then stepped in front of her, effectively blocking her way. "What's the rush?"

She placed one hand on her hip, hoping she looked cool and calm—even though her insides felt like they were in a meat grinder. "You heard me. I have work to do."

"Really?" His voice seemed lower, huskier. He stroked her cheek with his fingertips.

Her blood rushed. "Yes, really."

"You look like you need to relax."

Her heart thumped so hard she was certain he could hear it. "Nighttime is when I work best. Besides, I have a deadline to meet."

He frowned, his mouth forming words that didn't come out, as if maybe they were too difficult to say. "What?" she asked.

Squaring his shoulders, he said, "I'm still wondering why you left me."

Oh, God. Her throat constricted. "Luke. Don't. Please." When he just stood there, she said, "You…you know why."

"But that's just it. I don't. I know what you said when you left, but I know there was more to it. And it's been eating at me for five years."

Her voice was barely a whisper when she said, "I can't get into all that again, Luke. I just can't."

"Was it me? I couldn't blame you there."

Her head came up. "Oh, no. God, no. It wasn't you, Luke. I promise." His drinking hadn't helped, but that wasn't it at all. On instinct, she rested her hand on his arm.

He looked at her hand, then placed his other one over hers.

Tears welled, but she pushed them back. She'd gone through therapy, learned how to live with her grief over losing Michael, thought she'd learned how to live with the breakup of the marriage. So why was she such an emotional mess?

Finally, she managed, "I can't do this, Luke. I've moved on. I hoped you had, too." She pulled herself up to her full five feet six inches. "Now please let me go."

Tears burned behind her eyelids as she

walked inside, trying desperately to hold herself together. Trying desperately not to turn around and rush into his arms.

CHAPTER FIVE

LUKE WATCHED Jules walk away, his jaw clenched, his fists kneading his thighs. If it wasn't him, then what the hell was it?

People who loved each other were supposed to stand united and support each other when bad times came. People who loved each other didn't run away and destroy everything good that they'd built together. Maybe she'd never loved him. Maybe the wonderful relationship he'd thought they had was a bunch of garbage. He'd convinced himself of that more than once.

And now, seeing the pain in her eyes as she ran inside to escape him made him feel even worse. He'd brought up things that hurt her. Damn. He banged the wood railing with the flat of his palm. He was like a fox in a chicken coop, tearing things apart because *he* wanted something. Because *he* needed to know. God, he was a jerk.

He stomped inside and on the way to his

room hesitated outside her door. He wanted to say he was sorry for hurting her. But the hurt was already there. Sorry didn't change anything.

Tomorrow. Tomorrow he'd apologize. Tell her he'd never bring it up again. Then he had to get outta here. Go back to work. Work was what he did best.

In his room, he punched in his partner's cell number. "Yo," he said when Jordan answered. "What's happening?"

"That's what I was wondering. When are you coming back? I've got a good lead on the Renfield case."

Luke's pulse quickened. "Does Carlyle know? He didn't want me on it until after the election."

"No. But I'm not doing anything to stir the pot as far as Thorpe's concerned."

"How good is the lead?"

"It's hot. I tracked down an old friend who'd heard Thorpe threaten to kill Michele Renfield."

"Who's the friend?"

"Betsy Stephens. Renfield's former college roommate."

"So why haven't we heard about her before?"

"She said she was questioned way back but nothing ever came of it. And in the back of her mind was the thought, if her friend disappeared, so could she."

"So, what changed?"

"She said she was cleaning out some of Michele's things and found something. An ultrasound photo."

"Renfield was pregnant?" *With Thorpe's kid?* Luke's nerves vibrated with excitement. All his instincts said Thorpe was guilty as hell and Luke wanted to get him so bad he could taste it. He hated politicians who thought they were above the law. Now they had motive and if they could get this girl's testimony… damn. He had to get back to L.A. "I'll be back the day after tomorrow. It's a full day's drive and I have to clear up some things here first."

"So how's it been?" Jordan asked.

"My dad needs help. I'm going to try to take someone on before I leave." Then he'd plead with Jules to get his father to a doctor. And she'd be overjoyed that he was leaving.

"That's good. But I meant how are you managing with Julianna in the same house?"

Luke rubbed the stubble on his chin. "No big deal. The past is in the past."

There was a hesitation on the line before Jordan said, "Yeah? So that's what you tell yourself."

Annoyed that his partner had him pegged, Luke gripped the phone tighter. "Yes, it is. But I fully understand your thinking. You have this pie-in-the sky philosophy that love conquers all, and because you're about to be married, you can't understand why everyone doesn't feel the same way. But take my word for it, in my case, love doesn't conquer anything. The past *is* in the past. It's done. Kaput. Finito."

Jordan coughed as if choking on what Luke had said. "Yeah, okay. Whatever you say."

"I'll call you when I get close to home."

When he was finished with the call, Luke stripped off his clothes and headed for bed. Dammit. The past was in the past. Except he kept seeing how Jules had looked when she came out and sat beside him tonight. She'd smelled clean and fresh and he longed to feel her in his arms again, to be as close as they'd once been.

The fat yellow moon and the brilliance of the stars had reminded him of all the other times they'd sat together simply enjoying the night.

Times he needed to forget. *Done. Kaput. Finito.*

THE NEXT AFTERNOON Julianna was taking a break from her research and making lemonade when she heard a noise outside. After taking the sheriff out to see the dead animal this morning, Luke and Abe had disposed of the carcass and then spent the rest of the morning working around the place. Though Abe had come in earlier, Luke was still in the barn.

Last night after she'd gone to bed, her emotions warred with her needs. She wanted to go to Luke and try to explain, but she knew going to his room wouldn't end well. She hadn't been with a man for six months, at least. Not since her one attempt at a relationship—post-Luke—fell apart. And right now, her hormones were working overtime. Getting too close to Luke could be a dangerous proposition. In more ways than one.

Luke was comfortable. She knew him, knew how to please him. He knew how to please her. But to do that would be misleading. He'd think it meant more, and even if it did, it wouldn't be fair to either of them. Because nothing would change.

Luke was probably staying outside so he wouldn't have to see her again. She couldn't blame him. Every time he'd tried to talk to her she'd cut him off.

She poured the lemonade into a large thermal container, placed some cookies she'd made into a Ziploc bag and headed for the barn. Luke was inside, replacing the hinges on the side door and didn't seem to hear her come in. Wearing jeans, a blue denim shirt and his Stetson, he looked the typical rancher. A far cry from the perfectly groomed, designer-suited detective she'd once been married to.

She knocked on a wooden box to alert him she was there. When he looked up, she said, "I made some lemonade." Putting both the cookies and the container on the box, she motioned for him to come and get some. Then she'd get the hell out of there.

Luke untied the bandana around his neck and wiped off his forehead. He seemed surprised to see her. "Sure. Thanks. It's hot in here."

"But it's nice outside." A crisp fall day and the sun was shining. She handed him a glass and saw his hands were covered with tiny cuts.

"Where's Abe?" Luke asked.

"Taking a nap."

"Great. Good time for me to call some people about the job. I'm calling a couple guys I know and see if they can recommend anyone, and I put a help wanted ad in the local paper."

Luke took a cookie, and then after another swig of his lemonade, said matter-of-factly, "I'm sorry about last night. I was out of line."

She glanced away. He shouldn't be apologizing. She was the one who'd fled. She was the one who couldn't explain herself. An irony that hadn't escaped her. A writer who couldn't express herself. How sad was that? But then the only time she had the problem was when she was with Luke. "It's okay. Let's just leave it alone. Okay."

His gaze caught hers again. "Deal. If I can hire someone, I'm leaving tomorrow morning, so I want to do as much as I can today."

She felt the tension in her shoulders ease. "Well, if you need anything, if you need my help—"

That got a raised brow.

"Okay," she said. "I know I'm probably the

most unmechanical person around, but I am good at helping if I'm told what to do."

He smiled, then picked up another cookie. "Great. I do have something I'd like you to help me with."

"Oh…okay." She hadn't really expected him to take up her offer.

He walked over and sat on a bale of hay, then gestured for her to have a seat, too. She sat on the bale opposite him, pulled up her feet and sat cross-legged. The scent of hay teased her senses, dredging up a long-ago memory of the time they'd made love in the hay loft. She wondered if Luke remembered.

Luke took one last sip of lemonade, then said, "It's about my dad. Since I'm leaving tomorrow, I won't have time to get him to see a doctor, but he needs a checkup."

"And you were wondering if I'd convince him to go."

He nodded. "That's it. I know it's asking a lot. He can be stupidly stubborn when he wants to be." He gave a half laugh. "Which, now that I think about it, is all the time. At least when I'm here. You might have better luck asking him after I leave."

"I'll be happy to do what I can. But you know—with Abe—there are no guarantees."

"If you can't, then we'll have to go to plan B."

"Plan B? What's that?"

"I don't know yet, but there'll be one if this doesn't work."

"If what doesn't work?" Abe hobbled inside. He looked at Julianna, a scowl on his face. "You scared the living crap out of me disappearing like that," he said. "You shouldn't leave without letting me know where you're going."

Luke glanced at his father. "Why?"

"She knows why," Abe said.

Julianna looked at Luke. "It's nothing. Really."

"Well, now that I know you're together, I'm going back to do some figuring on the books." He started to leave, then turned back and said, "Don't scare me like that again, young lady. It ain't good for an old man."

She smiled affectionately. Abe had been extra watchful of her since she'd told him about the voice-mail messages. She jumped off the bale, walked over and gave Abe a hug. Of course he'd be worried. "I'm sorry," she said. "Promise I'll be more thoughtful."

When Abe was gone, she gathered up the

things she'd brought, but Luke stopped her with a hand on her shoulder.

"You want to explain?"

She slipped from under his hand. "It's nothing really. Abe is overly concerned about me."

"That's easy to see. But the question is why?"

She crossed her arms, hugging herself. Then she shrugged.

When she didn't say anything, he said, "You might as well tell me because now that I know there *is* a reason my father's worried about you, I'm not about to let it go. And you know I can find out just about anything."

"Not this time." She didn't like his attitude…or being told she had no choice. Despite that, she knew he *wouldn't* quit until he did find out. Luke was a detective. But if he cared at all about her, he wouldn't spread the news she was hiding out, either. Maybe it would be okay. She dismissed the thought as quickly as it came. Knowing Luke, he'd call out the forces, the media would hear, Mark wouldn't like the publicity and she'd never finish her story.

He gently took her by the arms and sat her on the hay bale again. "Please tell me."

Maybe it would be better to tell him something. Something that would make him back off. She settled herself on the bale, then palms up, she said, "It's just that I received a couple nasty e-mail messages from some creep who didn't like the article I was writing. That's all."

Luke pulled back. "That's all."

She nodded.

"You're hiding out."

"Not hiding out exactly. Just taking a vacation to finish the last installment of a series."

Luke knew Julianna wasn't the kind of person to run from idle threats. It had to be more serious than that. "What didn't he like?"

"He didn't say. He said he wanted me to stop writing about missing kids." Almost as the words left her lips, his eyes darkened— and she knew. She should never have mentioned what the story was about. But just as quickly, he reined himself in.

"Or what? Did he threaten you?"

"I can handle it, Luke. People write letters to the magazine all the time." She stood, her back straight as a board.

"I'd like to see the messages," he said.

"I see no reason for you to get involved."

Luke gritted his teeth. She never saw things from his perspective, only her own, which in this case was clouded by her need to shut him out. "Sorry. That doesn't cut it. You're involving my father. That gives me more than a passing interest in knowing what you're getting him into."

He stood at the door blocking her way. "If my father is involved, I'm involved. Whether you like it or not."

Her mouth pinched. Her hands clenched at her sides. He felt as if they were in a war of wills. But if she knew him at all, she knew he wasn't going to back down.

"Okay!" she said. Then with a hint of resignation in her voice, "When you finish here, I'll pull up the messages."

He placed a firm hand on her arm, urging her forward. "Let's do it now."

Walking to the house, Julianna bristled at Luke's demands. She shrugged off his hand. So, big deal. She'd show him the messages and that would be that. What was he going to do? Tell her to leave? This was his father's house, not his.

Abe was waiting for her on the porch, pacing back and forth.

She glanced at Luke. "Give me a minute will you."

When he just stood there, she added, "Alone. Please."

Luke looked at his dirty hands and grungy clothes. "I'm going to take a quick shower. Then I'll be back."

When he was gone, she turned to Abe. "What's the matter, Abe?"

Abe stopped his pacing. "Did I screw things up?"

She forced a smile. "No, you didn't screw things up. I'm sorry I worried you." They went inside together.

"You sure?"

"Sure. I was going to tell Luke anyway."

Abe rubbed the gray stubble on his chin. "That's good. Keeping secrets is foolish. They always come out somehow."

"No more secrets, Abe. I promise."

It must've been a satisfactory answer, because then Abe said he was going to go take a nap. She'd noticed he was taking a lot of naps lately. "Are you okay?"

"I'm fine. I get this tired feeling once in a while, that's all." Then, he stood straighter, as if bolstering himself up. "Old men get

tired easier than the young studs, you know."
He winked at her.

"Not you. You can outwork anyone your
own age—and most younger men as a matter
of fact. I've seen you do it."

"I like how you think, young lady. Maybe
you can talk some sense into that son of
mine."

She frowned. "About what?"

He sent her a look that said she should
know what. And unfortunately she did. "No,
Abe. Luke and I are divorced. We've been
divorced for five years. We've made new
lives for ourselves. It's better this way."

On his way out, he said, "Maybe you've
made a new life, but I don't think Luke has.
And that can only mean one thing."

She didn't want to hear it. "Go, take your
nap, Abe. I have things to do."

Abe left and she headed for the den.
Sitting at the old oak table, she pulled up the
first e-mail message and got the creeps all
over again. What was it about the story that
threatened this guy? He had to be threatened
somehow, otherwise why was he so adamant
that she stop writing it.

She left the message on the screen and
picked up one of her research books, her

muscles tensing as she read the title. *Killing for Sport: Inside the minds of serial killers,* a necessary resource for the articles she was writing. It was important to know her subjects.

No sooner had she sat in the chair to start reading, than Luke returned. She got up and went to the desk and showed him the first message. The least threatening message. "Stop the articles about Renata Willis or you'll be sorry."

"And the other?" Luke glanced at the book in her hand. His face went ashen. She saw a muscle jump near his eye. "Nice reading material," he said through gritted teeth.

She tossed the book on the chair, then pulled up the next message. "Stop now or you'll be next!" Both messages were signed with a star at the bottom. Reading it again, a chill jagged up her spine. She'd been shocked when the first message had come, and she'd been a little scared when she'd read the second. Then something in her rebelled. Scared or not, she'd never acquiesce to threats.

She had notified the San Francisco police but all they did was write a report. That's all they could do, they'd said, and if she didn't like the heat, she should get out of the kitchen. Their attitude made her even more determined to finish the series.

As Luke read the message his body practically vibrated, the veins on his neck bulging. "You think this is nothing?" he spat out.

She pursed her lips. "The magazine gets nasty letters all the time."

"If you didn't think it was so bad, why did you go into hiding?"

"I didn't go into hiding. The opportunity to get away presented itself, and it seemed a better idea than doing nothing. A precaution—sort of."

He pointed to the book. "How can you read that stuff?" He snatched up the latest edition of *The Achilles' Heel* and shook it in her face. "How can you *write* this stuff?"

Julianna stiffened. "The same way you can keep working in Homicide."

His expression switched from anger to insult. "It's different. I'm helping people. Trying to find some kind of justice for victims and their families."

"And what do you think I'm doing?"

He shook his head. "I don't know. I honestly don't know."

"The stories I write are about victims who've been forgotten. Their cases closed because the police can't find the perpetrators. I'm telling the public that these children and their grieving families shouldn't be forgotten. I'm a constant reminder that these killers are out there, ready and willing to kill some more. By keeping the stories in the public eye, maybe someone somewhere might do something. Maybe even the police."

He winced at the comment, then squared his shoulders. "You know damned well a cold case is only shelved because there aren't any viable leads. If there were the police would be on it."

She chewed on her bottom lip. She'd hit a nerve by questioning his precious job. "Keeping the story alive is important."

"And your life isn't? Putting yourself in the line of fire for a story…how smart is that?"

She shrugged. "It's what I do." She hoped she sounded more confident than she felt.

Raking a hand through his hair, Luke spun around. "Then you need police protection."

She gave an ironic laugh. "Right. I tried that. But the police in San Francisco don't hand out protection to every woman who's been threatened or harassed. You of all people should know that."

"Yeah," he said on a sigh. "Well, then, you should stop writing the stories."

Her mouth fell open. "Excuse me?"

"The solution is simple. Stop writing the stories."

She gave a huff of indignance. "I'm not going to stop writing the stories. I can't do that. I need to finish the series." She turned away from him, her muscles drawing tighter and tighter. He had never understood her passion for writing, and he'd never grasp why she had to write these particular stories. If he could, he'd never have stopped looking for Mikey's murd— She caught herself midthought.

Don't. Just don't. Her pulse suddenly pounded in her ears. "Besides, no one would ever think to look for me here. I haven't told anyone. Not my editor. Not even my mother."

The sharp ring of Luke's cell phone interrupted. Why was she not surprised?

Luke pulled out his phone, glanced at the number of the caller, saw it was Jordan and then walked a few steps away before he answered.

"Yeah," Luke said, keeping his voice low.

"Just checking on your ETA. I'm going to make an appointment with the new lead on the Renfield case and I want you to be there."

Luke felt the usual rush of adrenaline. He needed to get back. He had a job to do. But…if he left, there'd be no one to protect Jules. Dammit. He couldn't leave her here alone.

"Some things have come up. You'll have to do the interview without me."

It was quiet on the other end of the phone for the longest time. Finally Jordan asked, "Something wrong with Abe?"

"No, something else. I can't talk now, but I need a favor."

"Sure—what's up?"

"A cold case." He searched his brain for the name of the child in the story. "Willis…Renata Willis. Pull it for me, will you? Then I'll get back to you as soon as I can."

Jordan agreed and Luke hung up. Julianna was incredibly naive if she thought there was no danger. It was obvious the articles had triggered some kind of hostility in the person who wrote the messages. She had to know that.

But why? What bothered this person so much he, or she, had to make threats? That's what he needed to find out.

He walked over to where Julianna stood by the window. It was dark now and there was nothing to see outside, but she stared out anyway.

Standing behind her, he said, "Tell me about the other threats."

She pivoted around to face him. "What other threats?"

"There are more, aren't there?"

She closed her eyes, rubbed her temples with two fingers. "If you're going to nag me until you find out, then yes, there were a couple of phone messages. I picked them up from my voice mail the night you arrived."

He touched his forehead where there was still a mark from her bashing his head with the butt end of the gun. "So that's why you reacted so violently when I came in. You were scared."

She pushed him away and went to sit on the couch. "Yes, I was scared. I thought you were a freaking burglar."

As he turned to look at her, he couldn't help the grin that formed. "Yeah. I guess you did."

He saw a tiny grin tip the corners of her mouth. "You have to admit, that night is kind of funny in retrospect," she said.

"Don't try to change the subject." He went over and stood in front of her. "What did the recorded messages say?"

"Just more of the same. You can listen to them tomorrow. Right now I'm tired and I'm going to bed."

She rose to her feet and as she started to walk away, Luke placed a hand on her shoulder. "Now. I want to hear them now."

CHAPTER SIX

SLEEP WAS AS ELUSIVE as Julianna's answers to Luke's questions. He kept thinking about the voice-mail messages. She'd told Abe about them, but she hadn't told him. And he was the one who could protect her.

He'd been taken aback when she showed him the e-mail messages, but the calls were serious threats. Whether the police did anything or not, the calls needed to be documented with the San Francisco police. Julianna would know that. She wasn't stupid.

But she'd always been unpredictable. Just when he thought he knew what she was going to do, she threw him for a loop. Which was why he had a bad feeling that she might not be telling him the whole story.

He remembered the first time he saw her across the room at Bernie's, the local sports bar where Luke and his buddies hung out whenever they could watch a game. He'd been a beat cop when they'd met, on the cusp of promotion to detective.

For him, it'd literally been lust at first sight. But she'd been with another guy and they'd left before he could find a way to introduce himself.

A week later he'd arrested her at an environmental rally that had turned into a riot. So started their tumultuous relationship. And it had been that way ever since.

The thought made him smile. Despite everything, she still made him smile. She'd affected him like no other woman ever had, and from the moment they'd met, he'd wanted to get her into bed. When he fell in love with her, the desire only intensified… and no matter how many times they'd made love during their marriage, each time was as exciting as the first.

He wondered how it would be now to feel her body against his again. She had the smoothest skin he'd ever felt. His pulse quickened, blood rushed to his vital parts. But he knew the danger of giving in to desire with Jules. He'd only open himself to more pain. He couldn't do that again. Not even if she was willing. If he did, he might never recover.

He checked the clock on the night table.

2:00 a.m. It was pointless to stay in bed when he couldn't sleep, so he pulled on a pair of jeans and headed for the living room. On the way, he grabbed a Coke from the fridge, noticing some Bud Light next to the soda. Jules must've bought the beer because his dad wouldn't be caught dead drinking light beer.

In the living room, he set his drink on the end table, clicked on the lamp and dropped into the worn leather recliner next to it. The chair had been there since Luke was a kid. Even though it was his father's favorite, his mother had threatened to torch the behemoth more than once.

He glanced at the pile of magazines next to him and his stomach knotted. He didn't want to read about missing children, but to know what was going on with Jules, it was something he had to do. He picked up the latest issue of *The Achilles' Heel,* and as he read, he could see why the caller might've been disturbed about the story. By putting all the facts and the interviews from the victims' families together, it gave a more complete picture. A human interest story that put faces to the cold statistics and made the tale more compelling.

And from his experience in working with

criminal profilers, she'd described the traits of a serial killer perfectly. If the person making the threats was the murderer, he might believe she could expose him.

In another part of the article, she'd stated her theory about the connections between several similar crimes, even indicating she knew the names of criminals with the same M.O.

Whether she realized it or not, she'd made herself a perfect target.

"Couldn't sleep either?" Jules's low sexy voice came from behind, making him jerk to attention.

He chucked the magazine back onto the pile upside down. "Something like that."

She came around and sat on the couch across from him, curling her legs beneath her. She was wearing a tight-fitting yellow top with barely-there straps, and loose yellow pajama bottoms with pictures of a cartoon bird on them. Tweety Bird, he remembered, her favorite. "So, what do you think?"

"About what?"

"The story. You were reading my story, weren't you?"

He raised his hands. "Guilty. But I didn't finish, so I won't be drawing any conclusions."

"Conclusions about what?"

"Whether the story's good or not."

"That's not what I meant. I thought maybe you'd find it interesting. Compelling. It's supposed to be compelling."

He shrugged. "I found it disturbing. In more ways than one."

She frowned, then said, "That means I've done my job. It made you think."

"It did that. It made me realize how serious the threats are. It made me think there's a lot of anger in your words." *Anger and pain.* Every word dripped with the pain of a parent who'd lost a child.

"It's a sensitive subject." She closed her eyes and leaned her head against the red-and-blue blanket covering the couch. When she opened her eyes, she looked directly at him. "Sensitive yes, but nothing I can't handle."

"You can handle a serial killer?"

She sat upright. "You don't know if he is."

"You profiled the guy perfectly. He could think you know more than you do."

She ran a hand through her hair, then with a shake of her head, flipped the long locks back over her shoulders. "Good. I wanted to wake people up. If I've done that, I've succeeded."

"So, where did you get your information?"

Her eyes sparkled. "Are you questioning my resources?"

"No, I'm just curious how you know so much."

"I don't know any more than anyone else. I've just put it together in a different way. In each case I write about, the profiles are composites garnered from the experts who wrote them. The rest is public information and interviews."

"You've been goading him."

"That wasn't my intent."

"But it's the result. That's why he's threatening you."

"So why didn't the police do anything when I told them? They thought I was a hack wanting publicity."

"I don't know, but I think you need protection, and if I'm going to help you, I need to know everything."

"I'm not asking for your help. And if I need protection, I'll…I'll call the police."

"The police are already here." He wanted to smile, but it was important she knew how serious this was. "In addition to letting your local police know, we need to contact the FBI. But…it might be more effective if I'm the one who calls."

She hesitated, stood and then paced in front of him.

"You can't blow this off, Jules." Luke felt his blood pressure rising. "Or are you just burying your head in the sand like you used to?"

She stopped dead in her tracks and glared at him.

He held up a hand. "I'm sorry. That was uncalled for. It's just that…I can't sit by and do nothing."

"Luke." She turned to him. "Please let it be. Whoever is making the threats thinks I'm in San Francisco."

Her words didn't fit her demeanor. She seemed edgy, more so than before. Maybe what he'd said was getting to her, but she couldn't…wouldn't admit it. Another of her traits he knew so well.

"I can't let it go. You may be putting my father in danger." He cleared his throat. "And *you* are definitely in danger."

Her expression went from obstinate to resigned.

"Abe knows about the calls and he insisted I stay. But if there's any chance it might put him in harm's way, I'll leave."

Luke rubbed his chin. "No…no, I don't think you should."

She turned, came over, snatched his Coke and took a long swig. She shifted from one foot to the other. "First you want me to leave. Now you don't. Make up your mind."

Ideas started falling into place. "I think if we take the right precautions, you might actually be safer here. Especially with me as your bodyguard."

"For once I agree with you. But not about the bodyguard part. I truly don't believe anyone could track me here. No one knows. I left no trail. I even used a different name on the plane."

"What name did you use?"

"I bought a fake ID from a reputable source who got it from someone else who got it from—"

"So someone else knows your fake name."

Frowning, she said, "Okay, maybe so. But it's someone who doesn't have a clue who I am. Too many people in between."

"But he knows the name and could track it, or give it to someone if they asked."

She whirled around. "Only if he wanted to be arrested. Believe me, fake IDs aren't the only illegal thing he traffics in. Besides, how would anyone know to even contact him?"

"You found a way."

She shook her head. "Someone else got the I.D. for me. I'm safe. Believe me."

Safe, maybe. But not a hundred percent. "Okay. Let's leave it at that. We don't know what anyone knows for sure, but to be safe, we have to assume they know everything and be prepared. Once I notify the FBI, I think we should talk to Sheriff Yuma as well."

"Even though nothing has happened?"

"Even though. I'll make the calls from my cell."

"Then what?"

"We need to take steps to find out who sent the messages." He caught her gaze to see her reaction. "Deal?"

She hesitated. Then, finally she said, "Deal," and she reached out to knock knuckles the way they'd always done.

Luke smiled. Funny how some things came so naturally.

Yet other things seemed so foreign. She did seem different now, but he couldn't put his finger on exactly what. Maybe it was simply the fact that she was older, wiser. More confident. More beautiful.

"I'm going back to bed. Don't strain your eyes reading in the dark."

"I don't read. Remember."

Julianna left the room feeling as if she'd achieved some measure of success. Once she sent off the last installment in the Willis story, she was off to London to visit her sister—and work on her next story. The only glitch was that she had to put up with Luke until he left. And now, she had no clue when that might be.

She carried her laptop into the bedroom, sat on the bed and flipped to her working file. But the words on the page might as well have been written in Russian. All she saw was an image of Luke's face, which now seemed embedded in the forefront of her brain. If only she could hibernate until she finished. Keep Luke out of her sight.

We. Everything he said was *we*. It looked as if he was involved whether she wanted him to be or not.

But his staying was a two-edged sword. Whenever she was around Luke, she couldn't stop looking at him, and when she wasn't looking at him, she was thinking about him. His mouth. His eyes. The muscles in his back that moved sensuously under her fingertips when they'd made love. She couldn't remember how long ago that had been, and yet, the image was as fresh as if it had been last night.

Forcing herself to focus, she typed a couple paragraphs, but when she finished, she knew it was crap. She switched programs to her calendar and noted the imminent deadline for the last installment and the date she was leaving for London. Then she typed in a reminder that she had to convince Abe to get a physical.

Sweet Abe. She hoped he was okay. Sometimes he was in good spirits, but other times he seemed to flag. He was also coughing a lot, and his energy level certainly wasn't what it used to be. But then he was getting older; he had to be seventy.

Abe had been over thirty when Luke was born, while Luke's mother had been a few years younger. Luke had idolized her and Julianna had always wished she'd had the opportunity to know his mother. She might've given Julianna insights into the man who still remained an enigma to her.

But none of that was important now. Luke wasn't a part of her life anymore, and barring any unforeseen incidents, they'd both go their separate ways. She should be happy about that, but instead, she felt sad. Spending time with Luke had been both disturbing and oddly comforting. She couldn't deny that his presence made her feel safer.

But safe was a relative term. She might be safer physically—but not emotionally. Since Luke had arrived, there'd been moments when the past seemed so vivid, she felt as if they were living it all over again. She'd heard that sometimes people fall back into relationships with an ex-spouse because it's more comfortable than finding someone new. She could easily imagine herself with Luke again, for just that reason.

But she was a realist. The reasons she'd left were still there—and always would be, no matter what. He'd married her because she was pregnant. She'd never really known if he truly loved her or if he'd felt obligated to marry her. Living with that uncertainty had made her insecure and needy. When he spent more time at his job than at home, it reinforced her worst fear.

After Michael's death, there was no reason to stay. She'd had to leave.

THE NEXT MORNING as Julianna was making breakfast, Abe came into the kitchen. Luke was working outside somewhere and later he was going to interview a man he might hire to help Abe.

"Morning, Pops." During her marriage to

Luke, Julianna had taken to calling Abe *Pops,* as Luke did. It seemed silly to change that even after the divorce. He'd always been the father she never had.

"I'm not sure it's good," Abe said as he lowered himself onto a kitchen chair.

"Oh, I bet you'll perk right up after some coffee."

"Maybe. Right now I feel sluggish." He coughed a couple times.

Julianna looked at him in surprise, her mouth half open. Abe would never admit to feeling ill. Maybe he didn't consider "sluggish" the same as being sick. "Well, what strikes your fancy this morning. Pancakes or French toast?"

A knock on the door startled both of them. As she walked over, Julianna saw a shadowy form through the sheer curtains over the glass of the door.

Opening the door, she was surprised to see Abe's neighbor standing there. "Hello, Mrs. Hancock."

Abe made a noise in the background, as if clearing his throat. Julianna ignored him and said, "How nice to see you."

"Nice to see you, too," the older woman said. "But please call me Stella. I came to see how Abe is doing."

Puzzled, Julianna looked at Abe, who waved her off, indicating he didn't want to talk to anyone. She stepped outside and closed the door behind her.

Julianna stared at the woman, not sure what she meant.

"His hand," Stella said. "When I saw you at the store, he'd injured his hand."

"Oh…oh, yes." Where was her head these days? "His hand is doing well, but he seems a little under the weather this morning, probably a flu bug, and he really shouldn't see anyone until we know for sure."

"Of course. I wouldn't want to bother him," Stella said, but the disappointment in her eyes was almost palpable. Brown eyes that looked as if the color had faded over the years, and once-dark hair now sprinkled with gray. Her long silver-and-turquoise earrings matched the multiple rows of rings she wore on both hands. An attractive woman, Julianna decided, but she seemed unusually concerned about Abe.

"I can have him get in touch with you when he's feeling better."

The comment brought a hearty laugh. "My dear, you don't know, do you?"

"Know what?"

"Abe hasn't talked to me for twenty-five years. I didn't expect he would now."

Julianna frowned, even more confused. "And yet you're concerned about him? Enough to come over."

Stella gave a big sympathetic smile, as if to say she couldn't expect Julianna to understand. "Of course I'm concerned. I've known Abraham a long time. We were important to each other once and when I realized he wasn't feeling well, I knew…I knew I had to make an effort before…"

She looked away, as if to compose herself. Then she said, "We have to let the bad things go if we want some kind of peace in our lives."

As Julianna opened her mouth to speak, Stella turned to leave.

"Stella, wait."

The woman stopped.

"Do you know anything about a corporation wanting to buy property around here?" she blurted, remembering her conversation with Luke.

"Yes, I do. They've asked me to sell mine. I think they asked Abe, too. I tried to talk to him about it a couple of times, but you can imagine how that went."

"What did you tell these people?"

"I said no, of course."

"Does Abe know that?"

"I don't know. But I think he'd prefer it if I did move." She gave a resigned smile, then continued. "But my friends and family are here. That means more to me than money."

Julianna wondered if she included Abe in the friends category. "Do you mind if I tell Abe what you said?" Julianna didn't know why she asked that, but she felt Abe should know.

"If you wish," she said. "And please tell Abraham I hope he feels better soon." Then she left.

The woman's words resonated in Julianna's head. *Peace.* Did people really ever achieve that state? She doubted she ever would.

Back inside, she was even more curious about Abe and Stella. Apparently they'd been *friends* at one time, but Abe had never spoken of it. "Stella wanted to know how you were, Pops. I saw her in town when we were there the other day and told her about your hand," she said crisply. "She said to tell you she hopes you feel better soon."

His expression switched from cranky to surprised. "My hand is fine. In fact I need to take this bandage off so I can get back to work."

"Oh, and she said she wasn't selling her

property to that corporation. She's not leaving."

His eyes sparked with interest, but the look dissipated quickly. Okay, he wasn't going to talk about it. Fine. She wouldn't either. At least not to him. But she would find out somehow why Abe and Stella hadn't talked for twenty-five years. Journalists were skilled in ferreting out information. Not unlike detectives.

"You leave that bandage on until tomorrow like the doctor said. Now is it pancakes or French toast?"

"I'm not hungry, but I'll have that coffee."

She poured them both a cup and as she handed him his mug, she said, "You have to eat. Breakfast is the most important meal of the day. And I'm not taking no for an answer."

He grumbled something under his breath that sounded suspiciously like *"women"* before he said, "Pancakes."

LUKE WALKED from the barn toward the house just as a battered green pickup kicked up a trail of dust down the road away from the house. He didn't recognize the vehicle.

But then why would he? He hadn't been here for a year, and the last time had only been a quick stopover. The thought produced a wave of guilt. If he'd known his dad was doing so poorly…

Yeah, what? What would he have done? If nothing else he needed to be truthful with himself. Fact was, he probably wouldn't have come any sooner. He'd needed to get his own head on straight. Get his life back to some semblance of normal. Not act like the walking dead. He'd been that way for too long and wasn't going to backslide, no matter what.

Staying here with Julianna was definitely a challenge, but after last night, he knew he couldn't abandon her while she was in danger. If she would just listen to him…

He kicked the dirt off his boots before he went inside. "Something smells good," he said, apparently to himself because when he glanced around, the room was empty. He felt a twinge of disappointment. He liked having breakfast with other people for a change. With Jules.

"Pops? You here?" He'd expected him to come out to the barn to help, but he hadn't.

"He's not feeling well." Jules's voice came out of nowhere.

Looking up, he saw her standing in the kitchen archway wearing a pair of low-rise jeans and a white T-shirt that didn't quite meet the top of the pants. He didn't remember her wearing such sexy clothes before.

"He had breakfast and then decided to lie down again."

Luke frowned. "That's not like Abe."

She walked to the stove and held up the coffeepot.

Nodding, he pulled out a kitchen chair, turned it backward and then straddled it. After pouring the coffee, she stood across from him, her hands on the back of a chair. "I know. He says it's a flu bug, but if it was he'd have a fever or something. And he's finding it hard to breathe."

"Who was driving the pickup?"

"The neighbor. Stella Hancock. She came to see how your dad was doing." When he frowned again, she quickly added, "I ran into her and told her about his hand."

"He doesn't need her concern."

"Maybe not, but he does need yours. I think you should talk to him."

Luke scoffed. "I could talk to that stone wall outside and get a better response. He doesn't want to hear anything I have to say."

Shoving the hair from her eyes, Julianna

came around and sat next to him, elbows on the table. "Don't be so sure."

"Why? Nothing's changed. My being here is more of an aggravation to him than anything."

Jules's expression turned serious. "Luke, I've never meddled in your relationship with Abe, but I know he needs you now." Her eyes pleaded with him. "Even if he won't admit it."

He lifted the cup to his lips. The coffee tasted strong, as if it'd been heating all morning, and it was so hot, it scalded his throat as it went down. What did she know about it? After a moment, he said, "I'll talk to him, but I know anything I say will fall on deaf ears."

She grinned. "He's only deaf in one ear. He'll hear you."

"Funny."

"But true. Whether he does anything about it is another story." She cleared her throat. "When I told Stella that I'd give Abe the message that she was here—" her gaze came up to meet his "—she laughed. She said she hadn't talked to your father in twenty-five years."

Luke shrugged. "So?"

"I wondered why, if they hadn't spoken for so long, she was coming over now?"

"You didn't ask? That's not like you, Jules. The journalist in you asks questions even when you shouldn't."

Julianna laughed. He knew her too well. "Okay, so I did ask."

"And—"

"She said something about being friends once and letting things go in order to be at peace with herself." As she spoke, Julianna studied Luke's face for a reaction. The woman's words had touched Julianna more than she could've imagined. Maybe they would touch Luke, too.

"Fine," Luke said. "Let her be at peace at her own place. She doesn't need to come around here stirring up more trouble."

"More trouble?"

Luke ignored the question, pushed his cup away and stood. "I've got to shower before I go talk to Clyde Davis."

"Clyde Davis?"

"Someone who might be able to help out here after I leave."

After I leave. The words should've made her happy. Instead she felt oddly let down. "Good. Where'd you get his name?"

"I called around. Got a few referrals."

"Well, I hope they're good referrals. Considering the calf and…other things, it pays to be careful."

The second she saw Luke's wide grin, she wanted to retract the words.

"That's what I've been telling you, sweetheart," he said, drawing out the last syllable. "I'm glad you're finally admitting I'm right."

If she'd had something to throw at him, she would've.

"ABE, WAKE UP." Luke touched his dad on the shoulder. "You're going to sleep the day away." Hell, the day was almost gone.

Abe tried to sit up, but fell back. "I'm awake, dammit."

Luke pulled a chair up next to the bed, the scent of tobacco lingering in the air, in the fabric of the furniture. "How do you feel? Julianna said you might have a flu bug."

"I feel fine and I'd feel a lot better if I didn't have people poking me in the middle of the night."

"It's not nighttime, Dad. It's dinnertime. I can bring your meal in here if you'd rather not get up."

His old man grumbled something and took another stab at sitting up. This time he made it.

"So what do you say?" Luke didn't like the way Abe looked. His face seemed ashen and his voice weak—even through the bluster. And he seemed disoriented. His dad had always been sharp, quick with the words and even quicker with his comebacks.

"I—I say you go ahead. I'll be there in a little bit. I have to wash up first."

More likely he wanted to go outside and smoke another cigarette. But Luke left anyway. His father was a proud man, too proud sometimes. Too proud to give an inch. Ever.

"He'll be here in a few," Luke told Julianna as he entered the room, then went to the fridge for something, but closed the door again.

"There's wine if you'd like that," Julianna said.

"No thanks. I've sworn off the stuff."

"Really? You used to love wine with a good steak."

Luke had offered to barbecue some steaks for dinner and Julianna had snapped up the offer. Why she thought it was her job to make meals, he didn't know. But he hadn't refused a single one. It had been too long since he'd tasted real honest-to-goodness home cooking.

"Merlot? It's been in the fridge for about a half hour. It's better with a tiny chill."

He raised a brow. "You're a wine connoisseur now?"

"No way. But living in San Francisco it's hard not to learn simply by osmosis."

Luke got out the wine and poured one glass and handed it to her. He grabbed a Coke for himself then raised the can. "To a great future for us all."

Her eyes met his. "To us all."

Luke felt an urge to step forward, to taste the wine on her lips. Instead, he took a sip of his soda. "Are the steaks ready to grill?"

"Ready as they'll ever be," she said. "I made a salad and I'm baking some potatoes."

"I'm salivating already." As Luke turned from getting out the steaks, he saw his dad leaning against the archway. "There he is," Luke said. "Glad you could join us, Dad. We've got some mighty fine steaks ready to throw on the grill."

Abe wheezed. "I don't think I can eat anything. I'm going back to bed."

Julianna rushed over, put her hand to his forehead. "You don't feel as if you have a fever, but then maybe you're just working up to it." She smiled sympathetically.

The woman could cajole a stone, and Abe wasn't immune.

"I just need to lie down for a little while longer."

"Do you want us to take you to the E.R.?"

He jerked away, stumbled and bumped the wall with his shoulder. "What the hell for?"

Julianna stepped back, her expression shocked. Then she glanced to Luke as if asking for help. Abe had talked harshly to Luke for most of his life, but he'd never snapped at Jules.

"No reason, Dad," Luke said, walking over to him. "You know women…they're always concerned and want to help."

Abe nodded as if repentant. He looked at Julianna like he wanted to say he was sorry, but they both knew he'd never get out the words. "Like I said, I'm going to lie down for a little while longer."

"We'll put a steak on for you and you can eat it when you feel like it," Luke said as he watched his dad make his way down the hall.

As soon as he was gone, Luke picked up the phone. "What's the name of the doctor you took him to for his hand?"

"Dr. Terry. His number is right there on

that pad." She pointed to the paper on the counter below the phone.

Julianna watched as Luke punched in the number. He waited, listening, then left a message.

"He's not there. And if he doesn't call back soon we're going to the hospital."

Nipping at a cuticle on one finger with her teeth, Julianna said, "I'll go along, too."

Luke's head came up. "I wouldn't let you stay here alone if you wanted to."

She should've bristled at the comment, but for some reason she felt good instead. It had been a while since anyone cared where she went or what she did.

The phone rang and Luke answered. He nodded at her that it was the doc. Thank heaven for small-town doctors who didn't wait days to respond.

After explaining his father's symptoms, Luke's end of the conversation was pretty much yes and no answers. When he hung up, he gave her a strange look. "Well?"

"He said to watch him tonight. If he develops any chest pain, pain down the arm, inability to put sentences together, we should give him an aspirin and bring him in right away."

"How will we know if Abe doesn't tell us?"

"I'll go check on him in a little while and see if I can get him to answer some questions. Other than that, the doc seems to think he's got a virus of some kind, and he's just not as resilient as he used to be. Illness is bound to affect him more at this age than it used to."

Julianna leaned against the fridge, relief seeping into her. She hadn't realized until now how worried she was about Abe.

As if he knew what she was feeling, Luke reached out and touched her arm. "He said there's no need to panic."

Something fluttered inside. She felt warm. No, she felt hot. "I'm glad," she said, her voice sounding low and froggy. "I—I don't know what I'd do if something happened to—"

Luke pulled her close, cradling her in his arms as if it were the most natural thing in the world to do. "He's okay. Don't worry." He lifted her chin with two fingers and stared directly into her eyes.

She thought his mouth moved closer, or maybe hers did. She felt he might kiss her and her heart raced as if she'd just run a marathon. He could probably feel it thudding against her chest. Suddenly she couldn't breathe, and pushed away.

"Thanks. I guess I do overreact a little."

His smile seemed guarded. Either he didn't like that she'd pushed him away or he didn't like that he'd held her in the first place. God, why was she second-guessing everything? What did it matter what he was thinking?

"I'll get those steaks on now," he said. "And why don't we eat on the patio. It's really a nice night."

She straightened. "Sure. I'd love to," she said. "I'll get the table settings."

Thankful to have something to do, she collected what they needed, a couple of straw place mats, plates, flatware and napkins. And the wine. Had to have the wine. She brought everything outside, to the area out back where the grill was located. It wasn't a fancy patio, but a big rectangle of adobe tiles, some chipped and worn, the outdoor fireplace in the corner, and the whole area covered by a crosshatched trellis with pink flowering vines growing over the top. The vines provided shade in the summertime and tonight, the twinkle lights left over from the previous Christmas made it utterly romantic.

A few potted cacti dotted the edges of the tile, plants Julianna had given Abe years ago because he couldn't kill them if he wanted. All were doing beautifully, as were the bright red bougainvillea that spilled over the adobe wall surrounding the patio. A hanging ristra and a rustic wooden table and chairs completed the decor. Her heart warmed just being here.

"What can I do to help?" she asked when she finished setting the table.

"Pour yourself some more wine and then sit down and talk to me. These will be done in a few minutes." He glanced over. "That's if you still like your steak medium-rare."

"I do," she said, feeling good that he remembered. She realized then that she'd hate it if they'd spent all those years together and he simply blotted everything from his mind. While she didn't dwell on the past, she did have some fond memories.

"Do you still hang out with Jordan and Rico and… who was that other guy? Oh, wait, don't tell me. I know. It's on the tip of my tongue."

Luke gave a hearty laugh. "You never could give anything up, could you."

"Tex. That's the guy. I only met him a couple of times."

"Yeah, they're all still there. Only the state of bachelorhood among them has been seriously challenged. Rico's married now and Jordan is about to take the plunge. Tex has been living with someone for a couple of years and I'll bet my paycheck that he's practicing marriage vows as we speak."

"Wow. That only leaves you, then, doesn't it?" She leaned a shoulder against the wall next to him and took a sip of wine. "Why did you never marry again?" She shouldn't have asked the question, but couldn't help herself.

His head came up. "You forget. I didn't do very well the first time, so—" He shrugged. "What's the point. I know what I need and what I don't."

His words stung, but she didn't know why.

"How about you?"

"I don't know. It just never happened."

"No steady or live-in friend?"

"Nope. Not now anyway. You?"

He shook his head. "Not for a long time."

"Wow, we're really a pair, aren't we?" she joked. But joking aside, she had to wonder. "Think there's something intrinsically wrong with us that we can't commit?"

Another hearty laugh. "Speak for yourself. My psyche is just fine. In fact it's taken years to hone my inner self to this state of perfection."

She pretended to choke. "Excuse me, I think I'm going to be sick."

"No hurling until after dinner," he said. "And right now I need plates."

She stood, handed him one plate and then the other. Leaning toward the grill, she inhaled the meaty scent. "Mmmm. The steaks smell wonderful."

His brows rose a tad, as if he'd just thought of something. "You do still eat steak, don't you?"

"Of course I do."

They sat down together. "Well, living in the same town as your mother, anything could've happened."

"True. She's always trying to get me to embrace the vegan life. With no luck, I might add. I'm still in search of the best hamburger in San Francisco. I haven't found anywhere as good as Bernie's." They'd spent a lot of time at Bernie's, with and without his buddies. Bernie's made the best hamburgers in L.A.

Luke raised his drink and she followed suit. The crisp ping of her glass touching his metal can seemed somehow symbolic. Glass was delicate, easy to break if you weren't careful. Metal was tough, resilient. And all the small talk wasn't going to stop the current of emotions that coursed between them.

As his eyes met hers, he leaned forward,

his face close—close enough for her to feel the warmth of his breath against her face. Her heartbeat quickened. Her palms started to sweat. Lord help her, she wanted to kiss him. Worse yet, she knew he knew exactly what she was thinking.

"Uh…we better eat or the steaks will get cold," she whispered.

As the words left her lips, his mouth met hers.

CHAPTER SEVEN

KISSING JULIANNA FELT as natural as breathing and it was a struggle for Luke to pull himself away. Especially as she leaned into the kiss, her lips warm and soft and willing. With their faces only inches apart, he said, "Bad move, huh."

His hands still on her shoulders, he said, "I'd say I don't know why I did that, but it would be a lie. I've wanted to since the day I got here."

"But you didn't." Her tongue darted over her lips.

"I don't always do everything I want to do. If I did I'd be in big trouble."

"Well, now that you've got it over with, you don't have to think about it any longer." She moved from under his touch.

He laughed. "True. I'm sorry, though."

"It's okay. I wondered what it would be like, too."

The admissions seemed to make them both

self-conscious. After another moment of silence, he said, "Let's call it a curiosity kiss and leave it at that."

"Deal," she said. "Now let's eat this steak."

By the time they finished the meal, they'd talked about the past five years: his career, though he didn't tell her the worst of it, her career, their mutual friends… they'd talked about everything. Everything but…Michael. The heartbreak of their lives.

Like a two-ton elephant in the room, they chose to ignore that part of their life altogether. Because they both knew the reality of their loss. It wasn't something that could be fixed.

"So," he finally said. "I think I'll go do a quick check on Pops."

Pensive, she nodded.

He placed his hand over hers, but the words he wanted to say wouldn't come out.

"Go ahead," she said. "I'll clean up here. Then I've got some work to do."

With that, he stood and walked down the hall, want and need nipping at his heels, regret replacing the emptiness he felt inside.

Abe's room was dimly lit by a small night-light glowing in the bathroom. He wondered if Abe had put it there so he wouldn't stumble when he got up at night.

Not wanting to wake his father, he lightly touched Abe's forehead with his fingertips. He seemed hot. His breathing was shallow. If he had the flu, he would have a fever. Unsure what to do, Luke went back to the kitchen where Julianna was just finishing up. "He's hot," Luke said, "and his breathing is labored."

She handed him the phone and the paper with the doctor's number on it. "Thanks," he said and punched in the number. He got the answering service again and left another message.

"Do you think he's had a flu shot?" Julianna asked.

Luke shrugged. "I doubt it." And they both knew the ramifications of that. Many seniors died every year from the flu, even some who'd been immunized. "We don't know if he has the flu either. Maybe it's something else."

"Perhaps we should take him to the clinic, just to be sure?"

"Yeah. But let's wait to hear what the doc has to say first." They stood there for another awkward moment before Luke said, "Why don't you go do whatever you need to do. I'll wait here for the doctor to call back."

"Okay," she said reluctantly, as if she knew he was trying to get rid of her.

And he was. He needed to be alone. He hadn't thought about his father dying. Ever. Somehow it played into his own feelings of mortality. A subject he avoided like he avoided going to church. His job made denial necessary, because any second of any day could be his last.

The phone rang. It was Doctor Terry who asked a bunch of questions, then told Luke to bring Abe into his office in the morning. "What about now?" Luke asked. "I'd feel better bringing him to the clinic now."

"There's only a nurse on call tonight and I can't get there until tomorrow."

Luke tightened his grip on the phone. Something told him they couldn't wait until morning. "Is there someplace else I can take him?"

"Saint Vincent's Hospital in Santa Fe," the physician said. "If you're going to do that, I'll call ahead so they'll be expecting you."

Luke thanked the man and hung up. He didn't know why this felt so urgent, but it just did. Getting Abe to agree to go along wasn't as difficult as Luke had expected. That's when he knew his father was really sick.

An hour and a half later Luke and Julianna

sat in the sterile white hallway waiting for Dr. Martinez to tell them what was wrong with Abe. Luke was reminded of another sterile, white room. The memory made his heart ache. He studied Jules, who sat quietly next to him reading a magazine. This had to be affecting her as well. But she seemed to have nerves of steel. A total switch from the woman he'd known five years ago.

"Mr. Coltrane." Dr. Martinez came over to sit in the chair next to Luke. "Your father should have some more tests but it looks like pneumonia, and his emphysema exacerbates the problem, making treatment more difficult."

"Emphysema?" Luke looked at Julianna who shrugged. Apparently she wasn't aware of it either. But it made sense. Abe had been smoking since he was fifteen.

The physician gazed sympathetically at Luke, as if apologizing that Abe hadn't told his own son what was wrong with him.

"He didn't tell you."

"I—I don't get home much," Luke said.

"Well, he needs to be hospitalized to clear up the virus, and I also recommend that he stay a few days extra for observation and tests."

Luke shot from his chair, clenched and unclenched his fists at his sides as he paced the confined area. "I can't believe he didn't tell me he had emphysema."

"I'm not surprised," Julianna said. "He's a proud man."

"Well, that won't help him one bit if he's a proud dead man."

The physician stood. The skin sagged beneath his eyes and Luke remembered the man had been ready to go home but had stayed to see his father.

"Emphysema gets worse, doesn't it?" said Luke.

"True, but slowly. Depending on the outcome of the tests, he may have to use oxygen at some point, but with treatment, I'm sure he'll be fine for a while. He's a strong man."

Luke felt relief seep through him. "That he is."

Dr. Martinez said, "I suggest you go home and call him tomorrow. I've already talked to him about the tests and further evaluation, and he's sleeping now. Don't plan on taking him home for a few days."

Before Luke and Julianna left the hospital, he peeked in on Abe and despite the oxygen tubes in his nose, he did seem to be sleeping peacefully.

"I'm so glad we took him in tonight," Julianna said on the ride home. "That was a good call on your part."

He looked at her. "I still can't believe he never said a word about being sick."

She arched one eyebrow. "Really. I think it's typical Abe."

"Yeah." He hit the steering wheel with the butt of his hand. "But this is serious. People die from emphysema."

After that they were silent, the only sound the hum of the tires against the asphalt. The night was cool and the stars shone brightly above them. As he drove, Luke thought about Abe and how he'd been going through all this health stuff alone.

His father had told Jules Luke stayed away because when he was a kid, he couldn't accept authority and that somehow soured everything. Only that wasn't the half of it. And dammit, his father knew that.

The past few years had separated them even more because Luke had been too stuck in his own quagmire to pay attention to anyone else.

Yeah, they had issues all right. But if his father had died leaving things as they were, Luke would never have forgiven himself. He made a silent vow to change things when his dad came home.

"You missed the turnoff, Luke."

He screeched to a stop. It was late, there were no highway lights and theirs was the only vehicle on the lonely back road. If it weren't for the headlights, all they'd see was an inky blackness. "Yeah, I did." He turned the car around and sought out the road where he should've turned.

"I'm sorry about Abe," Julianna said, her voice choking a little. "I was really frightened."

Luke realized he'd been thoughtless. Jules loved his father and must be just as worried as he was. Probably more. He reached to place his hand over hers. "I know. I apologize for being so self-absorbed."

"He's your father, Luke. Your concern *should* be for him, not me."

Yeah, just like the concern he'd had for Michael. Only he'd failed in his quest to find his son. Pain stabbed in his chest. Taking in some air, he forced his own torment away and squeezed her hand. He wanted to say thanks for being so understanding, but couldn't get out the words.

After another long silent stretch, he said, "I'm sorry…."

She looked over at him, questions in her eyes.

"I'm sorry for being such a...bad husband... for being gone all the time—"

"Don't, Luke. Don't say any more. Please."

Yeah. The time for apologies was years ago. He couldn't blame her for not wanting to listen to them now.

THE HOUSE SEEMED EMPTY without Abe, and though it was late, Julianna couldn't sleep. She got out of bed, threw on a baggy sweatshirt over her pajamas and went to the kitchen. The nearly full moon shining its buttery light through the high windows made it easy to navigate and, with the added light from the fridge, she poured herself a glass of wine left over from dinner. She headed for the back door, hoping the crisp fall air might help her think more clearly.

It was obvious she was going to have to make some decisions. Staying here with Luke had her doubting herself. She'd worked too long to learn how to trust her own instincts and she wasn't going to throw it all away because she had feelings for Luke. Yes, she admitted it. But those feelings didn't mean squat in the whole scheme of things.

Luke's personality was so strong, he could overpower a weaker person in ways he didn't even realize. Like he'd overpowered her. During therapy, she'd realized that regardless of what had happened to Michael, their marriage had been doomed from the beginning. It's why she'd left. So what was the problem? Why did she keep thinking of him, wondering if—

Dammit. She was not going there again. Though Luke had said he wasn't staying, things had changed drastically and it was obvious he wasn't going to leave anytime soon. Certainly not by tomorrow.

Despite all that, she felt a sense of satisfaction in proving her point that she was safe here. With her hand on the knob, she saw a shadow of movement through the curtain on the door. She gasped and jerked back. Muscles taut, senses on high alert, she gulped some air and inched toward the window again. Probably an animal. God knew there were enough of them out here.

Taking it extra slow, she slid the curtain aside. A man's face appeared on the other side of the glass. She lurched back, stumbling over her feet before realizing it was only Luke. Oh, God, it was only Luke.

The door burst open. "What are you doing?"

She tried to breathe, but could only draw a few jagged breaths. She didn't know whether to be relieved or mad as hell. In short spurts, she said, "You…scared…the bejeebies out of me." Okay. Angry it was.

His expression went blank. "I didn't know you were here. You should've turned on some lights."

She closed her eyes in an effort to calm herself. "I couldn't sleep. I was going to have a glass of wine, hoping it would help."

He held up a glass of milk. "Great minds think alike."

"What were you doing outside?"

"Looking at the stars." He grinned. "Wondering how in the world things got so screwed up with my dad."

Yes, she wondered too, only she didn't mean with Abe.

"You need an ear?" she offered, though she knew he'd say no. Why would he want to talk to her now when he hadn't during most of their marriage?

"Sure," he said. "Let's sit outside." He opened the door and gestured for her to go first.

Surprised that he'd actually agreed, she hesitated, noticing he wore pajama bottoms and a navy sweatshirt.

He plucked a black leather jacket from the closet near the door and dumped it on her shoulders.

She went ahead, but something told her this wasn't a good idea.

"Steps or rockers," he asked.

"Rockers," she answered as she walked over to the two wooden chairs at the opposite end of the patio. Rockers were safer. There'd be some distance between them.

Sitting in the chairs, they rocked together, the curved runners making a rhythmic clacking sound against the adobe-tiled floor.

"Just like a couple of old people," Luke said.

"Speak for yourself, Methuselah."

"I remember when my dad made these chairs and how my mother loved them. They'd sit out here every night in good weather."

"That's a lovely memory."

"Yeah. One would think."

Frowning, Julianna stopped rocking and looked at him. "So, even though you said before that your mom and dad had problems, they were happy together."

He closed his eyes and kept rocking. "I

guess there were good times and bad, like any marriage. Anyway, I was thirteen when she died and maybe what a kid thinks isn't always the way it is."

"I know what you mean. I always had this fantasy image of what my father was like, what my parents were like together. Then when I was about ten, I learned he'd deserted us without a thought and my fantasy took a nosedive. It took me the longest time to come to grips with that whole thing. Sometimes I wonder if I ever really did." She glanced at him. "But I've told you all this before, haven't I."

She'd bared her soul to the man she'd loved—and he'd returned next to nothing.

"You did. That whole thing sucks."

She moistened her lips.

He turned to gaze at her and his blue eyes looked like moonstones against the dark of the night.

"A child should be able to keep a few fantasies."

She sighed. "It would be nice, wouldn't it. But things never seem to work out that way." Before they'd married she'd had a fantasy or two about what their life would be like, but she'd learned a lot since then. "Fantasies are simply a way for people to delude themselves, to pretend life can be what they want it to be."

Luke felt the bite of her words. He'd promised her everlasting love, and dammit, he'd never wavered from that promise. She was the one who'd left…the one who'd torn their marriage apart. And he still didn't know why. Not the real reason. "Things work out one way or another, depending on the choices we make."

"And when there is no choice? What then?"

He didn't want to get into this. He really didn't. But he couldn't keep from saying, "People always have choices."

"Yes, I suppose. Even if they're bad ones."

"So, then we adjust."

She looked into his eyes. "Sometimes that's impossible."

"Well, I see things differently. If you want something you go for it."

"Sometimes what we want isn't what's best for us."

Now she was talking in riddles. He hated when she did that. He stood, walked to the edge of the patio and shoved his hands in his pocket. "Speaking of impossible," he said, "Dad will go ballistic if I tell him I hired someone. I'm not sure how to approach it."

"You hired someone?"

"Not yet. But I hope to tomorrow. I had to call the guy and tell him I couldn't make it today. I'm hoping he's still available when I see him."

"So what will you do if Abe refuses the help?"

Luke gave a futile shrug. "I'll cross that road when I get there."

"Maybe you could convince Abe that since you won't be here, he'll need a hand while he recovers. If he thinks it's temporary, then he might be more accepting."

"And then, after a while, he'll realize he really does need help and may ask the guy to stay on."

She nodded. "Exactly."

Luke had to laugh. "You learn those devious methods in San Francisco?"

She grinned. "I'm a journalist. You learn to be creative. I think this is one of those times."

"Maybe so." She'd been right about several things. But one thing still bothered him. The threats she'd received. He felt an ominous dread about it. Like the ominous dread he'd felt one horrible night five years ago.

CHAPTER EIGHT

THE NEXT MORNING on the way to Santa Fe to see Abe, Luke pulled into a Circle K gas station. While he filled the tank, he scoped out the area, his senses on alert since hearing the calls Jules had received. Two cars were parked in front of the store, one black, one silver-gray.

Just then Jules got out of the car and came around to his side. "I'm going inside to get a coffee. Would you like one?"

"A giant Coke with no ice would be good."

She stuck her hands in the pockets of her low-rider jeans and laughed, a light teasing laugh. "Same old, same old."

He shrugged. "Gotta have my fix. And it's not as expensive as a Starbucks."

She turned and walked toward the store. And he kept watching, not just to keep an eye on her, but because he couldn't tear his gaze away from the quick swing of her arms, the subtle movement of her hips. He felt a primal urge. Looking at Julianna had always been a turn-on. The passage of time hadn't changed a thing.

When she reached the entrance, he was about to look away but just then a guy wearing a Stetson got out of the silver car and followed Jules inside.

Odd. Had the guy been sitting there…waiting? Luke dropped the nozzle and sprinted across the asphalt, his heart racing. Inside, he scanned the store for Jules. Where was she? And where was the guy in the cowboy hat?

He went down one aisle and the next until he reached the beverage section at the back of the store. He stopped. Jules stood with her back to him, talking to the man who'd followed her in. She turned when Luke walked up, surprise in her eyes.

"Luke? What's wrong?"

He grabbed her arm and herded her toward the door.

"What's going on?" she said, wrenching away. "Are you crazy?"

"Who was that guy and why were you talking to him?"

"He asked for directions, that's all. Sheesh! Stop acting like a cop all the time."

Luke gritted his teeth. "It's what I do," he said, throwing her earlier words back at her. But was she right? Was he overreacting? It was natural for him to be suspicious of everyone. If he wasn't it could cost a life—his or someone else's. "Just get your stuff. I'm ready to go."

As he returned to the pump, another vehicle chugged up into the next stall. A faded maroon Pontiac with steam rising from the hood. The driver got out and nodded at Luke.

"I think I'm overheating," the man said, pushing back his battered baseball cap.

"Looks that way," Luke answered as he watched the door for Jules to come back out. "Or maybe you have a leak in your water hose."

"Well, whatever it is, it's not good. I've got business to take care of."

Still agitated, Luke didn't respond. The guy wanted to chit-chat because that's what people did here. They had nothing better to do. Well, he wasn't going to get sucked into a conversation he didn't want to have. He had more important concerns—like keeping an eye on Jules who thought chatting with anyone who asked her a question was no big deal.

Finishing, he closed the gas cap. Julianna returned. "Here you go," she said handing him his drink. "Cola with no ice."

"Perfect."

On the road again, Luke turned on the radio and found a country station. Jules gave him a skeptical gaze.

"What?" he asked. "You don't like country?"

"I've never tried. I didn't know you liked it either."

He shrugged. "I didn't until I won some free tickets to an Alan Jackson concert."

"Uh-huh. Did you stay for the whole thing?"

Zing. She was good at that. "I did. Not one call out," he said. "That only happened when I was with you."

"Well, I'm glad I was so special." She smiled. "What is it that you like about the music?"

"Honest lyrics straight from the heart. It's music that tells a story."

"You mean like 'My girlfriend dumped me when I crashed my pickup and now I'm so lonely I could cry'."

He laughed. "Hey, it happens."

"I did like that girl Carrie on American Idol. She sang country."

Now it was his turn to be skeptical. "You watch reality shows?"

She shrugged, grinning. "My dirty little secret."

"I listen to country and you watch reality shows. So much for thinking we're the same people we were five years ago."

"Thank God," she said.

He didn't know if she was referring to him or herself, but it was a can of worms he wasn't going to open. He drove on—silently—until he felt her watching him.

"What?"

"Well, now I'm wondering what else has changed."

He waggled his eyebrows and gave a lecherous grin. "Some things never change."

"Oh," she said dryly, "I figured that out already."

"Me, too." He kept his eyes pinned to the road. "But don't worry. I've learned self-control."

That brought another long silence.

Finally she said, "I'm curious. Do you think I've changed?"

He glanced at her. "Some."

"In what way?"

Luke tightened his grip on the wheel, unwilling to give voice to what he really felt. *Keep it light, Luke. Just keep it light.* "Well, some things are still the same. You're still in great shape."

She turned, touching the collar of her shirt. "You think so?"

"Uh-huh. And you still answer a question with a question."

She grinned.

"You still have a weird sense of humor and your laugh is the same."

All traits he admired. Traits that had drawn him to her from the first day they'd met. He scratched his chin. "As to what's different, you used to wear your hair pulled back most of the time." He fixed his eyes on the road, only glancing over once in a while. "And the lipstick. I don't remember you wearing any kind of makeup before."

He wondered if he should say more. Could be risky. But what the hell. "You seem more at ease, more self-assured." He smiled. "I like that. It's…sexy."

She tagged him on the arm. "Damn. It's always about sex with you."

He turned to glance at her. "I seem to remember I wasn't alone in that thinking. In fact—"

She averted her gaze. "That was a long time ago."

"True." He had to remember that. "Yeah, five years can make a big difference in a person's life."

"True. But *you* don't seem all that different."

If you didn't count the years he'd spent trying to forget how she'd ditched him when he needed her most. For him, it'd been four years of hell and another year of clawing his way out of the inferno. "Same old, same old. That's me. Same job…same friends."

"Well, I have noticed one thing that's different about you. You seem more concerned about your dad than before."

A skunk darted across the road in front of them. Luke pulled the wheel to the left, swerving out of the way. "For all the good it'll do me." He sighed. "I came here with an idea that maybe we could clear the slate and attempt a normal father-son relationship, but I know now that isn't going to happen. Whenever we're together—it doesn't matter what we're talking about—I feel this undercurrent of disapproval."

"But you're trying to change things. I think that's admirable."

"No, it's not. It's selfish, something I need to do for me."

He gave a wry laugh. "Well, I know now

it doesn't matter. You can't change people and you can't change the past."

"Don't I know it," she said, her voice so low he barely heard her. The pretty smile had switched to a frown. She pinched the bridge of her nose with her thumb and forefinger, as if she might be getting a headache.

Damn. He'd probably stuck his foot in his mouth again.

Reaching the hospital, he cranked the steering wheel, swung into the parking lot and into a visitor's space. "Come on. This can't take too long because I've got to interview that guy at eleven."

"GET ME OUT of here," Abe demanded the instant Julianna and Luke entered the room. Nothing they hadn't expected.

Julianna saw Luke's jaws clench. She elbowed him in the ribs, urging him to say something. Something nice, she hoped.

"We've got to talk to your physician first. In fact, I'm going to see if I can track down Dr. Martinez right now." Luke turned and left the room.

Abe still had the oxygen tube in his nose, but seemed feistier than the day before. He also had an IV in his arm.

"What's that for," Julianna asked.

"They say I'm dehydrated, but I think they're pumping me with drugs."

She raised a brow, then sat in the chair next to Abe's bed. "But you're looking better, Pops."

He placed a hand over hers. "You and Luke getting along?"

"We're doing fine," she answered. "We're adults. We can be civilized for a little while."

"That's not what I meant."

"Oh." She realized Abe had some misguided notion that she and Luke should still be married. It had taken him a long time to accept their divorce, and when he finally did, he blamed Luke. She'd tried to explain it was no one's fault, but that wasn't Abe's mindset. If something happened, someone had to take the rap for it.

Just then Luke came back in with Dr. Martinez.

"Good morning, Abraham," the doctor said.

"When do I get to go home?"

The silver-haired man walked over to the bed and picked up the chart. "Nothing's changed since last night. As I said then, I want you to stay for a few days until we get the infection under control."

The physician took Abe's pulse. "You can go home when we're sure you're one hundred percent."

The older man grumbled something about the food being terrible, the beds being hard, and that there was nothing good on television. By the time Julianna and Luke left, they weren't sure he wouldn't bust out of the place.

"He's so…ornery," Julianna said on their way down the hall.

"So, what's new?" Luke opened the door for her to go out. "We've still got some time before I have to be back for the interview. Want to have coffee in the plaza?"

The plaza. It had been one of their favorite places when they came to visit Abe at the ranch. She didn't want to see it, but maybe she should. Her therapist had said she needed to face the past before she could go on. She'd disagreed and thought she'd done just fine. So what was holding her back? "Sure. I haven't been there for years," she said.

It wasn't far from the hospital to the old plaza square in downtown Santa Fe. The air was crisp and the sun was shining, a perfect fall day. They parked on a side street and walked into the courtyard lined on three sides with tiny boutiques and upscale art galleries.

More galleries and trendy restaurants filled the narrow streets that jutted from the plaza, the heart of Sante Fe.

Local artisans were setting up shop on their blankets and tables under the Palace of the Governors' portico, a building that dated back to missionary days. Displays of turquoise-and-silver jewelry, Navajo pottery and handwoven blankets and baskets were laid out on sidewalks on both sides of the portal, leaving space for customers to walk down the middle.

Some people said the displays of jewelry weren't really the Native American handcrafts they purported to be, that most were just knockoffs imported from China or Malaysia. Having grown up in the area, Luke was pretty astute when it came to knowing the difference.

As they strolled past, a bracelet caught Julianna's eye, and even she was pretty sure it was the real thing. She stopped to look at it, but Luke kept walking. As she gazed through the crowd to see how far ahead Luke was, she had the eeriest feeling that someone was watching her.

She gave a furtive glance around. No one was even looking at her, except for one woman urging her to examine her crafts.

Luke was ten feet in front, obviously more interested in getting coffee than checking out the displays. She turned back to the bracelet again, then saw a man standing near another vendor quickly avert his gaze. It struck her that she recognized him. But that was silly. She'd been to Santa Fe only a half dozen times and all of them more than five years ago. She didn't know anyone in the city.

Still, the edgy feeling persisted. She hurried to catch up with Luke then touched his arm to get his attention. He slowed his pace. "Don't look now, but there's a man back there who I think is watching me." Luke stopped at a blanket at the end of the walkway, bent down to look at some belt buckles. She bent down, too, and whispered, "Black hat, black outfit, silver belt."

He cast a surreptitious glance back.

When she looked herself, the man was gone.

"You sure," Luke said.

Feeling stupid and a little paranoid, she shrugged it off. "Must've been my imagination. My brain has been working overtime lately."

His eyes widened…as if he'd never expected her to admit she'd had any misgivings about her situation.

"Any other defining features?" Luke scanned the area, his gaze like a camera on motordrive, clicking off images to file away.

"He was tall. Six feet, maybe. His face was shadowed by his hat, but something about him seemed familiar." She shrugged. "I don't know anyone in New Mexico except Abe, so…so, it's probably nothing."

He took her arm and led her down the street toward Zele's coffee shop. "Basic instincts are usually right. When your gut tells you something, you need to listen. Especially now."

Maybe. But she felt a little foolish, and she'd flat-out admitted she wasn't as blasé about her would-be stalker as she'd like to think. "Right now my gut is growling from hunger. Do we have time for breakfast with that coffee?"

The restaurant was less than half full, a hangout for locals, apparently. Julianna could always tell the locals from the tourists by the way they dressed. Tourists favored Native American knock-offs.

"Table for two," Luke said. "Preferably by the window."

When they were seated, Luke sat facing the door where he could see everything, a habit she'd gotten used to long ago. The fragrant scent of sopaipillas filled the air. Her salivary glands kicked into action just thinking about filling one of the fried pastries with warm honey and gobbling it down, but her sensible side won out. Too many calories.

After they ordered, huevos rancheros for him and a chili pepper omelet for her, Julianna said, "It really isn't necessary for you to stay, you know." She peered at him over the rim of her cup. "I mean, I know you need to get back to L.A. and I can do whatever is necessary for Abe."

He kept looking around. "Stop trying to get rid of me. I'm staying until Abe is out of the hospital. After that, we'll see."

Good Lord, that could be days, a week even. Could she handle that much time with Luke?

After that, she had nothing more to say and after breakfast they were soon back on the road, arriving home ten minutes before Luke had to leave for the interview. As they drove up to the house, she saw Stella Hancock's truck parked in front.

Luke cursed. What did she want now? And why was she so damned persistent? As far as Luke knew, Abe had made it clear he didn't want anything to do with her, and considering how she'd torn their lives apart before his mother died, he didn't want anything to do with her either.

Luke and Julianna climbed from his car. He opened the rustic wood doors to the front entry and found the woman sitting in the shade of the ruby-colored bougainvilleas that tumbled over the adobe wall. "Can I help you with something," Luke asked, striding toward the front door.

She stood and Luke noticed her eyes were a bit red, as if she might've been crying.

"I had this…feeling that something awful had happened to Abraham and I couldn't get it out of my head. Is he okay?"

Her pewter-gray hair was pulled back at the nape and she wore flared pants, boots and lots of turquoise and silver on her hands. For a second he wondered if all the rumors were true, that she had some kind of sixth sense. She was part-Navajo, an *alni* he'd heard, one who walked the line between traditionalist and modern culture. There were rumors that she came from a long line of healers.

Luke had his own views on the tradition of Native Americans on the res using their own healers to treat their tribes' illnesses. To him it was like practicing medicine without a license, and the result could be fatal for someone who needed immediate care. Like his mother. His father knew the dangers and yet he'd done it anyway. This woman was as much to blame as Abe.

Jules spoke up. "Abe is in the hospital. He has pneumonia and will be there for a few days. But the doctor says he'll be fine."

The lines in the woman's face softened. "Oh, that's why he was having trouble breathing."

Luke exchanged glances with Julianna. How did *she* know that?

"I thought it might be due to his smoking."

This was getting more weird all the time. The most logical explanation was that Mrs. Hancock had called the hospital to find out about Abe. Even though they weren't supposed to give information to nonrelatives, she might've sweet-talked one of the nurses into telling her. But how would she have known he was even there?

Hell, he didn't have time to stand out here jawing. He had only a few minutes to get to Pecos to meet the guy he was going to interview for the job.

Having his father hospitalized had made Luke more aware that it was important to find someone good, someone who could do more than just help with ranch chores. If Abe was alone and got sick, or injured himself in some way…it could be disastrous. The solution was obvious. Abe's hired hand would need to live at the ranch.

"I've got to go," Luke said to Julianna.

"Sure. Good luck."

STELLA HANCOCK STUDIED Julianna, hoping to get some positive feelings from her. She'd had a disturbing vision about the young lady, but she'd learned long ago that disclosing her special gift to non-natives usually made them think she was a witch who practiced voodoo or something.

She'd had a similar vision about Abe and had felt such an urgency, she'd been compelled to come over.

"Would you like some tea?" Julianna asked.

Stella smiled. "I'd love some. Thank you."

"Come with me," Julianna said. "Since it's so nice out, we can sit on the patio if you like."

They went inside, and walking through the darkened rooms with their thick walls and small windows, Stella felt a lump form in her throat. Everything seemed just as it had been so many years ago when she and Lizzie had been close—as close as sisters.

When they reached the kitchen, Julianna said, "Go on out to the patio. I'll bring the tea."

Stella went outside, forcing herself to stay focused. She was here to find out about Abe. Not to visit old memories that should have faded long ago—like the dried bouquet of flowers her lover had once given her.

She found a chair with cushions that were of the same Kokopelli design that seemed to adorn so many New Mexico homes. A few seconds later, Julianna appeared with a tray holding a teapot and two cups.

"Is it warm enough out here?" Julianna asked as she set down the tray. "I can start a fire."

"It's lovely. And I'm quite used to the out-doors."

"I can see why. I live where it's damp all the time and I love the arid climate here."

"Where do you live?" Stella asked, hoping the answer might give her some insight about the disturbing image she'd had about the young woman sitting next to her.

Julianna hesitated. "Uh…California."

"So," Julianna said. "How did you know Abe wasn't well?"

She poured two cups of tea and handed one to Stella. "It was a feeling I had. A strong feeling." She reached for the cup offered her.

Julianna nodded, as if she might understand.

"I learned a long time ago not to ignore my strong feelings, even if they turned out to be wrong."

"Uh-huh," Julianna said, pensive, as if deciding whether she should buy into what Stella was saying or not.

After all these years, Stella was used to that kind of response and paid no mind to it. "I'm happy to hear Abraham is going to be okay."

After another thoughtful moment, the younger woman looked directly at Stella and asked, "Why haven't you and Abe talked for twenty-five years?"

Stella suppressed a smile. She liked the girl's forthrightness. "Our families had a falling out," she answered. It wasn't a total lie, but she saw no reason to tell a stranger the whole story.

"So you were friends once?"

"A long time ago."

"You and your husband?"

Surprised that Julianna continued asking questions, she said, "Abraham and I went to school together. We were…good friends at one time. Lizzie and I were, too."

Julianna's eyes widened. "Really. You knew Luke's mother? I'd love to know more about your friendship with her."

She hesitated. "I'd rather not talk about it, if you don't mind."

The look on Julianna's face was priceless. She obviously hadn't expected a refusal. Few people could resist talking about themselves, but she wasn't one of them.

"Oh, I'm sorry if I seemed to be prying. I'm a journalist and asking questions is what I do. And in this case, whenever I ask Luke or Abe about…Elizabeth, I get nothing. It's as if talking about her would hurt too much."

Stella took another sip of tea. "I can understand that. I don't think either one has ever been able to deal with the fact that Lizzie's death was inevitable—that it was her time, and they couldn't do anything to help her."

As she said the words, Stella noticed the younger woman's face pale. She reached for her hand. "We can't always help those we love, no matter how much we want to. Some things are out of our hands."

When Julianna didn't reply, Stella said, "I suppose I better leave now. I'm sorry if I said anything to upset you."

Julianna squared her shoulders. "Uh—no.

You didn't. I appreciate you coming by to check on Abe. Even if—"

"It's okay," Stella said quickly. "I know how they feel, and it's okay." She cleared her throat and stood to go. But before she left, she said, "Please be careful while you're here."

THE GUY WAS LATE. Luke ordered a cola and decided to give him ten more minutes, hoping he had a legitimate excuse. He had no other leads on a hired hand for his dad, but he wasn't going to hire a slacker either.

When the guy didn't show, Luke paid the waitress and got up to leave. As he walked to his car, his cell rang. He fished it from the pocket of his leather jacket and glanced at the number. Not one he recognized. "Coltrane," he said.

Nothing. "This is Luke." Then a crackling sound and the dial tone. Dammit. He hit a couple of buttons. No call back number, but his phone was working fine. Maybe the call was cut off on the other end. Maybe it was the guy saying he'd be late. Or maybe it was Jules. He punched in his dad's number.

No answer. An awful awareness came over him. He'd left when the Hancock woman was there, not thinking that Jules would be on her own when she went home. Fear sent a spurt of adrenaline into his veins. Someone could've drawn him away under the guise of an interview to get at Jules.

He got into the car, caught his jacket on the corner of the door as he sat, then yanked it off and heard a rip. He slammed the accelerator to the floor and hauled ass down the highway, his heart hammering triple time. If something happened to Jules—dammit! How could he be so stupid as to leave her alone.

All he'd wanted to do was get away from Stella Hancock. He'd reacted on emotion. He never did that. For once in his life, he hoped the neighbor hadn't left and they were simply talking and hadn't heard the phone. Or maybe Jules was in the bathroom.

But whatever scenario he came up with didn't ease his mind and when he barreled up the road to the house, dust and dirt spiraling behind him, his heart felt as if it would burst from his chest.

He'd barely set foot from his vehicle before Jules met him outside. "Back so soon?" she asked. "Did you hire him?"

His stomach did a belly flop, but he sucked

in some air and tried for nonchalant. "No. He didn't show." His words came out sharper than he wanted.

"Really? You think something happened?"

She hurried alongside as he stormed toward the house.

"It doesn't matter if something happened. He showed his character by not bothering to call." Irresponsible people annoyed the hell out of him.

"Is something else wrong?"

"No—" he tried to soften his voice "—nothing else is wrong." Except that he'd been rookie stupid and if something had happened to her… He slammed open the door.

"Do you have some other leads on someone to hire?"

"I put the word out with some local people, and I hung a notice at the Circle K. And there's the ad in the paper. We'll see what comes up."

As they walked inside together, Luke half expected Abe to greet them, then realized he wasn't there. They were alone. "I need something cold to drink. How about you?"

"I made some lemonade."

"Fine."

Luke watched Julianna as she went to the

fridge and then poured two glasses of lemonade. He liked to watch her. She moved with an easy grace that he found sexy as hell.

But what he thought one way or the other didn't matter. How he felt about her didn't matter. He couldn't let any of it matter. "I'd like to see those e-mail messages again."

"Why? You know what they say."

"Yeah, but I had some ideas. I thought of a way to find out where they came from."

"I tried that already. The messages are scrambled somehow. I even asked a friend who's a computer geek and he said to forget it."

"I know an expert."

"Someone here?"

He shook his head. "No, Rico. Remember?"

"But he's in Los Angeles."

"Go ahead. Pull them up. Then I'll call him and see if he can help us do a search."

Luke followed Jules into her bedroom. The laptop was on the unmade bed, and as she sat and turned on the machine to pull up her e-mail, he stood opposite her, staying his distance. He couldn't guarantee what might happen if he didn't. Just being close to her made him aware of how good they'd once been together.

He watched as she clicked on the keys,

then used the mouse. The soft light from the screen illuminated her pale, beautiful face, but hid the intensity she carried inside. He knew what she was thinking, her brain ticking off the moments until he left. And that only made her more desirable. Why the hell did he always want what he couldn't have?

He sat on the end of the mattress, still keeping his distance. Her unique scent rose from the bedding like an aphrodisiac, like opium, sucking him in. He wanted to pull her down between the sheets with him, bury his head in her silky hair...bury himself inside...

"Oh, God," she whispered. Her face went white.

He jumped up and came around behind her. "What?"

She didn't speak and simply waved at the computer.

He looked down to see a new message on the screen. *"I know where you are."*

CHAPTER NINE

"Yeah," a sleepy voice answered when Luke made the call to Rico.

"Sorry to wake you, buddy, but I need your help."

"Luke? Where are you?"

"I'm still in New Mexico. I've got a favor to ask. A couple favors as a matter of fact."

"Shoot."

Luke could always count on Rico and Jordan, LAPD's finest detectives and the best friends anyone could have. No matter where, when or how difficult the task might be, they were there. "I need your computer expertise. I have some e-mail messages and I need to find out where they came from."

"You have a computer with you?"

He cleared his throat. "It's not mine. But I need to track the messages to find out who sent them."

"Did you click on Reply?"

"Click on Reply," Luke directed Julianna.

"I did. The reply address is garbage."

"Doesn't work. What else?"

"Nothing that I can do from here. If I had the computer I might be able to figure it out. There's always a way."

Luke thought for a minute. "That's not possible. At least not right this minute." He shoved a hand through his hair, his frustration rising. "There has to be a way to do this."

"Sounds important," Rico said.

"Yeah. It is." Luke quickly explained the threatening e-mails, and that Jules's life might be in danger.

There was a long pause on the line before Rico asked, "Can you express mail it to me?"

"That's a thought. I can do it tomorrow morning."

"You said two things."

"Yeah."

"What's going on?" Rico sounded more awake now.

"Renata Willis. Seven years old. Abducted and murdered fifteen years ago."

"That's an old case. Really old."

Before either Luke or Rico worked in the RHD. "I understand there were no viable leads and the case went cold."

"You got a lead on it now?"

"Not exactly. I asked Jordan to pull the old file."

"You think the e-mail is connected to the case?"

"Maybe. Keep that in mind when you're working on it."

As Luke hung up, he contemplated what to do. "Rico thinks he can find out where the messages came from but he needs the computer."

Her eyes widened. "*I* need my computer. I can't finish my work without it."

"Would that be the worst thing in the world?"

When she didn't say anything, he knew the answer. "If you want to track down this guy, you'll have to do without your computer for a while."

"I have a deadline to meet."

"What's more important, a deadline or your life?"

"It's just an e-mail. It doesn't mean he really wants to hurt me and it doesn't mean he really knows where I am. He probably thinks I'm still in San Francisco. For all we know he's just a crank who gets his kicks scaring people."

"But we don't know any of that and we won't know until we find out who this creep is. We have to assume he means what he says. So, save your stuff on a CD and we'll get you another laptop."

Lines formed around her mouth, the way they always did when she dug in her feet over something. She closed the lid on the laptop.

Scrubbing a hand over his chin, Luke stood, paced, then stopped in front of her. "I have a better idea. Pack your things."

"What—"

"We're going to L.A."

"L.A.? But…what about your father?"

"I'll call the doc and find out how long he's going to be there. If we leave early in the morning, we'll be there in a couple hours and on a plane back by evening."

"I—I don't know."

"What don't you know? You do want to know who this sicko is, don't you?"

She nodded. "But if the police already refused to do anything, what good will going to L.A. do?"

"We'll take the laptop to Rico. Then I can check the Willis file myself."

"So, you go then. I'll stay here in case anything comes up with your father."

"I'm not leaving you here alone. Your only other options are to get another computer or to quit writing the story."

She gave him a look that could've wilted steel.

"That's what I thought. So, we'll leave first thing in the morning. You won't lose a minute of writing time."

She realized Luke fully believed whoever was threatening her meant business. Otherwise he'd leave her here and go to L.A. alone.

Feeling a chill, she rubbed her arms. She'd wondered more than once how serious the guy really was, but she always thought she was overreacting because of the past.

After losing Mikey, every noise, every look from a stranger had seemed threatening, every person she passed seemed sinister in some way, and she'd spent her days in a perpetual state of suspicion and fear.

She'd finally had to seek more grief counseling to help her crawl from the abyss of sorrow that almost destroyed her.

Now, a feeling of dread came over her. Was the threat as real as Luke thought it was? Or was she relapsing?

"You okay?"

She nodded. Rubbed her arms again.

"It's okay to be scared, you know. I'm scared every day when I go out on the streets."

Her head came up. His admission surprised her. "I—I didn't think it bothered me, but tonight it feels…eerie. We're so far away from everything."

He reached out, lifted the laptop off the bed and set it on the night table. Then he sat next to her and slipped an arm around her. "I'll stay here with you tonight."

It was a bad idea, but an offer she couldn't refuse. It wasn't like she'd never slept with him before, and tonight, she needed to feel the physical warmth of another human being. She needed to draw on his strength. To be close to someone who cared about her.

Despite their divorce, she believed he did care, if for no other reason than their history together. The fact that they'd had a child. She leaned into him, resting her head on his shoulder.

Still holding her, he leaned against the pillow, his face nestled in her hair. She felt him draw in a long, deep breath, then he stroked her head. "Go to sleep now," he whispered. "We've got a busy day tomorrow."

MORNING CAME too soon, and after a drive to Albuquerque and the short flight to Los Angeles, they were in a rental car speeding down the freeway to Rico Santini's house in Anaheim.

A wave of apprehension swept through Julianna. She'd last seen Rico not long before she and Luke had separated and it hadn't been pleasant. She felt embarrassed just thinking about it. She'd found Luke and his friends at Bernie's and she'd gone inside and stood there shrieking at them like a banshee, telling them that sitting around watching football wasn't going to help find her son. She'd said some horrible things, including that they were to blame for not finding Michael. She'd totally lost it.

Apparently Luke sensed her nervousness and took her hand. "It'll be fine," he said.

"The last time I saw Rico, I was so horrible to him… to all of you."

"Don't worry, guys get over things like that. They know you were emotionally stressed. I was, too."

She inhaled. "I don't know how you can handle what you do all the time. I'd be a wreck."

"That's why you're not a cop," he said,

trying to diffuse her nervousness. "Hey, come to think of it, I used to know a good remedy for stress."

Julianna couldn't help smiling. Whenever things got too bad, they'd wind up in bed. And he was right. It was the best stress-buster around.

But even good sex hadn't been able to save their marriage—or mend their broken hearts.

"Here we are," Luke said, pulling into the driveway of a small cottage that sat back from the tree-lined street. She'd been to Rico's home many times before and felt a twinge of nostalgia. Rico had always liked big barbecues and coming from a large Italian family, he knew how to cook and did it well. They'd had many memorable times at Rico's.

"I can't believe Rico, the quintessential playboy, is married now. It's so…unlikely."

"Yeah, I couldn't believe it either. They adopted a little boy that Macy had in her charge as a ward of the court and voilà, instant family. Billy's great, too."

She couldn't help but wonder if Billy reminded Luke of Mikey. If every time he saw a child that age, the pain swept back, again and again.

Luke smiled, then reached across her lap to open the car door on her side. "Life is full of surprises."

Julianna climbed out and hoisted the strap of her laptop case over her shoulder. "Do you think Rico can do it?"

"Rico's brain is a computer, so if anyone can do it, he can."

"Do you think it'll take very long?"

"No clue. But you know me and computers. Two left hands."

Rico opened the door almost as they reached it. "Yo, buddy," Rico said, doing one of those handshake hug things that guys do. "Hi, Julianna," he acknowledged and gave her a quick hug too. "Really great to see you again. Come in."

As they went inside, Julianna noticed the house seemed brighter, more homey than before.

"Macy's made a few decorating changes around here."

"It looks wonderful. She has a designer's touch."

"Where's Macy now?" Luke asked.

"She's at work and Billy's at school. I've got to leave shortly, too. Just had a call from the boss."

Julianna looked at Rico. "Do you have any idea how long this will take?"

Rico shrugged. "Could take an hour or a couple days. I won't know until I get into it."

"She's worried about a deadline on a story."

"No problem. Follow me." Rico led them down the hall to one of the bedrooms that he used as his office. Three computers were lined up across the oak desk that took up most of the room. "Here," Rico said, picking up a laptop from one of the bookshelves. "You can borrow this. I never use it."

"Oh, I couldn't—"

"Yes, you can. Take it with you. Really."

"Geez, Rico. What do you do with all these computers?" Luke looked befuddled, which wasn't a surprise. He had no clue why anyone needed a computer at all except at work to catch bad guys.

Rico shrugged. "One belongs to Macy."

"So, when will you be able to work on mine?" Julianna asked.

"Later tonight. I'll give you a call when I get back and let you know if I need any information."

"I'll be down later to take a look at the Willis case," Luke said.

"Where are you headed now?"

Luke avoided looking at Julianna when he said, "My place. You can get me there or on my cell."

When in the car and on the 405 toward Venice, Julianna was as silent as a stone, the tension in the air palpable. He knew she might be worried about going to the home they'd shared, a place where memories were embedded in every room, in every knick-knack and piece of furniture. "We have to go somewhere," he said. "We might as well be comfortable."

After that, he couldn't think of anything to say that might assuage her fears. He'd had his own misgivings about staying in the house after the divorce. It had been the place where they'd shared their dreams and fantasies—and the place where they'd lost Michael.

But for Luke, the house was comforting. They'd lived there as a family, and every day since then he felt Julianna and Michael's presence there. For him, that was a good thing. But if she hadn't felt the same, there was no point trying to explain. She'd been intent on leaving. Intent on putting him and their life together behind her.

"It's apparent we're not going to get out of

here until tomorrow, and it's the safest place I know. If someone is trying to find you, he's not going to look for you at your ex-husband's house. But…if you are uncomfortable with going there, we can check into a hotel."

When she looked at him, her eyes were dark and unreadable. "No, it's okay."

He wasn't convinced. But he didn't push it. They rode the rest of the way in silence, but then on the way past the beach, Julianna said, "Can we stop at the pier?"

Surprised, he said, "Sure." He made a sharp turn and pulled into the public lot. Even though it was fall, the tourists still loved coming here, many of them to gawk at the unusual, visit the funky shops and be entertained by the jugglers, dancers and musicians. It took a couple circles around to find a parking spot.

For Luke, the uniqueness of Venice Beach was what made it appealing. Jules used to feel the same way, and he hoped that was why she wanted to stop. When they got out of the car, she didn't say a word, but simply stood with her eyes closed, inhaling the salty sea air.

A cool breeze ruffled her hair, blowing it back from her face. "It's…revitalizing," she said, then started walking toward the sand.

Luke followed. "Do you want my jacket?"

"No, thanks. I need a jolt of fresh air."

They walked leisurely over the hard-packed sand, then she stopped at the water's edge and kneeled down to pick up something embedded there. "A sand dollar," she said, then looked up at him, wistfulness in her eyes. "I—I came here a lot with Michael so he could play on the beach."

"He loved the water." Luke had been teaching Mikey to use a boogie board and Jules had had a fit, thinking her little boy was going to get hurt or washed away.

"On the way here I didn't think I could do this. I thought all the reminders would make me fall apart."

"And now?"

She turned away, but not before he saw, her eyes well with tears. "I—I don't know. It's…almost like I can feel him here. Like the wind is Mikey, wrapping his arms around me."

Luke swallowed hard, put his arm around her and they slowly walked back to the car. No words were necessary. They both knew what they'd lost.

JULIANNA HAD BEEN nervous about going into the house, but her fears were quickly quelled when she stepped into the kitchen. Luke still had her photos, yellowed and curled as they were, pinned on the cork board.

She asked him to wait in the kitchen while she walked through the rest of the house. It was something she had to do. Alone. She had to dispel her demons right away, or she'd regret it. She knew that about herself as well as she knew her own heartbreak.

As she moved slowly from room to room, like ghosts the memories whispered from every corner. Upstairs, she stopped in front of their bedroom. Luke's room now.

The family photo was still on the dresser, the furniture arrangement was still the same, even the lace coverlet that she'd so desperately had to have was on the bed. And the horribly distorted afghan she'd made when she first learned to knit lay over the top of the rocker in the corner. She brought her hand to her mouth, her fragile emotions threatening to spill over.

Luke had kept everything as it was before she left.

Except for Mikey's room. Only that had been her doing. During one particular despairing rage, she'd gone on a rampage and cleared everything out of Mikey's room, giving away her only son's clothing and toys to the children at the shelter. It had seemed a good idea at the time, a way to purge the reminders.

But afterward, when it was too late, she'd regretted it like nothing she'd regretted since.

The only things she'd saved were some pictures, some shells Mikey had collected on the beach, and a jar full of colorful stones worn smooth by the water. Odd stuff, she realized now. Later, after her cleansing streak, looking at his empty room had been devastating. She couldn't believe what she'd done. By getting rid of everything, it felt as if Mikey had never existed. She wanted to take it all back. But she couldn't, and her despair grew even darker.

Luke had never said a word to her about what she'd done. She guessed he was battling his own demons. The irony was that she'd always heard families drew together to get through the bad times, that sometimes a crisis made them stronger.

But they'd failed the test. Neither of them had been able to help the other.

"So," Luke said when she came back into the kitchen. "You okay?"

Apparently he knew he had to let her work

this out on her own. "I'm fine. The place feels more like you than before."

"You mean it's messier."

She managed a tiny laugh. "Something like that."

"Are you hungry?"

They'd left so early this morning it felt as if it should be bedtime already, but it was only early afternoon and they hadn't had lunch and she was starving. "I'm famished."

He peered into the fridge. "Well, I didn't buy any groceries before I left for New Mexico, so maybe we better go out and get some fast food or something."

"Okay. Or I can look and see what you have that I can whomp up."

He looked surprised, then gestured toward the cabinets. "Be my guest. But I think all you'll find is that stuff to mix with hamburger."

She stuck a finger in her mouth in a gagging gesture. "Maybe you're right. But instead of going out, why don't we order takeout?" She pulled open the drawer where they'd always kept the restaurant menus, took a couple out and started to look them over. "What's on the agenda after we eat?" she asked absently.

"I need to go to the station to look at the Willis file."

She stopped reading. "You're really going to look into it?"

"As much as I can. But no guarantees. The case went cold for a reason."

"But it's important. Why don't you go ahead right now and grab a bite to eat along the way. I'll find something here and that way we'll save time and I can get some work done, too."

He shook his head, his expression puzzled. "Work doesn't always come first, you know."

She stood straighter. Taller. "Well, it always did before."

He winced, almost imperceptibly, but she saw it.

She felt as if they were fencing, parrying and lunging, repeating the same moves over and over until one of them stabbed too hard. She was as much to blame as he was. But she couldn't seem to help herself. "And in case you've forgotten, *I* didn't always work so much."

"Touché," he said, looking directly at her. Then he turned and walked toward the door. On his way out he said, "I'll be back later. Put the security alarm on and lock the door after me."

ARRIVING AT HEADQUARTERS and feeling a need to release his pent-up energy, Luke took the stairs two at a time. At the top, he unzipped his leather jacket, then palmed open the door into the RHD.

About half the detectives in the unit were at their stations in the open room. Rico's desk was across from his and Jordan's was butted up against Luke's in the back of the room. Walking toward his desk, Luke saw the captain glance up. Carlyle waved him in. "I'll be back," Luke said and gave Rico a pat on the shoulder as he passed by.

Inside the captain's office, Luke held up a hand. "I'm not here to work on the Renfield case."

"Then what are you doing here?"

Luke sat in one of the oak chairs. Since Julianna's problem involved an old LAPD case, he told the captain everything Jules had told him. "If we can find the guy who's threatening her, we may solve the other crime as well."

"You mean if he's not some idiot wanting attention. You know how often that happens."

Too often. Every homicide case generated dozens of calls from people who thought they knew something. Some were legit, many weren't. But they had to treat each one as if it were the real thing.

"How's your father?" Jeff asked.

Luke wasn't aware the captain knew anything about Abe's illness.

"Jordan told me."

"Oh." Luke nodded. "He's in the hospital with pneumonia. I talked to his physician this morning and it looks like he'll be there a few more days. I'm going back tomorrow morning. I have to make sure he gets some help on the ranch."

The captain steepled his fingers.

"So, what do you think about the Willis case," Luke asked.

"It was before I came to the RHD, but I do remember the media coverage. The FBI was involved."

"Initially they were, but it was so long ago, I don't know what procedure they followed."

Luke thought for a second. "You could contact the suits." He gave his boss one of his best smiles.

"You mean if I agree that we move forward on this. And I'm not sure we have the jurisdiction to do that. You said the threats happened in San Francisco and New Mexico." Carlyle gave him a hard look.

"The Willis case was ours and it still is. We can open a cold case anytime we want, especially if we have a new lead. It's a long shot, but the threats are about the Willis story, and I call that a new lead."

The big black man rubbed his chin. "A lot has changed in fifteen years."

"A lot that may finally help solve this case."

"You still have a week left of your vacation."

"I know. If you give me the go-ahead on this, I'll keep track and switch out the time."

Carlyle grinned. "You're like a dog with a bone. You never leave anything alone." He tapped his pen on a stack of papers on his desk. "Yeah, go ahead."

Luke's blood pumped. "Thanks, boss." On his way out, Luke said, "I'll let you know what I find."

Between Rico tracking down the person making the e-mail threats, and researching the old file and the old evidence, to see if any was still viable, they just might get lucky.

As he passed Jordan on his way back to his desk, his buddy stopped him. "I hear you brought Jules back and she's staying at your place."

Luke frowned. "Who said?"

Jordan nodded at Rico.

"Uh-huh." Luke gave Rico the evil eye and in turn, Rico shrugged, palms up. "Then I assume he also told you she's there under my protection until I can find out who's making the threats on her life."

His partner smiled. "I pulled the Willis case." He indicated the three boxes on the floor next to Luke's desk.

"Oh, man," Luke groaned.

"So you're back?"

"I'm not on the clock. But I want to get things moving because we've got to go back to New Mexico in the morning."

"Okay. I'm in. Let's get started."

Luke and Jordan culled the files, reading notes and searching for anything that might signal a connection with Julianna's caller. The only thing Luke found was that little Renata's mother and stepfather had split about a year after the discovery of the child's body. It happened frequently in cases like this. Some traumas were too big to be overcome.

He knew that only too well.

Another entry said the mother's brother had visited earlier in the month, but he'd been questioned only briefly since he'd gone back home before the child's disappearance.

Luke noted that the stepfather had been the most likely suspect, which was usually the case. Family members were always the first to be scrutinized when someone was the victim of a violent crime. He made a note to interview the main parties again, and also the neighbor's boy, who'd said he saw a man around the house a few days before.

It was after six when Luke realized everyone else had gone home and the next shift was straggling in. Jordan and Rico had been long gone on a call-out. Quickly he wrote down the numbers he needed and stuffed the notepad into his pocket.

On the way home, he called Jules to see if he should pick up anything. It felt strange, almost like they were married again. After five rings, he clicked off and searched his pockets for her cell phone number. When he found it, the waning light made the number difficult to see. Finally deciphering his scribbles, he punched in the number.

No answer there either, so he left a message. But why wouldn't she answer her cell phone? He hit the redial to call again, just in case he'd gotten it wrong. One ring. Two rings. Three—he stomped on the accelerator.

"Hello."

Relief swept through Luke. "It's me. Everything okay?"

It took a moment for her to answer. "Yes, everything is fine. Why?"

His heart still thumped like a drum. "No reason. Just checking in."

He heard her breathing heavily.

She didn't sound right. Maybe she was more bothered about being there than she wanted to admit. "Do you want me to pick up anything at the store?"

A long silence. "Yes. Can you get some coffee? I…I couldn't find any."

CHAPTER TEN

SOMETHING WASN'T RIGHT, Luke decided, as he sped home through the lines of traffic, darting in and out of clogged lanes to capture a few extra seconds. He was probably overreacting to the hesitancy in her voice, but that he'd heard it at all put him on edge. Despite his NASCAR driving skills, it took another half hour to reach the house.

He didn't bother pulling into the garage and bounded up the front steps. Before he reached the door, he could see there were no lights on inside. Jules wouldn't be sitting in the dark. Unless maybe she was working in the bedroom. Logical reasons flitted through his brain as he searched each room, calling out for her as he went. "Jules? Dammit, answer me will you!"

The moment he realized she wasn't there, panic tightened in his chest. He hadn't imagined she'd leave the house or even where she might go without a car. His gaze darted. An empty cup on the kitchen counter next to her purse, the coffeepot with the cover off. Had she decided to get the coffee herself? He rejected the idea. She wouldn't go to the store without her purse. And she knew the closest one was near the beach. *The beach.*

He launched himself down the front stairs.

The multicolored lights and signs along Venice Boulevard gave an eerie circus quality to the night, and the people in various states of dress or undress only added to the surreal image.

His heart in his throat, he pushed past the tourists and the regulars, inadvertently knocking the balls out of a juggler's hands. "Sorry, bud," he said, shouldering forward through the crowd. He circled around a couple of guys twisting their bodies into contortions for whatever money onlookers tossed in a box.

Despite the crispness of the evening, sweat beaded on his forehead and he felt the dampness under his arms as he barreled ahead, eyes scanning the crowd, searching faces. He saw a woman with long dark hair, but when she turned, it wasn't Jules. He tapped another on the shoulder, not her either.

Then he realized that if she was here, she would be down by the water. She hated crowds.

As he headed toward the beach, he noticed a bench ahead with a lone person on it. A woman, he could tell by the silhouette. But he couldn't tell if it was her. "Jules," he called out. The woman's head came up. Yes! His blood rushed. Thank God.

He walked over and dropped onto the bench beside her, relief filling his chest. "You scared the hell out of me, Jules. What were you thinking coming out here alone?"

She stared at him, a frown forming. "I thought you said this was the safest place for me. Either I'm safe or I'm not."

His muscles tensed, his annoyance spiraling. "I said my place was safe. I didn't expect you'd be wandering around out here alone. That in itself is dangerous, even without the other stuff. Why didn't you call and tell me?"

She pulled back. "I just stepped out front for some air. I wasn't planning to come down to the beach, but suddenly, here I was. You didn't tell me not to leave, so I never thought twice about it. I'm sorry if I worried you."

Worried? How about frantic? He leaned

against the wood slats and draped an arm over the back of the bench. "It's just that…I brought you here under my protection. It's my job to worry. It's what I do." And if anything had happened to her… He felt his chest constrict.

"Would you like to walk a little?"

Standing, he shrugged to ease the tightness in his shoulders and neck. "Sure," he said, stuffing his anger. It was true, he hadn't told her not to leave. He should be mad at himself for neglecting what should come naturally. The woman was driving him insane. Or at least causing him not to think sanely. That happened when a cop was emotionally involved. It was the reason cops didn't work a case when it concerned their family. But he'd always thought he was immune. That he could always keep a clear head. No matter what. Yeah, so much for that theory.

As they started toward the pier, he asked, "Did you eat?"

"I found some peanut butter and crackers."

"That's it?"

She nodded.

His gaze circled. "I didn't have time to eat either, so let's go find something."

JULIANNA REMEMBERED a café near the pier, but restaurants in the area changed like the shifting sand. "The Venice Whaler. Is it still there?"

"Yeah, good thought. I'm up for that."

He placed his hand at the small of Julianna's back, directing her toward Washington Square. The warmth of his hand against her felt comfortable and natural… and it stirred deep longings. Longings that conjured memories of sweaty passion-filled nights and fun-filled days. When had all that ended? Long before they lost Michael, she realized. But what good did it do to think about all that now?

As if he knew what she was thinking, Luke stuffed both hands in his jacket pockets and glanced at the horizon between sky and sea. A fat yellow moon seemed suspended just above the water, lighting their way.

"Do you go to the Whaler often?"

"Nope. Not since—"

"Oh," she interrupted. "Sorry. It's a bad idea."

"No, it's an excellent idea." He put a hand on her shoulder and they kept walking. "I'd probably have gone before this if I'd thought about it, but…you know me…always busy someplace else."

Yes, she knew. Only too well. And while

she understood what his job entailed when they'd gotten married, she'd been so young, so blinded by love, that she never imagined the LAPD would disrupt their lives so much. That was her fault, not his.

There was a line in front of the restaurant. Nothing unusual; the place was as popular with locals as it was with tourists. She glanced at the people waiting, mostly young couples, but there were a few older people sitting apart on a bench, some in their thirties talking and touching, and some gen-Xers ready to party and who had no qualms about a little PDA. She smiled. Luke never had a problem with public displays of affection either—and way back when, neither had she. God, that seemed so long ago.

The thought made her feel old and staid. She'd give anything to have that carefree feeling back again.

"It'll be ten minutes," Luke said after putting their names on the wait list. "Can you make it that long?"

"I think so." If she could forget about the past. Turning, she walked to the balcony overlooking the water, stood at the rail and Luke came up beside her. The sound of the waves slapping against the pylons underneath them seemed to echo the rhythmic salsa music vibrating from the restaurant. The music underscored the nature of Venice Beach. Party city. And while she didn't feel like partying, the music energized her and she was glad they'd come.

They were seated near a window that overlooked the ocean. If the weather had been warmer, she knew Luke would've preferred sitting outside on the deck. After returning with their drinks, a Bud Light for her and a nonalcoholic beer for Luke, the waiter took their dinner orders. Luke chose his usual. The surf, steak and jumbo shrimp. Rather than thinking about the menu, she requested the seafood platter, an assortment of fish, crab, shrimp and scallops. Too much food, she knew, but Luke would eat what she didn't.

"I can't believe everything is exactly as it was," she said. "Right down to the fish net on the wall."

Luke lifted his drink. "Why mess with a good thing?"

"Hear, hear." She lifted her beer in a salute.

"To friendship," he added.

"Yes," she said, then took a big swig. But they weren't friends anymore. Friends had contact, they kept in touch. Friends shared the ups and downs of life and supported each other no matter what. They'd been best friends once, and it made her sad to think that the most wonderful part of her life had ended so badly. In that one moment she wanted it back again…wondered if they could ever… The thought faded as quickly as it came. Nothing had changed. Nothing would be any different now.

"So, what's next? Did you have any success today at the department?"

"Yes, I did. Jeff supports taking another look at the Willis case." He kept his voice low so she could barely hear him over the music. She switched chairs to sit beside him instead of across the table.

Smiling, she said, so he didn't get any crazy ideas, "Hard to hear over there."

His shoulder touched hers as he leaned in to talk. "I'm going to try to interview a couple of people in the morning before we head back to the ranch."

The ranch. She realized she was anxious to get back. To see Abe. "Have you talked to your father or the doctor?"

Luke pressed closer, close enough for her to smell his aftershave, a light, woodsy scent.

"I spoke to Pops a little while ago and told

him the doc said he had to stay a couple more days. Barring any new problems, he'll probably be able to come home on Friday."

"Oh, boy. I can imagine his response."

Laughing, Luke said, "Right. I'm glad I wasn't there to tell him in person. And since we're out here, he can't insist I take him home."

The waiter brought them big plates of steaming seafood, bowls for the crab shells, extra napkins and some wet wipes.

When he was gone, she said, "I feel bad that Abe has no one to visit him."

"Nothing he hasn't brought upon himself."

"Maybe Mrs. Hancock will visit? She's really concerned about him."

Luke grunted, then picked up one of her crab legs and snapped it in half.

When he didn't respond to her question, she asked, "Why do you hate her so much?"

His head came up, a surprised look in his eyes. "I think *hate* is a little strong."

"So, you don't hate her. You could've fooled me."

"I don't *like* her. There's a difference."

"Which means she's done something you don't approve of, otherwise it wouldn't be important enough for you to dislike her."

"It's not important." He leaned back in his

chair and took a gulp of his O'Doul's. "Leave it alone. Okay? We've got more significant things to worry about."

She bristled. She felt as if she were five years old again, chastised like a child. Going back to her meal, she said, "Sure. You never told me about it in five years of marriage, I don't know why I was dumb enough to think you'd tell me now."

LUKE WISHED he could snatch back the words, but as usual, it was too late. And he wasn't going to apologize. His feelings about his father and that woman had nothing to do with Jules.

After a long silence, she finally said, "I'm sorry. It's none of my business and I should know better. I'd blame it on my journalist training, but I'd be lying. I really wanted to know more about you."

He stopped eating midbite. "Jules, if anyone knows about me, it's you. You know me better than anyone."

"Better than Jordan?"

"Yes," he said without hesitation. "Better than Jordan. And better than Rico."

Stabbing a piece of crab with the tip of her fork, she looked over. "Things change." She dipped the meat in melted butter and lifted it to her mouth.

As he watched her slowly nip the succulent morsel between her perfect white teeth, his groin tightened. "Some things never change, no matter how much we want them to." Like his pure animal lust for her. Like his love. His need. Which suddenly seemed overwhelming.

She glanced away. "Do you want me to check on a flight out tomorrow?"

"Yes, but we can't go until after I talk to a couple people."

Between Rico getting the computer information and making arrangements to set up a wiretap on Jules's home phone in San Francisco, he figured he had all bases covered. If the guy threatening Jules was truly serious, they'd soon find out.

After dinner, they decided against coffee and opted to walk off their meal by going the long way home down the boardwalk. As they strolled, Jules popped into one tiny store after another, marveling at all the funky items for sale. They stopped to watch an artist named Tony who'd been selling his work on the beach ever since Luke moved there.

Tony's hands glided over the paper as he created pastel sketches of tourists who wanted a memory of their visit to Venice Beach. When the last person got up, Tony urged Julianna to sit for him.

She balked at first, but then she said, "What the hell," and plonked down in the director's chair.

Luke watched as the artist sketched her fine cheekbones, her wide-set brandy-colored eyes and long sooty lashes. The artist captured her perfectly and when he finished, he held the sketch up for Julianna to see.

"Oh," she said, blinking at the sketch.

"You don't like it?" Tony asked.

She reached out for the picture. "Oh, no. I love it. It's just that…"

Luke paid the man and said, "Just nothing. It's beautiful."

They walked home without saying much. The night was crisp and the air snapped with potential. He hadn't been so relaxed…hadn't felt so alive, since…since before Jules left.

Getting out his keys, he stopped at the front steps. "What is it about the picture you don't like?"

She climbed to the top step, gave him a quizzical look and unrolled the picture. "I do like it…only it doesn't look very much like me." She tipped her head for another glance. "The woman in this picture is beautiful."

He remembered she'd always thought she wasn't as pretty or as smart as her sister, but he'd never taken it seriously. How could she not know what she looked like? He stepped up next to her, took her by the arms and looked directly into her eyes. "It looks exactly like you, Jules. You are beautiful."

She'd been pretty before, but now she *was* beautiful, and he wanted to kiss her in the worst way, wanted to hold her in his arms again, and just as he was thinking it, her lips met his. Warm and soft and inviting.

It was all the encouragement he needed. He deepened the kiss, breathing in the scent of the woman he'd never been able to forget. When she melted into him, he couldn't help the moan that escaped, couldn't help thinking she wanted this as much as he did, and even if this was going to be the most stupid thing he'd ever done, he couldn't stop. The only way that would happen was if she objected.

She didn't.

Still kissing her, he fumbled to get the key into the door with his left hand and the second it was open, they moved inside as one. He felt her heart beating like a drum against his chest, her breathing came in short passionate spurts, and he crushed her against him, unable to get enough of her. When she reciprocated, he scooped her into his arms and headed for the bedroom. She felt hot, he *was* hot.

His need was so intense, they didn't make the bedroom. He dropped onto the couch in the living room with her still in his arms. She unbuttoned his shirt, her hands like an inferno on his chest. He kissed her mouth, her ears, her eyes, her neck and her fingertips. So long. It had been so long. He wanted to devour her, to get inside her and never leave.

Dammit. He'd told himself he wasn't going to let this happen, that he wouldn't fall back on old feelings. But he hadn't anticipated that she'd be so willing. And that she would fuel the fire that burned inside him. The emotional fire. It wasn't all about sex. It was about sex with *her.*

Her small moans of pleasure spurred him on. He wanted to feel her, taste her, plunge inside her. Some part of his rational mind said he should stop. Get up and walk away. But when her legs wrapped around him, he kissed her long and hard, condensing the passion, desire and frustration of all the lost years into this one moment.

"Take off your clothes," Julianna whispered. And as he stood to undress, she began removing her clothes, too. He was stunned at her beauty and for a moment, simply stood there watching her.

"Do it," she reminded him.

As Julianna watched him remove his pants, some basic instinct took hold. She loved looking at him, always had. His body was perfect, except for two scars he'd gotten from a bust gone bad. His hard muscles were evidence that he took great care to keep them that way. Workouts. He'd always been vigilant in his workouts.

Watching him, she knew this was insane. One kiss and she was disrobing him. She felt wanton and wild and wet, and she ached to have him inside her. She might as well admit it. She'd wanted to make love with Luke from the moment she'd seen him again. She'd been convinced she had enough self-control to keep her wits about her when he was around. And she had. She'd maintained her distance, both physically and emotionally. Or thought she had.

What made tonight different? As she thought it, she knew. Luke had shown a side of himself she hadn't seen before. It wasn't the fact that he'd said she was beautiful, but more that he'd cared enough to say it to make her feel better. And at this moment, all the self-convincing in the world couldn't make her feelings for Luke disappear.

Without a word, he dropped down next to her, his eyes hungry and filled with something primal, as if he wanted to consume her. And, oh, man…she was more than willing to let him do it.

Still gazing into her eyes, he touched her breasts with his fingertips, gently, almost reverently. He hadn't forgotten that she liked their lovemaking slow. Slow and seductive. Tantalizing. But tonight, she didn't think she could stand the waiting.

As they lay side by side on the couch, she reached to touch him and almost fell onto the floor. "Bedroom," she said quickly, then got up and pulled him to his feet along with her.

The next thing she knew they were on the bed, their bodies entwined. He kissed her mouth, her earlobes, her neck, her breasts, taking time to tease the tip of one nipple with his tongue, then he kissed her belly and her thighs, all the way to her toes. On the way back up, he stopped midway, right there, pressing his lips and his tongue against her in a way she remembered oh, so well.

Her muscles contracted, her body thrummed with anticipation until she thought she might explode. He continued to tease her, bringing her just to the edge…and then he stopped and she felt his fingers, alternately stroking, then slipping inside.

A small moan of desperation escaped her throat. The combination of emotion and physical pleasure took her to another plane where the frenzied sensations brought her to the brink of ecstasy. Within seconds, her body convulsed with pleasure and she closed her eyes, giving in to the insatiable need inside her. A primitive need. A need for *him*. And only him.

He'd been watching her, she realized, but there was no embarrassment on her part. No repentance. She reached for him, wanting to make him desire her as much as she desired him, to need her as much as she needed him. She had to have him inside her. Now.

As her hand curved around him, she knew her memory hadn't played tricks. He was exactly as she remembered. When he moaned, she smiled.

In the next instant, he was on top of her, spreading her legs. He reached to get something from the nightstand. "I hope those aren't from five years ago," she teased.

"Nope. But they're not new either. I've been saving myself."

"Me, too," she said, her voice low and husky. She hoped they were both talking about the same thing, but right now, it didn't matter. All that mattered was this moment. Everything else faded into the background.

Finished sheathing himself, he kissed her again, his tongue exploring her mouth, and she kissed him back in exactly the same way and at once she was lost in the passions she remembered so well.

She'd never imagined their lovemaking could improve, but she'd been wrong. So very wrong.

His mouth raged over hers and she felt him against her, hard and ready as he entered her. It took two seconds to find the familiar rhythm they knew so well and not much longer for her to reach the point of climax again. Her body stiffened under him, muscles taut, desire rising and rising to that pinnacle when she shuddered and a thousand searing sensations ripped through her.

He moved slowly inside her, and her muscles again tightened around him as he brought her amazingly quickly to another point of no return and simultaneously gave a guttural moan, stiffened and erupted in a tempest of liquid heat.

Her heart pounded wildly, his eyes raked over her with blistering intensity. Then he lowered himself next to her, resting at her side, their breathing heavy. Making love didn't get any better than this.

LUKE LAY AWAKE watching Julianna sleep, her dark hair splayed across the pillow, her lips parted. Moonlight streamed through the dormer windows, highlighting her flawless skin. He reached to touch her, wanting to feel that smooth flesh under his fingers once again, then resisted and pulled his hand back.

He'd thought that quenching his desire for her would be the end of it. But it wasn't. He wanted her again. And again. Nothing had changed in that respect.

It was stupid, but where Jules was concerned his hormones had never listened to reason. Why should they now?

They'd both succumbed to desire, to the need of the moment. It wasn't the first time that had happened and it was stupid to make any more of it. Once after they'd separated, they'd bumped into each other at a friend's party and at her coaxing, ended up in a hotel room together. The sex had been great and he'd thought it was her attempt to mend their relationship.

Two days later he'd been served with divorce papers.

He wasn't going to make the emotional assumption that one night together had some deeper significance. Not again. Whatever need had driven her to make love with him five years ago was probably the same as last night. He'd be kidding himself to think of it as anything more. But he'd damn sure enjoyed it.

While he hadn't been celibate for the past five years, he'd stopped trying to find solace through sex a long time ago, and it'd been over a year since he'd slept with a woman. He had needs and so did she. Last night they'd *needed* each other.

Still asleep, she snuggled closer. On his side, he spooned himself against her and rested his arm across her waist. Her hair smelled good and he wanted to bury his face in it. God, he missed this.

Luke's chest constricted in pain, as if a giant vise wrapped around him and was squeezing the life away. He missed being with her, missed the way she touched him, the way she used to look at him. He missed being a family…and the closeness they shared. He missed the feeling he got knowing that someone knew everything about him… and loved him anyway.

The longing filled him with sadness.

But she was here now. They were together now. It didn't matter what happened in a few hours when they returned to business as usual. Right now he just wanted to feel. To feel her next to him…to ease the ache in his soul.

JULIANNA ROLLED OVER, stretched her arms out on the other side of the bed. Empty. She touched his pillow. Cold. Apparently Luke had been gone a while, though his scent still lingered in the sheets. She'd slept so soundly, hadn't awakened even once as she usually did, and she hadn't even heard Luke get up.

She glanced at the clock on the nightstand. 7:00 a.m. Because she worked mostly at night, she usually slept until about nine, but since Luke was already up, she figured she should do the same, see what his plans were.

His plans. The thought made her tense up. He was making all the plans, and while it felt good not to be in this alone, she'd gotten accustomed to doing things for herself, making her own decisions. It was part of the personal transformation she'd desperately needed to make in order to go on.

Her blood rushed as another thought hit her. What was she going to say to Luke about last night? Maybe it was best not to say anything. Their lovemaking had filled a need, she wasn't going to make it into any more than that. And she hoped he wouldn't either. Still…

Rolling over, she snuggled in for few more minutes and couldn't help smiling. Her libido had been dormant for so long, she'd felt as if his every touch, every kiss, was more intense than the one before—as if each one might be the last and it had to be memorable. The irony in that didn't escape her.

Being with Luke had felt wonderful, like being with an old friend…and yet everything about last night seemed new and exciting.

She could see why some people got back together after a divorce. The familiarity made it easy. She didn't need to worry about being on her best behavior or engage in all the game playing that single people did when getting to know one another. There was no pretending. They had history.

But just because they'd found comfort in each others' arms for one night didn't mean anything else had changed. They were the same two people with the same baggage as before.

Soft light filtered through the gauzy curtains covering the narrow windows, reminding her of other mornings in this room. The morning when she told Luke she was pregnant. The morning of their first anniversary when he brought her breakfast in bed. Mornings after Michael was born when he slept in a bassinet at their side.

Good memories, she realized, as she glanced around the room. It was a small room, with the big king-sized bed taking up most of the space. The old rocker that belonged to Luke's grandmother, the dressing table where Julianna used to sit and comb her hair and…she glanced to the wall beside the door…the matching chest of drawers with the silver-framed photo on top. Her mouth went dry.

She tore her gaze away. She had many old photos herself, but in an effort to get on with her life, she'd packed them away. Except one of Michael that she kept in her wallet.

She stared at the photo, until drawn like the proverbial steel to a magnet, she slipped out of bed and walked to the dresser. Her hand shook as she picked up the picture.

In the photo, Luke had one arm around her and was holding Michael in the other. It was a simple snap, taken in the back yard by one of Luke's friends during a party. Michael's toys were strewn in the grass around them.

With the pad of her little finger, she lightly touched Michael's face. Her heart wrenched. Tears filled her eyes.

Mourn him, and then let him go. Her therapist's words intruded. With a jerky motion, she put the photo back, then walked across the hall to the shower.

Love him. Then let him go.

CHAPTER ELEVEN

"DR. MARTINEZ SAYS Pops will be ready to go home Friday by noon," Luke said, hanging up the wall phone. He came over and sat next to her at the kitchen table again. "If we get a flight to Albuquerque early Friday morning, we can get the car and then pick up Abe on the way back to the ranch."

Friday morning? Julianna bit off another piece of toast. A hot shower had helped her shake off the heartache she'd felt after looking at the photo in Luke's room, but it hadn't diminished her need to get away from here. The place was a reminder of everything she'd once had—and of everything she'd lost.

Luke had showered already and was dressed in black pants and a tan mock turtle-neck. Work clothes. His black sport jacket and holster hung on the back of the chair. A familiar scene that flung her back to the past.

For one fraction of a second, she felt as if the last five years hadn't happened. Even his familiar scent had the same effect on her. Desire spasmed between her legs. "Are you saying you want to stay here another day?"

Luke looked at her nonchalantly. "Is that a problem?"

Julianna shifted. She shook her head. "I'm thinking of Abe. He probably hasn't had a visitor since we left."

Luke picked up his plate and took it to the sink.

"And didn't you want to find someone to help him?"

"I do. But I could use an extra day here for more research on the Willis case." Studying her, he frowned. "What's wrong?"

"Nothing," she lied.

He didn't believe her. She could see it in his expression.

"I hope you don't want me to say I'm sorry about last night because I'm not."

She shrugged. "No more than you want me to say I'm sorry. Let's leave it at that."

He looked at her. "Y'know you enjoyed it as much as me."

She cleared her throat. "Yes, I enjoyed it— for what it was."

He frowned. "And what, exactly, was it?"

Julianna stood. She'd wanted to forget about last night, pretend it hadn't happened. "I don't know. Two needy people. A one-night stand. Whatever it was, it won't happen again."

He arched a brow. "Uh-huh. Well, if you say so." He grinned lasciviously as he put a cup into the dishwasher.

A *Number 1 Daddy* cup Mikey had bought with his piggy-bank money so he could give Luke a present on Father's Day.

She closed her eyes. Everything here reminded her of Mikey. Her head started to throb. She rubbed her temples with two fingers.

"What's wrong?"

"Nothing. I—I'm just better away from here." She looked away. "Too many bad memories."

Luke's shoulders stiffened, eyes darkening as he studied her. "Good ones, too. You can't forget all the good things."

His words hit her like a blow to the solar plexus. She tried to catch her breath, but suddenly it seemed as if all the oxygen had been sucked from the room. Finally she managed, "No…but good or bad, I can't live in the past." Just being here brought it all back in spades. Her voice felt hoarse when she said, "I don't know how you can do it."

He leaned against the counter. "Do what?"

"Continue to stay here. Doesn't everything remind you of…what happened?"

He crossed his arms, sadness reaching his eyes. "Yes. Sometimes. But mostly I'm reminded that Michael was a beautiful little boy and one of the best parts of my life. Our life. I don't ever want to forget that."

She didn't want to forget Michael, either, but through therapy, she'd finally been able to accept that he was gone forever. That she had to let him go. In order to do that, she had to relinquish their life together.

"Walking on the beach yesterday reminded me of all the times I'd taken Michael there. It reminded me of how he'd collected shells and put them in a jar and gave them to me on my birthday. But I can't build a life on memories." Remembering meant sadness and pain. She couldn't deal with any more pain.

Luke turned, his lips moved as if he were going to say something, but nothing came out.

"I'll make flight reservations if you want me to," she said softly.

He straightened, shrugged. "Sure. Try to

get one early tomorrow morning. Six o'clock if you can." He was trying to be nonchalant, but the sharp edge in his voice gave him away. He grabbed the holster hanging on the back of the chair and slipped it on. Then the sport coat. "I'll call in a little while."

As Julianna watched him go out the door, he turned and said, "Stay inside until I get back. And lock the doors."

She stared at the closed door, emotions warring inside her. She hugged herself, as if that might ward off the bone-deep loneliness she knew would come. She felt it now more than ever.

Luke didn't understand the decisions she'd made. He never had. When she'd left him, he'd accused her of running away. He'd told her a change of scenery wasn't going to solve anything. But he'd been wrong. She'd made another life for herself and was getting along just fine…until she saw him again.

Staying with Luke would've destroyed her. And in turn, destroyed him. Last night she'd allowed herself to enjoy the warmth and comfort of Luke's strong arms, had told herself that's all it was.

But in the bright light of morning, she realized she couldn't escape the truth.

She wanted to feel again, passion, love…
even anger. She wanted to feel something—
anything. And she wanted to feel it with
Luke.

LUKE HEADED FOR the RHD, his shoulders
tight and his mind reeling. He couldn't get
Julianna out of his head. Couldn't stop
wanting to shake some sense into her. Tell her
the divorce was a mistake. But regardless of
what they'd once been to each other, he knew
now he was just another ugly reminder of her
past.

He remembered vividly one of their last conversations as a married couple—the night
before she'd left him. The scene was embedded
in his brain like a faulty microchip that kept
playing the same program over and over.

They'd come home from a group session for
parents who'd experienced the death of a child.
He'd wanted to make love with her because the
one thing that made him feel whole again was
being as close to Jules as he could possibly be.
Loving her salved his ragged soul and gave
him a reason to go on, and he'd thought it was
the same for her. But that night when he'd
reached for her, she'd batted his hand away.

"None of them know what we've been

through," she'd spat out. "Our situation is unique. How can anyone say they understand?"

"They may not have had the exact same experience, Jules," he'd said. "But they've all lost a child. They know what that's like."

"But none of them had the opportunity to save their child. We did. We didn't try hard enough. That's on us." Her face had twisted in anguish. "No one knows what that's like."

Luke knew when she said *we,* she meant *he.* He was an officer of the law. He had the whole police force at his fingertips. She believed he'd had the ability to find their son. And he hadn't.

She blamed him. She would always blame him. Because it was true. He hadn't found their son. And that was a truth that would haunt him every day of his life.

Realistically, logically, he knew what happened to Michael wasn't because he hadn't tried hard enough. He couldn't have done any more. But logic wasn't going to change Julianna's belief that he could've. It wouldn't change the guilt he felt.

Entering the RHD, Luke heard his buddy Jordan's voice.

"Hey, Coltrane. I thought you'd gone back to New Mexico."

Luke walked over to Jordan's desk and lowering his voice, he said, "Tomorrow morning. I've got some stuff to do on the Willis case." Luke had told both Rico and Jordan about Julianna's *situation*. "I don't want it to get out that I'm working on the case. Not yet anyway. Someone could easily make the connection between me and Jules."

"You saying the stalker and the Willis kid's killer are one and the same."

"It's a possibility."

"What's the plan?"

Luke pulled the numbers from his pocket for the child's mother, stepfather and the brother. "We need some stats run on all of these people. Current addresses, phone numbers, et cetera. Then interviews."

"Under what premise?"

"Let's say we're going through all the cold cases for DNA evidence. We have more high-tech testing methods now, tests that weren't available fifteen years ago. See what reaction we get."

"I'm on it," Jordan said.

"I'm going to pull the physical evidence file."

Jordan picked up his phone and Luke went to the evidence room, brought a box back to the desk and started sifting through the plastic bags of blood-stained clothing and envelopes with who knows what inside. Apparently the preservation of evidence wasn't a top priority fifteen years ago. Bags weren't sealed properly and several items had been taken out and never put back in their containers, contaminating evidence they might've provided.

An hour later, Luke had culled a few things he thought might be possibilities for further research. In particular, two pieces of fabric with spots that could be blood. Evidence in hand, he headed for the Scientific Investigation Division downstairs. The techs were always busy and with the number of cases that went through the department, most results took several weeks. Unless it was a high-profile case or threatened the public at large. A fifteen-year-old cold case wasn't going to the top of the list. But he had to start somewhere.

At the SDI desk, he saw Tex with Cecilia Deleone, one of RHD's newer detectives, chatting and looking more friendly than two detectives in the same unit ought to look. So caught up in conversation, they didn't even notice him. Luke cleared his throat.

Tex turned, his expression guilty as a thief. "Luke. Hey."

"What's up?" Luke asked, trying not to smile.

"Uh, I'm doing some research on the Studio Killer's first victim. Deleone has a theory…" Tex glanced at the young detective. "We're going to see if it holds water."

The detective pulled herself up, shoulders back, head high. She was an attractive woman. Dark hair and almond-skinned, she'd gotten a lot of flack her first few weeks in the department, but she'd handled it well.

She reminded Luke of Julianna. Smart, determined and just a bit unpredictable.

"Thought you were on vacation," Tex said.

"I am. But I have to clear something up first." Luke and Tex, aka Will Houston, who just happened to be from Texas, were good friends, but Luke wasn't as close to the Texan as he was with Rico and Jordan. Tex waited for Luke to explain, but he didn't. The fewer people who knew about Julianna, the better. No one knew she was at his place except Rico, Jordan and the captain.

"It's a cold case. Nothing urgent." He leaned closer to Tex. "Vanessa know about this?"

"I'm going back," Deleone said. "Let me know what you find out." With that she left.

Watching her walk away, Luke said, "Bad idea, buddy."

Tex shrugged. "Maybe. But nothing ventured, nothing gained."

"What about Vanessa?" If there was one thing Luke couldn't tolerate, it was infidelity. If a guy did that, how trustworty was he?

"It's not working with Van," Tex said, "everything's off." Then he leaned against the counter, and in his lazy Texas drawl, said, "I learned early on when opportunity knocks, you gotta answer. You may not have another chance."

His buddy had a point. How many chances had he thrown away with Jules? "Still, it's a bad idea. You work together."

Tex lifted his hands, palms up, and walked away. Luke took his evidence into the lab. The tech filed Luke's request in a slot next to a dozen others, which meant he wasn't going to be getting a response back anytime soon. On the way out, Tex's homespun philosophy played in his head. *You gotta answer when opportunity knocks.*

Yeah. He'd done that last night. For all the good it did him.

JULIANNA CLOSED her laptop, got up and went into the kitchen. Though late evening was her preferred time to write, she'd spent the day working on her story. Getting up so early, she knew she'd better take advantage of the time since her deadline for the last article was looming and she didn't know what Luke had planned.

Having been cooped up all day, she opened the back door and stepped out onto the redwood deck, a new addition since she'd lived there. Five years ago, there had been only a small porch out here with screens all around. Now the weathered redwood sprawled across the entire back of the house. A barbecue, table and chairs took up one corner and assorted pots and flowering plants made the area seem garden-like. Odd. Luke had never been one to putter around the house when they'd been married. When had he developed a green thumb?

Or maybe the plants were someone else's idea. A friend maybe. A woman. She hadn't thought about him having a girlfriend, and as she wondered about it, a strange possessiveness coursed through her. Because he'd never married again and never mentioned dating anyone, she'd assumed he had no one special. What if she was wrong?

Last night she'd felt connected to Luke in

a way she hadn't before. If he had someone else, he wouldn't have been with her. She knew Luke wouldn't cheat.

Not that it mattered. They'd spent one night together. No commitments had been made, no words of love murmured in the throws of passion. They'd had sex. Hot and sweet. That's what she'd wanted. Nothing more. Apparently, he felt the same.

Forcing the thoughts away, she crossed to the railing. The sun had just barely dipped below the horizon, the palm trees and rooftops were silhouetted by the gray of twilight, a familiar image that sent a wave of nostalgia through her. She felt for a moment as if she were caught between the past and the present…and then a brisk gust of wind blew her hair back, and she breathed in the crisp Pacific air. It was so quiet, she could hear the breeze rustling through the palm fronds.

There was one last installment to the Willis story; then maybe the crackpot who'd been the bane of her existence these past weeks would quit bothering her. And her life might just go back to normal.

Another sharp gust made her suck in her breath. In her peripheral vision, she caught a shadow…something moving. Her heart skipped a beat. She jerked around, scanning the pink flowering oleanders that stood over six feet tall and served as a barrier between Luke's property and the Baxters' next door. Suddenly a cat screeched and darted from the bushes. Jules let out a choked cry and jumped back, her heart beating triple time.

God. It was just a cat. But suddenly she felt chilled, and pulling her sweater closed in the front, she opened the sliding glass door and stepped inside, nearly colliding with Luke.

He caught her with both hands. "Hey, nice to see you, too."

She pulled away, her pulses racing. "You could make a little noise or knock or something rather than scaring a person to death," she said breathlessly, then shoved a hand through her windblown hair.

"Sorry. It wasn't intentional."

"Those bushes are too tall and need cutting."

He frowned, as if he hadn't a clue what she was talking about. But that wasn't unusual, either. He held up both hands. "Whatever I did, forgive me." He lowered his head to look into her eyes. "Something wrong?"

Moving past him to go inside, she said, "No. You surprised me, that's all."

"Okay." He went to the fridge and pulled out an O'Doul's and a Bud Light. Handing her the Bud, he said, "I seem to be doing that a lot lately."

"I—I think my nerves are on edge with all this crap going on. I'm so sick of it. I just want to write my stories and hope that they do some good."

Luke motioned her to the door to the deck. Once outside, they sat at the table together. Silent. After a moment, he said, "What kind of good do you expect your stories to do exactly?"

She shrugged. "I'm hoping that they'll provide some kind of solace to the victims' families. That they'll know their loved ones haven't been forgotten. I'm also hoping that by keeping these stories in the public eye, the police will continue investigating instead of dumping them in a cold case warehouse somewhere." She lowered her chin. "Michael's case included."

"But you didn't write a story about him?"

She looked away, ran a hand through her hair.

"You didn't." Standing, Luke stared at her,

his face visibly hardening. "You didn't write one on Michael, did you?"

Suddenly it was hard to breathe. She gave a reluctant nod. "My first."

He sprang to his feet and slammed a hand on the table. "Why? Why in God's name…"

Oh, God. She'd expected anger, but not this. Not the pain she saw in his eyes. "I—I used fictitious names. I thought it would…help. That it would be cathartic." She squeezed her eyes shut, unable to look at him. "I thought that by detailing everything that happened, I could somehow purge myself. It didn't work that way, though. I just became more—"

"Obsessed."

"I guess."

The tension was palpable. Luke's jaws clamped tight, the veins in his neck popped out, his body tensed. He tipped his head to one side and then the other, as if trying to release the stress.

"Well," he said, "you've achieved one of your goals in the Willis case." He clicked his fingernails against the side of the beer bottle. "And…you've achieved some other things that I doubt you wanted."

She'd thought he was going to lambaste her for writing about Michael and when he didn't, she released a silent sigh of relief. "You're right there. I never in a million years expected someone to start threatening me over one of my stories. And not knowing whether it's just some crank or if the guy's serious, makes me really nervous. I seem to be jumping at every little thing."

LUKE STUDIED HER as she spoke, squelching the anger that mushroomed inside him. *Clear head.* Keep a clear head. He sat at the table again.

"And what if this guy *is* Renata Willis's murderer?" she asked.

"If it is, we'll catch him." He didn't know exactly how, but he was certain they would.

"You'll catch him?" she said, her tone doubtful. "Just like that?"

Yeah, he knew what she was thinking. If they hadn't caught the guy in fifteen years, what made him think they'd get him now. He cleared his throat. "If he's the one, we've got a lead, something to go on now. We didn't have that before. And we didn't have the testing methods we do now."

He saw a flicker of hope in her eyes.

"You think it's actually possible? Because if it is, that would really be something."

And along with that hope came the inevitable question.

"Do you think—"

He placed a hand on her knee. "No, I don't think. I take it one step at a time. We've got to finish what we started here, so don't get ahead of yourself. Right now the most important thing in the equation is keeping you safe."

She glanced at his hand on her leg. "Most important to who?"

He retracted his hand. It wasn't a question he was going to answer. "Rico and Jordan are working on some things behind the scenes. We'll see what comes up."

Scraping her long hair back, she forced a wobbly smile. "Thanks."

"For what?" he said as he raised one foot to the rung of the chair she sat on. "I haven't done anything."

"Right. Except keeping me out of trouble and making an effort to track down whoever is threatening me. I think that's something."

He shrugged. He didn't like taking credit for doing what came naturally. Protecting people, seeking justice, was what he did. It had nothing to do with any feelings he might still have. Right. Who the hell was he kidding?

He took a swig of beer. "Have you had any more messages on your home phone?"

"No. Nothing."

"Hmm. Not sure that's a good thing."

"Why on earth not? I was hoping that since he wasn't getting the response he wanted, he gave up?"

"I'd like to think that, but my experience tells me different. When is the next installment coming out?"

"Soon. A week maybe."

He nodded. "So it's logical that he'd wait until after that to call again."

"There's one more in this series, next month."

"What then?"

"I write another, of course."

"Same subject?"

She picked at the label on her beer bottle. "Yes, same subject. I have it started already. And I'll continue until I'm asked not to."

Luke felt his muscles bunch. "What if we don't get this guy, and…and this continues to happen?"

"This? You mean if the caller keeps calling?"

"Uh-huh."

She raised her head, pushed her hair

back from her face. "I don't know. I don't have a plan. I guess I'll just keep playing it by ear."

And if she did, she could end up dead. "Well, you know what I think of that."

"Yes, I do," she said, giving him a big smile. Her quick smiles used to make him feel ten feet tall. Now he felt as if she did it to placate him.

"So…" he glanced at his watch. "I have to go out again. I have one more thing to do before tomorrow. Did you get the flight reservations?"

"I did. Six a.m."

"Great. And—" The jangle of his cell phone interrupted them. "Coltrane."

"I'm near your place," Jordan said. "I've got the stats you wanted."

Luke pushed to his feet, then glanced at the time again. "Great. I've got an address, too. Mrs. Jenner. I'm going out to do the interview. Want to come?"

"Man, I'd really like to, but Laura and Cait are with me." He paused. "Hey, would Julianna mind if they hung out with her for a little while?"

He glanced at Julianna. "She's not going anywhere."

When he hung up, he said, "Jordan's

going to stop by with his fiancée and her daughter. Do you mind if they stay here until we get back?"

Her eyebrows arched. "And if I did?"

"DO YOU HAVE any kids?" Caitlin asked.

The question caught Julianna off guard. It wasn't the first time since Michael died that she'd been asked the question, but the years hadn't made it any easier to answer. "I did once, Caitlin. But he's in heaven now."

The child looked amazingly like her mother with strawberry-blond hair and big eyes, though brown not green like her mom's. Laura Gianni hardly looked old enough to be anyone's mother.

"My daddy's in heaven, too," the child said, matter-of-fact.

Cait was sitting next to Julianna on the couch. "I'm sorry to hear that," Julianna said, but after those few words, she couldn't think of another thing to say. She hadn't been around children much since moving to San Francisco and when she was, she was always at a loss.

"Would you like to watch television?" Julianna looked to Laura for a response. "I don't know if Luke has anything else here for kids to do."

"She'd love to, I'm sure," Laura said, motioning to the child who had already picked up the remote. She clicked on the TV and went right to the cartoon channel.

"Would you like something to drink?"

"Sure," Laura said.

"Iced tea? Coffee? Soda? Something stronger?"

"Iced tea is great."

Julianna got up and went to the kitchen. As she took the pitcher of tea from the fridge, Laura followed her.

"I apologize for Cait. I should've told her but didn't think."

"It's okay. Can you get a couple glasses from over there?" She gestured to the cabinets with the glass doors. "So," said Julianna, changing the subject, "I hear a wedding is on the horizon."

Laura nodded, a big smile forming. "Yes. And I have to say I'm getting more than a little nervous."

After filling the glasses with ice and pouring the tea, Julianna handed one to Laura. "Would Cait like something?"

"She's okay for now. I'm sure she's happy." Laura sat at the table instead of going back into the living room.

Leaning against the counter, Julianna took a sip of her drink. "Will it be a small wedding?"

Laura rolled her eyes at the ceiling. "I wish. I wanted it small, but somehow it got out of hand. Jordan's family... well, they have lots of people to invite. The wedding party is fairly small, though. Just three bridesmaids and three groomsmen, Luke and Rico and Jordan's brother Harry."

Sitting across from Laura, Julianna smiled. "That's big to me. Mine was half that size."

"Oh," Laura said, looking surprised. "You're married now?"

Julianna felt a sudden heat in her cheeks. "Oh, no. I meant when Luke and I were married." She shook her head. Why the hell had she even mentioned that? "It was a small wedding. Just family. My sister was the maid of honor."

Laura tipped her head, questions in her eyes. "I guess Luke told you I was married before."

Jules nodded, not sure what to say to that. Before Laura and Cait had arrived, Luke had mentioned that Laura had withheld information about her ex-husband's death from the police to protect her daughter, but finally she testified against her ex's uncle, a Mob boss. But Julianna wasn't going to bring that up.

"And did he tell you the other stuff...

about Cait's father's death? That I had to testify?"

"A little," Julianna answered. "He told me how you'd met Jordan." Lord, it felt awkward talking about such personal things with someone she barely knew, and yet it made her feel closer to Laura. She hadn't been close to anyone in such a long time.

"Regardless of the circumstances, I was so lucky to meet Jordan," Laura said. "He literally saved my life. And he's wonderful with Caitlin. She adores him."

Laura beamed when talking about Jordan, and Julianna couldn't help but be happy for her, though a little envious. Would there ever be a time when she'd feel like Laura did?

"Luke's great with Cait, too. I was hesitant to bring her here when I found out—" She stopped, as if aware she'd said the wrong thing.

"It's okay. You can say it. My son is gone. I've learned to live with it." It wasn't totally true, but it was easier than admitting there wasn't a day that went by when she didn't think of Michael. Few people knew what to say to someone who'd lost a child. Herself included.

Laura smiled at Julianna. "I can't imagine," she said. "You're a stronger person than I'd be under the circumstances."

Laura's compassion touched her. Here was a woman who'd gone to hell and back to protect her daughter and she thought she wasn't as strong as Julianna. What a laugh! Julianna was only as strong as she could act, and that varied from moment to moment. Sometimes she felt as if she had to push herself just to make it through a day.

Luke had once said running away wouldn't solve anything. And there'd been many times in the past week with him that she'd wondered if he wasn't right. Had she only kidded herself that she had to leave to start a new life?

"What I was going to say," Laura went on, "was that I was hesitant because I'd made such a big blunder with Luke. Did he tell you about that?"

"No, he didn't. What happened?"

"There was a point during the investigation when both Luke and Jordan seemed to be questioning what I'd done to protect my daughter. I got angry. I lashed out and said they didn't have kids and couldn't possibly know what it was like to want to protect their child. I had no idea."

Julianna felt a wave of empathy for Laura. "Luke's got a thick skin. I'm sure he didn't think anything of it."

"No, he was deeply hurt. I saw the pain in his eyes. He left the room, wouldn't even tell me what was wrong. I heard later from Jordan that Luke had had a few bad years after the divorce. That he'd almost lost his job."

"I—I didn't know that." She knew Luke had been drinking too much. He'd told her that himself. But she couldn't imagine he'd do anything to jeopardize his job. He was a dedicated officer. He lived for his badge.

"I apologized, and since then, we've become good friends."

Julianna smiled. "That's great. If Luke's your friend, you've got a buddy for life." As she said the words, she felt a far-reaching sense of loss. She and Luke had once been best friends.

Tears suddenly welled behind her eyes. She blinked them back, and then asked Laura about her job and the shelter she ran. After Laura explained how she helped runaway girls get off the streets, Julianna felt an even greater connection with the woman. They were much alike in their desire to help others. Soon they were talking about all kinds of things and found they had many common interests. The rapport was so easy, Julianna felt as if they'd been friends forever. She regretted that, after today, she'd probably never see Laura and Cait again.

CHAPTER TWELVE

LUKE KNOCKED on the door of the upscale home in Pasadena, and within seconds a woman answered. Midfifties, short and plump.

"Mrs. Jenner?"

"Yes."

Luke flashed his shield. "I'm Detective Coltrane and this is my partner Detective St. James. We'd like to talk to you for a few minutes. Can we come inside?"

The woman stared. "Uh…what's this about?"

"It's about your daughter's case."

"But…that was fifteen years ago." She finger combed her graying hair but she stood back to let them in.

Glancing around, Luke noticed Mrs. Jenner's standard of living had greatly improved in the past fifteen years. At least compared to what he'd read in the file.

"We're taking another look at the case and we'd like to go over some facts with you."

"Okay. If I can remember."

How could she not remember! Luke recalled every minute following his son's abduction, the searching, the calling, the seesaw of emotion, one moment hope—and then the soul-wrenching devastation when they didn't find him. The unbearable heartbreak when they did. "I know this is difficult to talk about, but it's important."

She indicated the couch, but Luke took the chair. Jordan preferred to stand. The woman sat on the couch. "You remarried a short time after Renata's disappearance—is that right?"

"Yes. Rennie's stepfather and I weren't doing all that well before…what happened, and it got worse afterward."

"How did Renata get along with her stepfather?"

"I told the police before that they had problems, but Fred would have never done anything to hurt her."

"We're only asking questions, Mrs. Jenner. Not accusing anyone."

She wrung her hands together, her lips thinned. "Well, the police did before! They wouldn't leave us alone, kept asking us questions and more questions. They even hunted down my brother who only stayed with us for a little while."

"I understand." More than she could know. Even though he'd gotten a bit of a break when Michael went missing because he was a police officer, he and Jules were still questioned ad nauseam. Jules had nearly had a breakdown because of it. "It's standard procedure to start an investigation of this type with the family. Most crimes against children are committed by family members—or someone close."

"While the real murderer gets time to escape."

Jordan glanced at Luke. "Can you tell us where your brother is now?" Jordan asked.

Luke studied the woman. The mention of her brother made her sit up straighter. They'd been able to get an address for the ex-husband and for the girl's biological father, Terrence Willis, but they hadn't been able to locate Mrs. Jenner's brother.

"He's a good man."

"Do you have his address? We'd like to get in touch with him."

She shook her head. "He's a restless sort. Moves around a lot."

"So how do you contact him? Do you have his number?"

"No. He calls collect."

"How often?"

"Once a month maybe. He's called more lately though since I told him about that magazine that's doing stories about Renata. He worries about me."

Luke felt the hairs on the back of his neck prickle. "So, have you talked to the person writing the stories?"

"A few times, then I decided not to anymore. It was too upsetting."

"When did your brother last call?"

"A week ago."

"Do you know if the writer talked to him?"

"I don't think so. I told him she wanted to, but he didn't want to speak to her. It made him mad that she was digging up all this after so long."

"Do you keep records of your phone bills and payments? You could easily tell where his phone calls came from."

Her eyes narrowed.

"Can I see your last couple of bills."

Without answering, she got up and went into another room. The woman was gone so long, Luke was about to go see what she was doing, but just as he stood, she came back.

"No, I don't have them. I'm sorry."

Jordan gave Luke a disbelieving glance. Finally, after another half hour of questioning about her ex-husband and other people who were in their lives at the time Renata was murdered, they had little more information than when they came. "One last question," Luke said. "Your brother wasn't married when Renata disappeared. Is he married now?"

"Not anymore."

"Do you know where his ex-wife lives?"

"Of course. Marion was my sister-in-law."

"Did they have children?"

"A boy and a girl."

"Why did they divorce?"

Mrs. Jenner pulled back. "I'm sorry, Detective, but I don't see the point."

Luke wasn't sure there was one. Except that his ex might know more about Beau Thatcher than anyone else. Before they left, Luke made a point of getting the sister-in-law's name, address and phone number, gave Mrs. Jenner his card and told her to call if she remembered anything else.

Backing out of the driveway, Luke said,

"It's suspicious that her brother refused to be interviewed for Jules's story."

Jordan shrugged. "It's natural for a brother to be protective and not want to see his family hurt again. What I don't get is the no address thing. The brother calls her, but she doesn't know where he lives. How bogus is that?"

"My take, too."

"On the other hand, maybe he's avoiding support payments. People do odd things, but it doesn't mean they're serial killers."

Luke glanced at Jordan. His buddy always gave people the benefit of the doubt. A great quality, but sometimes Jordan's analyzing slowed the process. Luke's mode was action—as quick as possible. "Right. Now let's see if we can get Mrs. Jenner's phone records."

"What about the mother's ex-husband. I've got an address for him."

Luke stopped at a traffic light. "Right now, I'm more interested in the brother's ex-wife."

"Because?"

"Because he called his sister more often after hearing about Jules's story. Because they have kids together. He may have visitation rights or send support payments. She might know where he is. Because this guy was barely looked at in the previous investigation."

"It's late. Let's do it tomorrow," Jordan said.

"I have a flight out in the morning."

"So, I'll do it then."

Luke tightened his grip on the wheel. Damn, he hated when his personal life interfered with his job.

But his father wasn't in any shape to go home on his own. And there was no way he'd send Jules back alone.

CAIT WAS SLEEPING on the couch and Julianna and Laura were in the kitchen when Luke and Jordan returned.

"Sorry we were gone so long," Jordan said, greeting Laura with a kiss.

Julianna looked away. The adoring glances between the two only magnified the gaping void in Julianna's life—a void she hadn't realized was there until she'd seen Luke again. Until she'd witnessed a normal loving relationship.

For the past five years, her career and her friends at work had filled her days and many nights. She'd gone out on assorted dates, most of which were pleasant, and she'd even dated one guy for a couple months. But mostly it was just something to do.

But whenever a guy wanted to get serious, she immediately stopped seeing him. She wasn't ready for that. She doubted she'd ever be. But why not?

Maybe Luke had been right. Maybe she had run away. Maybe she was still running. At least in the romance department.

Loving someone meant opening yourself up for more heartbreak. She couldn't put herself through that again. Couldn't even chance it. She felt anxious just thinking about it.

"I'll carry Cait to the car for you," Luke offered.

Laura gathered Cait's things, Jordan wrote something on a piece of paper and left it for Luke on the desk, and Luke gently picked up the sleeping child. The wistful look in Luke's eyes as he cradled Cait in his arms tugged at Julianna's heart.

He'd so wanted another child. But she'd been adamantly against it. She'd told him they couldn't simply replace their son. Told him no one could take Michael's place in her heart. After that, the crevice in their relationship kept widening and widening until it was a canyon neither could cross.

They said their goodbyes to Jordan and Laura and when Luke came back inside, he went to the fridge and grabbed a Coke. "You want one? Or something else?"

She and Laura had already had tea and later some wine. Enough so that she was a little sleepy. "No thanks."

Luke shifted the bottle of soda from one hand to another, bounced around the kitchen as if looking for something to do, then went to the back door and peered out. He was wired, a familiar pattern when he'd just come off the job. Sometimes it took hours for him to wind down.

"I'm going outside," he said, opening the door.

He didn't ask her to join him, he wanted to be alone. In the past, she'd allowed him his time—but not tonight. She wanted to know what had happened with the people he'd talked to.

Luke stood at the rail, his gaze straight ahead.

"Did you and Jordan get what you wanted tonight?"

Slowly, he turned to face her. "Some things. Not all. I have to go out again."

"But it's nine o'clock."

"I know."

Luke's cell phone rang, cutting off her protest.

He pulled the phone from inside his jacket, looked at the number then answered. "Yo, Rico. You got something good, I hope."

Luke listened. "Which means?" Then he nodded and looked off into the distance. "Okay. Enough." Chuckling, he said, "Too much information, dude."

She wished she knew what he was talking about. Had Rico uncovered who sent the e-mail messages?

Looking at her, Luke said into the phone, "Bottom line, we've got squat, right?"

After he hung up, Julianna waited for him to explain. But he didn't. Instead, he paced, his thoughts elsewhere.

"You're going to wear out the wood if you don't stop. What did Rico want?"

He banged the back of a chair with the palm of his hand. "The guy uses Anonymizer sites for his e-mail messages."

"What?"

"Web sites that are located in other countries. They receive the e-mail message, strip its ID, then send it to another site in another country that does the same thing. The message goes through the process up to a couple dozen times. Most Anonymizer sites don't keep records. That's why the messages are almost impossible to trace unless someone makes a mistake."

"That's it, then?" she couldn't hide her disappointment.

"Yeah. Rico said it's how some computer viruses are sent and that's why it's so hard to track them down."

"For someone who never gave a rat about that kind of thing, you sound quite knowledgeable."

"I've learned a couple things over the years. Mostly through necessity." He gave her a tired smile. "But I still rebel at the intrusion. How did the world ever get along before computers?" he said sarcastically.

"So, we're back at square one?"

"Not completely. The fact that he uses the sites says he's experienced. That he doesn't want to get caught. That he's playing a game with us. With you."

Luke was still holding his cell when her own rang. Fear sent a quick chill down her spine. Dammit, she should've turned off her phone. But it was too late now. Most likely it was nothing. Could be her mother or her sister. Her editor, Mark. None of them knew where she was, but all had her cell number. She pushed the On button and raised the phone to her ear. "Hello."

"I know where you are."

Her heart raced. She closed her eyes, digging deep for strenghth she doubted was there. It was just a voice. *Just a voice.* Suddenly a strange calm enveloped her. If he really knew where she was, wouldn't he have done something by now? He wouldn't just keep calling, would he? How could he know anything, anyway? He was bluffing. She tightened her grip on the phone. "I don't believe you," she spat out. "If you know where I am, then prove it."

A second later, she couldn't believe what she'd done. but dammit, she was sick of the games this weirdo was playing—and they had to stop.

She waited for a response and when none was forthcoming, she handed the phone to Luke. "It's him," she mouthed.

Luke took the phone, listened, then shook his head. "He's gone." His eyes met hers. "And that was a pretty stupid thing to do."

A HALF HOUR LATER, Luke exited Highway Five on Jeffrey Road on his way to Marion

Thatcher's house in Irvine. "It won't take long," he said, glancing at Jules in the passenger seat.

The last thing Luke ever wanted to do was take a civilian along on a job. But he needed to interview the woman and he needed to do it tonight. After that phone call, leaving Jules at home wasn't an option. The guy knew her cell number. He had to know what he was doing to get it. He had to have the means. The thought made Luke's mind go nuts.

But, stubborn as she was, Jules wasn't happy about going along either, and she sat like a statue in the seat next to him, arms crossed, lips compressed.

"So, what am I going to do while you're interviewing this woman," she asked finally. "Sit in the car?"

He gritted his teeth. "No, you're coming in."

She glanced over, her mouth half open. "Won't you get into trouble?"

Yeah, he might. But it didn't matter. Jules's life was worth more than any reprimand. Worth more than his job. "Not if I play it right."

"Who is this person again?"

"Renata Willis's uncle's ex-wife."

"Oh, that explains it," she said facetiously.

"The ex-wife of one of the suspects in the Willis case."

"Ah, the guy I couldn't find."

When Luke looked at her, he didn't even try to hide his feelings. Exasperation or irritation, she wasn't sure which. Probably both.

"What? I tried and I couldn't find him," she said indignantly. "You think the ex-wife knows something?"

Luke grinned. "I don't think anything. I keep an open mind and put the pieces together later."

"And what are the other pieces?"

Glancing at the signs, he turned on Alton Parkway toward Lake Forest. "I can't say. It's a case. It's confidential."

"So, I can go along on the interview and listen to whatever happens, but you won't tell me anything more."

"Actually, I was hoping you'd make yourself scarce while I do the interview. Go to the bathroom or something."

"You're joking."

"No. I'm very serious. I'd like to keep my job." And he wanted to keep her safe. He hadn't realized just how much until that phone call when he'd seen the fear in her eyes. He'd noticed her hands trembling. For all her bravado, she was scared to death. The thought pissed him off. Made him want to punch something. Preferably the son-of-a-bitch causing it all. In fact he'd like to do more than that.

"He said he knows where I am, but I don't believe him. If he did, wouldn't he have done something to prove it?"

Luke tried to calm himself. "Not until he's ready."

"What do you mean?"

"He's playing with you. Sociopaths have huge egos. They don't want anyone forcing them to do something before they're ready. If they think they're going to be caught, they want it to be on their terms."

"That's sick."

"Yeah."

"So, why are we going to see this woman?"

He grinned. "Nice try, sweetheart, but my lips are sealed."

Luke drove up and down three streets before he finally found the right one. All the lights were out but, too bad, it couldn't wait.

When they reached the door, he said, "Just follow my lead, okay?" He rang the bell, then knocked for good measure.

Jules nodded her agreement, though he could tell she wasn't happy. It felt really weird having her there while he was working. He'd always made a point of keeping his personal and his work lives separate.

"No one's going to answer," Jules said.

He rang the bell again, and as he did, a light flicked on inside.

"Who's there?" a female voice came from behind the door.

"Police, Mrs. Thatcher. We need to talk to you." He held his shield up to the peephole.

The door slowly creaked open. A woman peered out. "What do you want?"

"I'm Detective Coltrane and…this is my partner. We'd like to come in and talk to you about your ex-husband, Beau."

"My children are sleeping. Can't this wait until tomorrow when they're in school?"

"No, I'm sorry, it can't."

Reluctantly the woman opened the door and let them in. Standing in the entry, Luke saw the house was sparsely furnished and the woman was so thin he wondered when she'd last had a meal. "We're really sorry to barge in like this, but we'll make it quick."

"Do you want to sit down?"

"Can I use your restroom?" Jules asked.

Good going, Jules.

The woman pointed down the narrow hallway. "First on the right," she said, then led Luke into the living room.

Luke sat on the lumpy couch. The only other piece of furniture was a small television set that looked as if it had been around since the Stone Ages. "When was the last time you saw your ex-husband, Mrs. Thatcher?"

"It's been a while. He doesn't see the kids, so there's no reason for him to come around here."

"Why doesn't he see the kids?"

Thatcher raised a hand to her mouth. Her dark eyes were large in a painfully gaunt face. "I had a restraining order during the divorce and for a while afterward."

"Was he abusive?"

"Not with the children. But I didn't want to take the chance that he might be."

"How long ago did you see him?"

"A year maybe."

"And do you know where he lives?"

She shifted in her seat. "Has he done something wrong?"

"No, we're just looking into an old case, his niece's abduction several years ago. I'm sure you know about that."

"Oh, yes. That was so terrible. We weren't married then, but he told me about it."

"What did he tell you?"

"He was worried that someone would think he had something to do with it."

Luke's interest piqued. "Did he say why?"

Rubbing her hands over her bare arms, Thatcher said, "Because he spent a lot of time with her and he'd been there visiting right before it happened. Funny they never found who did it."

Yeah. Funny. "Where does he live?" Luke repeated.

"I don't know. Last I heard he lived somewhere near San Francisco."

Luke looked up to see Jules standing behind Mrs. Thatcher, her eyes wide.

"Do you have a phone number to reach him if there's an emergency with the children?"

"Yes, but I don't know if it's any good anymore." She got up and went down the hall, returning a few moments later with a piece of paper. "This is it. Are we done now?"

"Sure, just one more thing. Do you have a photo of your ex-husband?"

"I do, but it's an old one."

"That's fine. Can I see it please?"

Luke couldn't believe his luck. An old

phone number was better than no number. A photo was even better. At least they had a starting place, and the fact that the guy was near San Francisco was very interesting.

"Is this good?" Jules asked on their way to the car. "It's creepy that he lives near San Francisco."

"I don't know if it's good or not, but it's something." Luke slid inside, started the engine, then waited for Jules to get in before he pulled the photo from his jacket pocket and showed it to her. "Does he look familiar at all?"

She shook her head, frowning. "No. But he looks scary."

"Yeah, but the last I heard, looking scary isn't a crime." He'd been amazed that the woman had given him the photo. He'd fax it to Jordan and let him check it out. If the guy was in the system at all, it could help in locating him.

"So, what now?"

"We go home, sleep a little and then head for New Mexico in the morning." He gunned the motor and headed for home. Turning onto the freeway, he took out his cell and called Jordan. "Sorry to call so late, but I've got some information for you."

"Shoot."

Luke gave his partner the lowdown on Thatcher and asked him to follow up once he sent the photo. That's all he could do for now. He pocketed the phone.

After a few more minutes humming along the highway, Jules said out of the blue, "What if he really does know where I am?"

He turned to look at her. In the pale yellow glow of freeway lights, she looked drawn, tired. For the first time he noticed the dark smudges under her eyes. The tense set of her jaw. Though she wouldn't admit to being scared, nothing could hide the physical evidence.

"Don't worry. No one will get past me."

The doubt in her eyes made him feel like crap.

THE PLANE HIT the runway at seven-thirty the next morning, and they were on the road to the hospital in Santa Fe within a half hour. Julianna glanced out the window at the dark foreboding sky. The weather gurus had predicted rain and Luke had said he wanted to get his father and head back to the ranch before the high-ways got slick.

The narrow roads between Santa Fe and the ranch could be treacherous when wet, she knew and even now, Luke seemed to be concentrating heavily on his driving. Or was he figuring out another strategy?

"I've been thinking," Julianna said.

"Uh-oh. That means trouble." Luke kept his eyes riveted on the road.

He seemed in a good mood despite the fact that he'd spent the night sitting in a chair at the foot of her bed, his weapon at his side. Every time she'd awakened and looked at him, he'd been alert. Poor guy probably hadn't slept but a few minutes. But then, she hadn't either. It was amazing they hadn't snapped at each other more often when hurrying for the flight.

Always in the back of her mind was the knowledge that Luke was only there to make sure nothing happened to her. He'd given his word and she knew he'd try to keep it no matter what. If his father hadn't needed him, Luke would've split the same night he'd arrived at the ranch. A night that seemed so very long ago and yet was little more than a week.

"I have an idea. I've thought this over for most of the night and this morning. I want to run it by you." The lightness in her voice belied what she was about to say.

"O-kay. I'm listening."

Hesitant, she nipped at the soft skin on the inside of her lower lip. He was going to think she was crazy, but then that wouldn't be the worst thing he'd ever thought about her. "I have a plan to entrap the stalker."

Luke jerked so fast to look at her, he swerved over the center line. Fortunately, there were no other cars on the road and he quickly corrected the maneuver. "Excuse me?" he said incredulously.

"I have a plan that I think will work to catch this creep."

The sound that came from Luke was half laugh and half hysterical gurgle. "The LAPD is trying to find him. I have the best guys in the field working on it as we speak. *We* have a plan."

"Mine is better."

She saw his grip tighten on the wheel. Then he cleared his throat and said, "What's better than the LAPD?"

"Using me as bait."

He stomped the brake and skidded to a screeching halt and at the same time, his arm flew out and whapped her across the chest to keep her from smashing into the windshield.

Gravel crunched under the tires as he pulled off onto the shoulder and then killed the engine.

Before Luke had a chance to get a word out, and she knew what those words would be—nutcase, insane—she said, "Please listen to me. Don't shoot me down before you even hear what I have to say. I'm not some quack with a flaky idea. Someone is threatening me. It's my life. I'm involved, just about as involved as anyone can be. And I think I know a way to get this guy."

Luke shook his head. "It's a complicated case."

"That's the problem. I'm not talking about the Willis case. I'm talking about this psycho, this sicko who's driving me crazy. *You're* making it more complicated than necessary."

"What? By following procedure?"

"Yes. We both know how that can screw things up." She'd had no intention to throw their past into it, but if it made him understand… "I think I know how to lure him out. If he intends to hurt me as he's threatened to do, why shouldn't we be prepared? Why shouldn't we be proactive and get him on our terms, not his?"

Luke clamped his lips together, turned

the key in the ignition and started the car again. Looking both ways, he pulled back onto the highway.

"At least listen to me."

"That's the most ridiculous thing you've ever come up with. For crying out loud, Jules. He could be a serial killer."

"He probably is. All the more reason to entrap him."

"I don't want to hear any more about this. You're naive if you think this is some kind of game. And I'd lose my job if I agreed to do anything like that."

His job. Always his job. Years of suppressed anger threatened to erupt. Only she couldn't let it. "Naive or not, I can't sleep at night wondering when he's going to pop out of the woodwork. I can't sleep knowing that if he is the one who killed Renata Willis, he's probably killed again since then. He might even be the one who—" The rest of the sentence strangled in her throat.

She closed her eyes for a moment to pull herself together. "You can't tell me you haven't noticed the similarities."

His hands clenched so tight on the wheel, his knuckles went white. She saw a muscle working in his jaw, the way it always did when he tried to suppress his anger.

"That's just it," he finally spat out. "The similarity isn't just in these two cases. There are other crimes as well. This could be big. Really big. And if we get any evidence and don't follow procedure, none of it will be admissible."

"It will be if you listen to my plan."

Luke's face went red, and he started to say something, but a hospital sign appeared on the left side of the road and he swerved to make the turn. A few minutes later, he pulled into the visitor's parking lot. "I'm going to get my father discharged. You'll have to come with me."

She crossed her arms. "I don't *have* to do anything."

If looks could kill, she'd be dead. But she had the edge. He wouldn't leave her in the car alone and unprotected. His training wouldn't allow it. "I'll come with you if you promise to listen to my plan later." She smiled, a gesture she knew would make him even more furious with her. But sometimes pushing him to the limit was what it took to make him see that his way wasn't the only way.

He continued to glare at her. Then finally managed to say, "Okay. Now get out of the damned car."

CHAPTER THIRTEEN

"IT'S ABOUT TIME." Abe was sitting on the edge of his hospital bed, fully dressed and looking meaner than a snake.

Luke sauntered over, his nerves still taut from his conversation with Jules. Now he had to deal with his father, too. "You look great, Pops."

At that moment, Dr. Martinez came into the room. "I haven't discharged you yet, Abraham."

"Well, do it, then. I've been ready to go for hours."

The doc walked over with his stethoscope, placed it on Abe's chest, then on his back. "Take a big breath and let it out.

"Good," the physician said. "I'm going to give you a couple of prescriptions and I want you to take all the drugs as prescribed. Don't stop just because you're feeling better." He glanced at Luke as he talked, apparently thinking Luke could monitor his father. Man, was he wrong.

Jules, who'd gone to the ladies' room, walked in and went over to the bed. "You look fantastic, Abe. How do you feel?"

His old man harumphed loudly. "I feel the same as I did when I came here."

"Maybe. But you didn't look as good when we brought you in," Jules cajoled.

"Does he have restrictions of any kind?" Luke went to help his father off the bed, but Abe shrugged him off.

"No restrictions. He just needs to quit smoking and take the medication."

"Hear that," Luke said to his father, for all the good it would do. Abe did what he wanted when he wanted. Luke was surprised he'd actually stayed in the hospital.

"Okay. You're ready," the physician said. "You take care of yourself, Abraham."

As the doctor walked out, Abe slipped off the bed and carefully put his weight on first one leg and then the other.

"Who are the flowers from, Pops?" Julianna walked over to the table by the bed and smelled the purple-and-yellow bouquet. "They're beautiful."

Abe waved a hand in dismissal. "I don't

know. I don't like flowers. The smell gives me a headache."

"So why'd you leave them in the room?" Luke asked. He picked up the tiny card stuck in the middle of the arrangement. The card read, Get better. S.H. He tensed then tossed the card onto the tabletop.

"Let's go," Abe insisted. "I've had enough of this place. The food is bad and the room is always cold."

"What about the flowers? Let's take them along." Jules picked up the vase.

"He doesn't want them. Leave them here," Luke snapped as he followed his father out the door. When Jules caught up, she was carrying the flowers. Her expression dared him to say anything.

Silence filled the car on the ride from the hospital to the ranch. Luke's mind spun trying to sort out everything that had happened. He'd gotten a lead on the Willis case that could be big. Or it could be nothing. One thing was certain, it was more than they'd had before.

He had no clue if this guy was in any way connected to the threats Jules had received. But if he was their serial killer and they screwed up…everything could go down the tubes.

And Jules had a plan. He almost laughed. The woman was mad.

As if she knew what he was thinking, Jules reached out and turned on the radio to a soft jazz station. Her favorite kind of music. He remembered how she'd liked to soak in a tub of bubbles with a good book and listen to jazz playing in the background.

The thought made his groin tighten. He'd never been able to resist a naked woman in a tub of bubbles. But he wasn't going to let memories cloud his judgment.

What Jules had said about the similarities between the Willis case and Michael's triggered every bitter, vengeful emotion he'd felt five years ago. Fellings a cop couldn't afford to have. But if this guy was one and the same, and they could somehow get him… Adrenaline shot through his blood like an injection of speed.

But as he turned onto the road to the ranch, his sanity returned. He couldn't allow Julianna to act as bait to lure the guy in. He absolutely couldn't. Even if it meant catching Michael's killer. He'd already lost the two people he'd loved most in life. But at least one was still alive. There was nothing Jules could possibly say that would convince him to do anything that would put her life in danger. Nothing.

"THE FLOWERS CAME from Stella," Julianna said after Abe had gone to bed for the night. "Her initials are on the card."

Luke shrugged, then picked up the remote and clicked on the television, surfing channels until he landed on CNN.

It was 9:00 p.m., time for her to start working, but she had to talk to Luke first. They'd had no time before now because Luke had been on the phone most of the morning.

First he'd talked with Jordan and Rico, and then with some people who'd called about the job at the ranch. He'd had one guy come out to see him, but Abe had made such a big stink, the man had all but left a streak on the road in his hurry to escape.

Luke and Abe had argued and finally Luke stalked out. He was gone for the rest of the day and had come back only a few minutes ago.

Julianna went over and sat next to him on the couch. "So, if you don't want to talk about Stella and your father, let's talk about my plan."

He pressed the Up arrow for the volume on the remote and the newscaster's voice blared. She snatched the remote from his hand and hit the power button. Luke's eyes widened in surprise.

"I said I want to talk. You agreed."

He turned back to the blank television screen. "There's nothing to talk about."

She folded her arms across her chest. "I think there is and for once in your life I want you to listen to me."

His head practically spun around to look at her. "For once in my life?"

"Yes. I think my idea is a good one. I wrote something in the article that might force the issue."

Leaning forward, elbows on his knees, he rubbed his hands together. "What did you write?"

"This guy thinks he's smart and can outwit the police, so I insulted his intelligence. I intimated that he'd already slipped up and that it was only a matter of time before he was caught." She cleared her throat. He wasn't going to like the next part, so she had to hurry through it to finish. "So, the next time he calls, I'll egg him on some more, tell him I think he's a crank caller, all talk and no action. I'll play on his vanity. I already told him I didn't believe he knew where I was and it seemed to tick him off. If he really does know, that's where my plan comes in. We give him the opportunity to prove it."

Luke's eyes lit up. "How so?"

His question wasn't much, but at least he hadn't gotten up and left the room. "I do something predictable on a regular basis, like feeding the chickens or going out alone to the stable to tend the horses every day at a certain time. If he is watching as he says he is, he may do something."

"Like kill you."

"No. I'll be protected. I'll wear a wire every time I go to the stable. You'll be nearby and hear everything that goes on. And I'll carry a gun."

"You hate guns."

"I know. But this is different. I'll use it if I need to."

"The last I heard you didn't have a clue how to handle a weapon of any kind. Except to hit a guy over the head for no reason."

She ignored the barb. "You can teach me."

Almost before she got out the words, Luke pitched back on the couch laughing. "A gun-toting pacifist. That's a picture."

She had to admit, it was the last thing she'd ever have imagined doing. But some things called for change. She waited until he calmed down, then said, "I'm serious. Dead serious. And if you don't want to help me, I'll find someone else who can."

Luke sucked in some air. "Who? My father?" His frown deepened. "Which brings up another issue. How does he fit into your *plan?* Endangering other people's lives because you have a mission is ridiculous."

"Hearing you talk about me like I don't have a mind of my own is ridiculous." Abe's voice came from the doorway. "If I can do something to help, I will."

"And how long have you been standing there?" Luke snorted. "Do you always listen to other people's conversations?"

"Only when I hear my name mentioned." He came in and sat in his old leather lounger. He seemed to be moving around a little easier.

"Well, I'm not putting either of your lives in danger and that's that."

Julianna looked from Luke to Abe. "I don't know about you, Abe, but I don't need anyone's permission to do anything."

Abe laughed. "Ain't needed permission for more years than you've been alive, sweetheart."

Luke's face reddened. "You're both crazy."

"Crazy enough to want to see a killer go to jail," Julianna said. "And I can't believe you don't feel the same way."

Luke stood, anger bubbling like a cauldron inside. Yeah, he felt that way. With every fiber in his being he felt that way. But it wasn't enough to make him want to put Jules and his father within a killer's reach.

"If he's going to come anyway, why not be prepared," Jules said.

"Because we don't know he's going to do anything. Neither one of you have my experience and you need to listen to me. This isn't some action movie where you can take things into your own hands and the bad guys always lose. You'd be risking your lives. Someone could get dead. And even if you two don't care about that, I do." And then he stalked from the room.

As Luke walked toward his bedroom, rage made his stomach knot. How could Jules be so unrealistic? So stupid. And his father. He was a sick old man who couldn't even take care of his ranch. What could he do to help?

Three hours later he was still awake, his mind whirling like a blender on high speed.

But the more he thought, the more Jules's stupid idea seemed to make sense.

And he was an idiot. A delusional, sleep-deprived idiot. He rolled from the bed and headed down the hall. Seeing a soft glow of light radiating from under the door in the den, he realized Jules was still up…probably writing. Getting herself into more trouble.

Feeling an overwhelming urge to talk some sense into her, he paused by the door, then remembered that talking to Jules when she had her mind set was like talking to a statue. He went to the kitchen and on his way back with a Coke, he turned and headed for the living room.

He dropped into his father's chair and flicked on the floor lamp next to it. He glanced at the magazines in the basket. Several copies of *The Achilles' Heel* were on top. He reached, then drew his hand back. He didn't want to do this. He didn't want to read about abducted children. He didn't want to read about Michael.

He didn't want to…but he had to.

He picked up the stack and went through each magazine, searching for the first article Jules had written. The one about their son.

As he flipped through the magazines, he

noted that "Missing" was the name for the whole series. Each story had another title of its own. Usually it included the name of the child. When he came across one that was called "Michael's Story: with love, from his mother." Luke's heart lurched. She'd used a fictitious last name, but not the first. He started reading and noticed immediately that the story was told in a different way from the others he'd glanced at. It was in the first person.

By the time he'd finished reading three pages, his heart felt as if it were going to crack. Jules told of Michael's abduction from the first moment she'd noticed him gone, describing her panic, disbelief and fear in moment-by-moment detail.

I couldn't believe he was gone. I wouldn't believe it. I kept telling myself he had to be hiding, or playing a game.

As one realization after another hit him, Luke's heart ached for Jules. She'd been alone. He hadn't been there for her. When she'd told him how she felt, he'd said he understood, but had he really? She'd said he couldn't possibly know how it felt to be responsible for losing their son. How many times had she told him that? How many times had he told her it wasn't her fault, that it could happen to anyone. He'd seen it in his job more than once.

With every second that passed, with every negative reply from the department-store manager, panic clawed at my insides. But I had to stay in control. I had to find my son. Shivering with fear I called out. "Mikey, Mikey." I kept calling and calling. The security guards came. Someone phoned the police. When I finally realized that Michael, my four-year-old son, my only child, wasn't in the store at all, I felt a bone-chilling fear. A kind I could never before have imagined.

I ran out the door to search every inch of the mall, but the corridors seemed like tentacles reaching out in all directions. Oh, God. What should I do? If I left and Mikey came back, I could miss him. But I had to look. I ran…searching, calling out his name in every shop, asking everyone if they'd seen him, store clerks and people doing their shopping, people sitting on benches, eating at the food court. "Have you seen a little boy in a red shirt and blue shorts? Did a boy wearing a Dodgers' baseball

cap come by here? Please won't someone help me look for him?" Somewhere
in my purse I found a photo and went
back again, tears streaming, covering
the same walkways, the same shops,
asking the same questions of the same
people and showing the photo.

A tear fell onto the page and then another.
Luke felt Jules's panic as if it were his own,
her pain, her guilt, he felt it all. And by the
time he read the last paragraph, tears flowed
like rivers down his cheeks.

I see Michael every day in my fantasies—
and at night in my dreams—and in the
eyes of all the children I meet. I still
search for the person who took my little boy away. I will always search. I have
nightmares about what he did to my
child, and I won't give up until he's
behind bars. Not a day goes by that I
don't blame myself. Not a day goes by
that I don't think of my little Michael
and wish it had been me instead.

Luke's chest spasmed in despair, his grief
so great he couldn't stop the unconsolable
sobs that wrenched from within.

THE NEXT MORNING, Julianna heard Luke long before she saw him coming from the bathroom. He'd showered, but he looked drawn, his eyes were bloodshot as if he hadn't slept.

Because he wouldn't listen to her, she was at a loss as to what to say or do, so she just kept on heading to the kitchen. Abe had volunteered to help with her plan, but realistically, she couldn't endanger Abe. She had to think of something, maybe someplace he could go until all this was over. Abe leaving the ranch was about as likely as him winning the Boston Marathon.

Abe was already in the kitchen when she got there. The aroma of coffee tantalized her. Abe liked his coffee strong enough to grow hair on your knuckles, and she'd gotten to enjoy it that way, too.

"Coffee's ready," he said. "Been up for a couple of hours and had breakfast, too. But I can whomp up a batch of eggs if you want."

"I'm not very hungry, Pops, but thanks anyway." She poured herself some coffee and popped in a couple pieces of toast. "This will be just fine."

As she set the plate of toast on the table, Abe said, "I hate to say I agree with Luke, but you could get hurt if you go through with this idea of yours."

"I know that, Abe." She placed her hand on his. "But I need to try. This…perverted lowlife could be Michael's murderer. It would be worth my life to take him down."

Abe's rheumy eyes sparked. "Michael's—you sure?"

"No, I'm not sure. But there are too many similarities for me not to entertain the possibility. Regardless, the man is going to continue to threaten me unless something is done. But in all good conscience, I can't put you at risk."

"You let me worry about that," he said. "If you're going to insist on doing this, then I'm going to help. Just tell me what I can do?"

Could she? Could she even consider including Abe in the plan? It wasn't his mission, it was hers. If something happened to her, so be it. But not Abe. "The one thing you can do to help is let me find a place for you to stay for a little while. A vacation spot. Maybe someplace beachy and warm."

Abe frowned, then pushed to his feet, his chair scraping on the adobe-tiled floor. "I may be an old man, Julianna, but I'm not dead. I don't have a lot of years left and dammit, if there's something I can do, by

God, I'm going to do it. And that doesn't mean going somewhere to rot on a beach."

Luke was right. The whole thing was ridiculous. A bad plan. Not a bad idea, but a bad plan since it would inevitably involve other people. She couldn't justify that. Especially not Abe. Luke, yes. He had law enforcement experience. He had a stake in the outcome. In more ways than one.

"I heard you say you wanted to learn to shoot a gun. I can teach you."

Julianna's spirits perked. "Really?"

"Best teacher around. Taught Luke when he was a boy. He's won some shooting contests, you know."

She smiled. "I heard about his shooting skills, but not the contests." Luke had never told her. Funny how little she actually knew about the man she'd been married to for five years.

"I was a crack shot with a rifle in Vietnam, and I still am."

"I don't know, Abe. I'm thinking Luke might be right. It's too dangerous."

Luke stood in the archway listening. Since last night he'd done a lot of thinking about Julianna's plan and also about his contribution to the end of their marriage.

Instead of being supportive, he'd turned to a bottle. Instead of understanding, he'd said they needed to go on with their lives, start a new family. Truth was, he couldn't imagine anything worse than bringing a child into an unhappy home. And Jules had been right about another thing. They couldn't replace Michael. They could only begin again once they learned to live with their grief.

Neither of them had handled that part very well. But by writing her stories, Jules was doing *something*. He felt a pang of remorse. All these years she'd been focused on finding Michael's killer and doing it the only way she knew how. Instead of using his skills, he'd drowned himself in alcohol and self-pity. He was appalled at his own weakness.

The way Jules handled the loss was a testament to her incredible strength. And she wasn't going to quit until she found the bastard who killed their son. He hauled in a deep breath. Perhaps working together would bring some kind of closure for both of them.

"Maybe dangerous. Maybe not," Luke said, walking into the room. He strode over, poured a cup of coffee and set it on the table, pausing before he explained. He didn't want either of them thinking he was condoning Jules's idea of taking matters into her own hands. He needed to make it a police operation. He ran a hand through his still-wet hair. "I've been thinking."

Julianna and Abe looked at Luke. "What about?" they said in unison.

Luke pulled out a chair and sat. "I've been thinking that if this plan was done in the right way, it might just work."

Jules's mouth dropped open. His dad frowned. Luke sipped his coffee. "We'd have to have backup. Sheriff Yuma, if he's around. Jordan and Rico in L.A. Rico has already set up a monitoring system on your laptop that makes all incoming messages traceable in some way. It's complicated and takes a while to follow up, but it's not impossible. If we get a location on the guy and he's in their area, they'll handle it from there."

When Jules and his dad simply sat there staring at him, he went on. "First thing for us to do here is get a tap on this phone. If the guy's using disposable phone cards, it won't do much good, but if he gets sloppy and uses a private phone somewhere, we might get lucky and locate the source. Jules, you'll keep your cell off, so if he calls it has to be the land line. Jordan is sending me wires, so we can be hooked up and transmitting all the time. No one will do anything without the rest of us knowing what that is. Even at night. And Jules, I'll train you to shoot a handgun."

"I can do that," Abe said.

"A handgun, Pops. Not your expertise."

"I taught you."

Luke rubbed his chin. "And a good job you did. But I learned even more at the police academy and by practicing at the gun range."

"I'm a good shot."

Luke felt as if he were battling a five-year-old who wouldn't give in. "Dad. I need control of the situation or we're not going to do anything. Lives are at stake. It's critical that we have one person in charge and that's me since I have the experience and the connections." He looked from one to the other. "Can you two agree to that? If not, that's it. We're not doing anything."

"Sure," Jules answered without hesitation. "You're the expert."

Finally, Abe reluctantly said, "Okay."

"You're the sharpshooter, Pops. I want you to find a place from where you can give the most cover to Jules when she goes to the stable each day. The second she goes out the door, you're going to be in position. I'll have the stable and other outbuildings rigged with cameras so we can see the entire place."

"If he's watching, won't he see us setting all this up?"

"If he's watching, all he'll see is us working. We'll have to be discreet."

Just then, Luke's cell phone rang. He answered, "Coltrane." It could only be one of three people. Jordan, Rico or the captain.

"Yo," Rico said. "We've got another e-mail message."

"What's it say?"

"It's weird. It's like a poem, but it's not. You want me to read it?"

"Sure. Let me get a pencil and paper."

As Luke finished writing, Rico said, "We've also got a phone number for Beau Thatcher from Mrs. Jenner's phone bill. There were several calls but only one we can track."

"Go for it," Luke said. "What about the stepfather?"

"Jordan's on it as we speak. The guy's moved around a lot."

Luke took a deep breath. He had to tell Rico about their plan, and he knew exactly what his by-the-book buddy would say.

Better to wait until later when his dad and Jules weren't there. "I'll get back to you after I talk with Jules about the message. If we can decipher what it means, then we can send a response."

This was the perfect time to set the bastard up. Jules thought he'd likely respond after the article ran, so they had a week to put their plan together. But the sooner they got everything in place, the better.

After he hung up, Luke said, "Okay, are we all on the same page?"

Abe nodded. "What if this guy doesn't make a move?"

"Don't know. He's been pretty predictable calling after each installment and he's just sent another e-mail message." He picked up the paper. "It's some kind of rhyme. Jules, does this mean anything to you?"

"This is weird," Julianna said. She read the message out loud.

"In the cicada's cry
No sign can foretell
How soon it must die."

"It's like haiku, but I don't know for sure."
"What the heck's haiku?" Luke asked.

"It's a kind of Japanese poetry. I think there has to be a certain number of syllables to each line. I can look it up on the Internet." She got up and left the room.

"It's gibberish," Abe piped up. "And if that's all it says how do you know who it's from?"

"He sent it to Jules's attention, and signed it with a star, the same as the others."

Jules came back with her borrowed laptop, set it on the table and turned it on. "I'll Google it and see what happens."

Luke watched as she typed in the word *haiku* and instantly several references came up. One site explained the original construction of Japanese haiku poetry, that there needed to be seventeen syllables divided into lines of five, seven and five. After reading the explanation, Jules hit another link that showed popular haiku writers.

Luke shoved a hand through his hair. "This isn't doing us any good unless we know what he means."

"Since this has been translated, it doesn't seem to follow the exact description for Haiku structure, does it?"

Luke and Abe both shrugged.

"But I think he's telling me I won't know when he's going to strike. And by the way, it says here that particular poem was written by Basho, a seventeenth century samurai."

"So this psycho thinks of himself as a samurai? A warrior of some kind?"

Jules slumped back in her chair. "I don't give a rat what he thinks. It just creeps me out knowing he's probably not some Neanderthal idiot. Idiots aren't into poetry."

"Serial killers believe they're above the law, too smart to get caught. They'll even taunt the police like the BTK killer. They're narcissistic bastards."

"Another good reason for you to get out of that job, son."

Luke did a double take. He couldn't remember the last time his dad called him "son." He couldn't remember his father ever giving a damn about what he did with his life. Once he'd left the ranch, that was it. "I didn't know you cared," he answered, then wished he hadn't sounded so sarcastic.

Abe crossed his arms over his chest. "I don't. But other people do." He glanced at Julianna. "Maybe they shouldn't."

Julianna looked away. Started typing again. "This Basho guy wrote some two hundred haikus before he died. Weird, huh?"

"Do *you* know anyone who writes haikus?"

She smiled. "I know a macho guy who wrote a poem once. But he's no threat."

Luke blanched. One freaking time he'd tried to do something romantic and it comes back to bite him. He stood, pulled a gun from the back of his pants.

Jules gasped.

"You wanted to learn to shoot a gun. I'm ready to start now."

CHAPTER FOURTEEN

"ARE YOU SURE we won't be seen doing this?" Julianna eyed the tree in the distance where Luke had tacked up a homemade target.

"I'm sure. We're two miles out with nothing around but pasture and an occasional tree. How could anyone see us? Now stand still and get in position."

"Someone could've followed us."

He came up behind her. "Not the way we came. It was totally open. I would've spotted them. We've got a clear view all the way around. Both hands now."

She felt his body against her back. Warm and big and she fit perfectly against him. He placed his left hand on her arm, his face against the side of hers. Her heartbeat quickened.

"That's better," he said, his hot breath fanning her cheek.

There was no way in hell she could concentrate enough to hit anything with him so close.

Her mind flashed to the night they'd made love in Venice Beach and her blood rushed.

"You're not concentrating." He stepped away. "Your hand is wavering all over the place. You'll never hit anything like that."

"I will if you move away."

He smiled wickedly. "Distracting, am I?"

"Mildly."

"Well, get used to it. There will always be distractions, so you have to learn to focus. Keep the gun raised, with both hands on it and your eye on the target. Feet shoulder-width apart. Once you're ready, squeeze off a round to see how it feels."

"Don't I have to do something to prepare?"

"You are prepared. Now just do it. Think of this as a trial run to see if you want to continue."

She moistened her lips, took aim and squeezed the trigger. Blam! She jerked back and almost dropped the gun. Her hand felt as if a live grenade had gone off in it. "That's a mean kick."

"Only when you've never done it before. You'll get used to it now that you know what to expect."

She squinted at the target. "Did I hit anything?"

He grinned. "See that tuft of dirt sticking up? That's what you shot."

"I shot the ground. That's great."

"Do you want to go on?"

"Until I hit the bull's-eye."

He gave more instructions and she kept at it until her hand was red and swollen and by the time they rode back, it was late afternoon. But finally, she'd hit the target. Not dead center, but close enough. Taking the horses into the barn, Julianna looked at Luke. "Well, you haven't said how I did."

He smiled. "You did just as I expected you would."

"You mean I sucked." And maybe she did, but each shot had been better than the last.

"No, I meant that I knew you'd keep at it until you got it right. Now you'll have to practice or what you learned today won't mean a thing."

"I will. But isn't there a closer place to do it? I don't want to have to drag you with me every time."

Luke unbuckled Balboa's saddle and pulled it off. "Now how would you know if you were doing something wrong if I wasn't there to tell you?"

She laughed. "Believe me, I know when I'm doing something wrong. Don't you?"

He shook his head. "Nope. I leave that up to other people."

She wasn't sure if he was kidding or deadly serious. Didn't matter. There were more important things at stake than her relationship with Luke. *Relationship*. How ridiculous. She had no relationship with Luke. He was her ex-husband for God's sake.

"Besides, you're not going anywhere alone unless it's part of the plan."

That's what *he* thought.

But every day after that, Luke shadowed her. Whether she went outside to the patio or to the store, he went with her. When she practiced her shooting, Luke stood at her side. Or behind her. Or he lay on the grass a few feet away, studying her, critiquing when he felt the need. And the more he watched, the more acutely aware of him she became; his strong hands and long fingers, the way he tipped his head when he was thoughtful, the little dip between his bottom lip and his chin. His sensuous mouth. Luke was a hard man to ignore. Her heart raced just thinking about him.

On the third day, Julianna hit the outer edge of the bull's-eye. "Yes!" she called out and raised a hand in the air. She turned to Luke. "Hey, I think I'm getting the hang of this."

A rhythmic pounding sounded behind Julianna. She turned to see Stella Hancock galloping toward them on a brown-and-white pinto, slowing as she got closer. The older woman's hair blew free in the wind and for a moment, Julianna thought she looked much younger than her years.

Tugging the reins, the neighbor pulled the steed to a halt near Julianna. She smiled. "I was out riding and heard the shooting. I couldn't figure out why anyone would be firing a gun out here, so I came to see."

Luke scowled.

"Luke was just teaching me how to shoot," Julianna said. "Now, we're seeing who's the best shot."

Stella slid from the mare, stood next to Julianna and squinted at the target. "Not bad. I used to be a fair shot myself."

"Really." Julianna glanced at Luke who was now ignoring the woman. Being rude. "Want to try it?" Julianna held out the gun.

Rising from his spot on the grass, Luke all but growled, "We better go."

Stella shook her head at Julianna's offer of

the gun and reached for her own weapon hanging on a holster from the saddlehorn. She released the safety, took aim and nailed the target dead-on.

"Wow. You're better than Luke," Julianna said, smiling. "You've obviously done a lot of shooting."

"Since high school."

"You must've had a good teacher."

"The best. Abraham taught me." Stella took aim and squeezed off another shot. Another bull's-eye.

Julianna's mouth fell open in surprise but not because of Stella's superb shooting. "Really. You've known Abe since high school?"

Luke couldn't not look. But he didn't say a word.

Stella looked at Luke, then back to Julianna. "As I mentioned before, Abraham and I have known each other a very long time."

She knew Luke was probably smoldering because she was talking to Stella, but she didn't care. She wondered if Luke knew that Stella and his father had known each other for so long. He must've. But looking at him, he seemed as surprised as she was.

"Here, I'll show you a trick," the older woman said.

Luke launched to his feet. "We don't have time for tricks. We have to go, Jules."

Stella didn't say a word, but after a few seconds, gave a resigned shrug. "It was nice talking with you, Julianna." She turned, hitched herself up into the saddle and looking at Luke said, "You, too, Luke."

As Julianna watched the woman ride away, her mind spun. What a bizarre exchange. She swung around to face Luke. "That was rude."

"She wasn't invited."

She stomped over to him. "I was talking to her and whether you like it or not, I can talk to whomever I please."

He snatched the gun from her hand and holstered it.

"Whatever is with you, Luke, it's been going on for a long time. Get over it."

For the first time in years, Luke seemed speechless.

"Did you know that she and your father have known each other since high school?"

Luke kicked at a clump of grass, his expression odd.

He knew something. Enough to make him hate the woman.

"Did you know that Abe taught her to shoot?" she pressed for an answer.

"No," Luke snapped. "And I don't care."

They walked in silence to get the horses they'd tethered at the tree a few yards away.

Maybe he didn't care, but she did. Something had happened a long time ago that profoundly affected Luke's relationship with his father, and it had something to do with Stella Hancock. She was sure of it.

FOR THE REST OF THE WEEK, Luke barely spoke to Jules, but he dogged her wherever she went. The only time he allowed her to be alone was when she was in her room, when she went to the bathroom, or out to the barn at dinnertime to feed the horses. He knew she hated having him around all the time, that was obvious.

But it was part of the plan. And for the most part, it was *her* plan, so he knew she'd stick with it no matter how uncomfortable he made her feel.

Abe had taken on the job of feeding the horses in the mornings because he thought it might look suspicious if Jules did it all the time. Luke had to agree. And with something to do his father seemed more energetic and more eager to help around the ranch.

Normally his dad was a loner, but lately he seemed to thrive on conversation with Jules. But never with Luke, and that fact stuck in Luke's craw like a fish bone.

Waiting inside the back door for Jules to return from the barn, his mike on and his gun at ready, Luke scanned the area with binoculars. Nothing. Which was as he'd expected. The stalker had been quiet. No phone calls. No e-mail messages. Which could be a good sign or a really bad one.

Luke's natural instinct as a cop was to expect the worst, and he was even more vigilant where Jules was concerned. He wasn't going to let anything happen to her.

The surveillance cameras had arrived by special delivery at the beginning of the week and he'd set them up within a couple of hours. He'd also received more information from his partner. Rico and Jordan were putting together a location grid for all the abduction cases that had a similar M.O. A grid had been done in one of the previous investigations, but some cases were so old, they hadn't been included. The Willis case was one of them.

The plan was for Rico to e-mail the grid to Luke tonight. Now he just had to get Jules to pull it up on her laptop and then leave the room so he could discuss it with Rico and Jordan on the phone. Jules had always been piqued when he withheld information about his job, even though she'd known from the get-go that was how it had to be.

Watching from the back door, Luke fidgeted as he waited for Jules to come out of the barn. She was taking longer than normal. He checked his watch. His muscles tensed. Unnecessarily so. Both he and Abe were plugged in and would hear her if she breathed a word.

She did have her mike turned on, didn't she? He'd told her to make sure before she left. Dammit.

He flung open the door, heard it bang against the house as he loped across the yard. Halfway there, Jules appeared in the doorway. Feeling stupid, he slowed his pace.

Her expression switched from surprised to puzzled as he neared. "What's going on?"

He peered inside the barn. "Everything okay?"

She placed her hands on her hips. "Of course. You'd know if it wasn't." She zeroed in on his face. "Were you worried?"

"I—uh…wanted to see if the horses had enough hay or if I need to go to town in the morning." He stepped into the barn. Yeah, like she believed that.

A tiny smile formed as she followed him inside. "There's enough for a couple days. But no oats. Doesn't Abe ever work the horses?"

Luke leaned against a bale of hay. "He used to. I think it's too much work for him now."

"Then he should let them pasture more to get some exercise."

Jules sat on a bale across from him, legs dangling. "Have you had any luck with hiring someone?"

"I've got another guy coming out in the morning. He sounds perfect. But you know how that goes."

"What about Abe?"

"I talked to him, told him if he screws it up again, I'm washing my hands of it."

"But isn't that what he wants?"

He shrugged. "I can only do so much."

She didn't seem interested in his response; she seemed to be studying him. "Do I have food on my face or something?"

"No." She laughed, almost self-consciously, looked away, then picked at the bale of hay where she sat. He liked it when she laughed. Especially when he made her laugh. It had always felt good knowing he could affect her in that way. He wondered if she ever remembered things like that about him. Not that it made any difference now.

Once, they'd promised to be there for each other no matter what. But when it came to crunch time, she'd bailed. That bitter truth tasted like bile in his throat every time he thought about it. The solution was not to think. But it was very hard to do when she was right next to him. When he could smell the sweet scent of her.

She looked up again. "I was just thinking that the next installment of the story comes out in the next day or so. It could be out already in some areas."

He couldn't blame her for being anxious. He went over and placed an arm around her shoulders. "We can call everything off the second you say so."

She leaned against him. "Thanks. But I have to see this through."

Their microphones suddenly crackled and whined. Jules winced at the screeching sound and fumbled with the switch. "What the devil?"

"Abe," Luke said as he bolted out the door, pulling Julianna along. They ran to the house and inside met Abe in the kitchen, sitting in a chair, his wire on the table.

"What's going on, Pops?" Luke panted, his heart hammering. For one brief moment, he'd thought something had happened to his dad.

"This thing don't work right. Can't hear a thing."

Luke looked at him. "Where did you have it?"

Abe pointed to his right ear. His deaf one.

Luke exchanged glances with Jules, then squelched a smile. "How about trying the other side?"

"I took it out to answer the phone, and couldn't hear a thing there either."

Jules sat next to Abe and rested her elbow on the table. Her eyes suddenly dark. "Who was it?"

"I couldn't hear very well, but it was a man, I know that much."

"What did he say?" Luke leaned forward, both hands on the table.

"He said he'd be here soon."

"Did he give a name? Or say anything about why he was coming?"

"No. That was it."

Luke's nerves crackled. The caller was

either the guy he was going to meet with to-morrow…or the sicko bastard who was threatening Jules.

Jules shoved her chair back and stood. Her hands were trembling. "I'm going to bed."

"What about dinner?" Abe said.

"I'm not hungry."

Luke watched her walk from the room, her body stiff, her movements jerky. She was ter-rified. But if she wanted to continue what she started, she had to stay alert. Be on guard.

Later, he took her a sandwich and a Coke. Knocking on the door, he said, "Jules, are you awake?" When she didn't answer, he opened the door.

She lay on the bed staring at the ceiling.

"I brought you something to eat."

She kept staring at the ceiling.

"It could've been the guy I'm expecting to-morrow," Luke said as he set the tray on the night table.

"And it could've been someone else."

"Maybe. I was serious about calling every-thing off if you want to. I think we can get the guy without using you as bait. I never wanted to do this from the beginning."

She sat up, took half a sandwich. "Thanks for the snack."

He sat on the edge of the bed next to her. "I mean it, Jules. Don't ignore me."

After she finished chewing, she set the rest of the sandwich back on the plate, took a sip of Coke and blotted her lips with the napkin. She looked into his eyes. "I can't give it up, Luke. I have to go through with this."

He took her hand intending to comfort her, but at the same time, his frustration reached boiling point. "Why?" She was so damned stubborn it made him crazy. "Why, if we can do the same thing without putting you in danger? I don't understand."

She pulled her hand away and rested her head against the headboard. Sighing, she said, "I know you don't. You can't."

Luke launched to his feet. "What the hell is that supposed to mean? I'm looking out for you. I don't want anything to happen to you. How the hell does that translate into not understanding." Dammit. She was the one who didn't understand. She had no real clue what she was getting into and he wanted to shake some sense in her.

Instead, he stood there clenching his hands into fists. "Don't make this about us, Jules. It's about taking a killer off the streets. If you pull out, the result will still be the same. I'll still be doing my job and we'll get this guy."

She looked down, rubbed her arms as if suddenly cold. "I know what it's about. It's about making some psycho pay for the pain he's inflicted on his victims and their families." She moistened her lips. "Us included."

"You don't know that he's—"

"No," she interrupted. "And you don't know that he isn't. With all the similarities, my instincts say he is, and that's good enough for me. I'll give up my life to get this guy if that's what it comes to. And you're not going to convince me otherwise."

Anger and empathy warred inside Luke. God knew he'd give his own life to get Michael's killer. But he wasn't going to sacrifice Jules. No way.

She turned to sit on the edge of the bed, her feet dangling, her hands clutching the quilt at her sides. "I want your word, Luke, that if anything happens to me, if the plan backfires somehow, that you'll get him."

If anything happens to me. Luke just stood there. If anything happened to her there'd be nothing to live for. The realization hit him like he'd been slammed in the chest.

"Please promise me that."

"Nothing is going to happen to you. That's the only thing I'll promise."

"But if it does, please swear that you'll do whatever you can to continue this investigation. Not for me, for Michael."

Luke suddenly felt as if all the blood had drained from his body. He dropped onto the bed next to her again. "You know I'd do anything for Michael."

"And if anything happens to me, promise you won't blame yourself."

He grasped her hand. "How could I not? I'm here to protect you. If I can't do that then I'm even more of a failure than I thought." His voice cracked as he tried to finish. "I failed before. If that happened again—"

Her hand came up to press against his mouth. "You weren't allowed to be on the case. You did all you could. You had rules to follow." She turned away again, thrust a hand through her hair, brushed it back. "I'm the one to blame. If it weren't for me…not watching…not paying attention—" She leaned forward, her face in her hands. Her shoulders started to shake. "Please forgive me, Luke."

The words were muffled, but he heard the pain. He leaned over her, his body like a protective cover. "There's nothing to forgive, Jules."

Rising up, she waved him away, silent tears rolling down her cheeks. "It *was* my fault. I lost Michael. I lost our son. It will always be my fault and there's nothing you or I or anyone in the world or even God can do to change that. I will live with that knowledge every day for the rest of my life."

She curled over again, rocking back and forth.

He kept soothing her, rubbing her back, saying, "It's not, Jules. It's not your fault. Believe me, I know. I've seen it happen before Michael and after. It's not you."

A few moments later, he felt her go still. Then she abruptly stood, eyes red and puffy, her face drawn. "I'm tired, Luke," she choked out. "I need to be alone."

LUKE HEADED FOR THE DEN feeling as if his heart were in shreds. No matter what he said, he couldn't get through to her.

His mind tracked back to other cases he'd worked on. In almost every abduction, the mothers blamed themselves. If only they'd kept better watch, if only they'd not done this or if they'd done that. And he'd always assured them it wasn't their fault. Just like he'd told Jules.

He realized now his words had been like wisps in the wind. Words weren't enough. They could never be enough. Jules had never believed him. And how could anyone in that situation?

God knew, he recognized his own failures where Michael's investigation was concerned. And it hadn't even been his case. Jules may not have been paying attention when Michael went missing, but that didn't mean it was her fault. If he'd been more understanding, more supportive, maybe he could've made her see that. Instead he'd drowned his sorrows in a bottle.

Either way, Michael was gone. He was never going to come back. Instead of realizing that and being there for each other, they'd let the tragedy tear them apart.

In the den, he closed the door and sagged against it. He couldn't change the past, but the least he could do was honor her wishes. Though he knew whatever happened to her, happened to him as well.

He went over to Jules's laptop on the table next to his father's chair. Normally he wouldn't use her computer without permission, but now was not the time to have her looking at anything concerning Michael's abduction. Sitting, he opened the PC and pressed the On button. He clicked on e-mail and five messages popped up. He was torn between respecting Jules's privacy and seeing if the stalker had contacted her again.

Seeing Rico's name on one message, he opened it. Rico had attached a chart and the message read, "I think we're onto something here. Let me know what you think."

Luke quickly opened the attached file and an L.A. city map popped onto the screen. *Holy moly.* His eyes darted from one pinpoint to another. The lines connecting them made the shape of a five-pointed star. And Southern Cal University was dead center.

All the profiles he'd read of serial killers indicated most committed their crimes either in or near their own neighborhoods. Most took souvenirs, and many left clues of some kind to show how smart they were. The star had been the creep's e-mail signature. Yes, they were definitely onto something. Now he had to find out what.

He punched in Rico's number.

"Yo."

"It's Luke. I got your message. Any ideas?"

"No, but I'm doing another comparison of the evidence, the suspects and persons of interest in all the cases to see if there's anything that could possibly connect them with the chart. Did you show it to Julianna?"

"No. Why?"

"Since she's the one getting the messages, she might see something we don't. Something specific to her."

"Okay. I'll ask her in the morning. She's… asleep."

Luke was glad Rico didn't pursue it. "You get any other messages?"

"She has a couple right now on the new e-mail address."

"Better check them out."

Luke knew if he did, Jules would be furious. She protected her privacy like the CIA protected the President. "They don't look like anything. Spam maybe."

"Okay. Let me know if you get any information from Jules. Tomorrow, Jordan and I are going to the university."

"You got a lead there?"

"No, but since it's the center of the star, maybe it's symbolic in some way."

After he hung up, Luke glanced at the list of Jules's messages again. He shouldn't read them. But what if one was from the stalker? Jules wouldn't read it until morning and time was of the essence in any investigation.

He clicked on the first message. Spam. Someone selling Viagra. Another had a similar title. He clicked on the third message that was blank in the subject line. The message opened and he read, "I miss you. When are you coming back? Love, M."

Luke's heart felt as if it had dropped to his toes. *I miss you.* She'd lied when she said she wasn't involved. She had someone. Someone who missed her. For five years he'd wondered whether she'd found a new love. But it had always been in the abstract because they hadn't seen each other.

But this was here and now. He'd spent almost two weeks with her and he'd been encouraged because he… His heart skipped a beat. *Because he loved her.* He'd never stopped.

"What's going on in here?" Abe's gravelly voice came from behind Luke.

He turned to see his dad standing in the doorway.

"You need my help?" Abe said.

Luke smiled. He needed more help than anyone could give him. "Thanks, Pops. Not right now. In fact, the best help you can give is getting enough rest so you're alert in the morning."

"How long do you think this is going to go on?"

He shook his head. "I wish I knew. If this creep follows his pattern, I think we can expect to hear something within a few days."

Abe sat in the chair across from Luke. "I wasn't talking about that. I was talking about you and Julianna."

Luke frowned and scratched his head. "What about me and Julianna?"

"I always hoped I hadn't raised a stupid son, but lately I'm beginning to wonder."

"Lately?"

"Lately since you've been here with Julianna. She loves you, you know."

Luke stared. Finally he said, "No, she doesn't. We have a history together. She cares about me like I care about her. I want the best for her and I hope she wants the same for me. But that's it. There's no more."

His dad rubbed his chin in an exaggerated gesture. "That's the trouble with kids these days. Always looking for the logical thing. Always being realistic. Wouldn't know the truth if it gob-smacked you in the face."

"I'm no kid, Dad. And being realistic is

important in my job. People could die if I looked at the world through fantasy glasses. I know what Jules and I are to each other and I know what we aren't. No matter what you've imagined in your old age."

Abe simply smiled. "Love is there for the taking. You throw it away and you might never have it again."

Luke exhaled loudly. He heard the pain in his father's voice. The regret. "I know you loved Mom, even though—"

"Even though what?" Abe injected, indignance resonating in his words. "I loved her no matter what. That doesn't mean I never loved anyone else. It doesn't mean I always did the right thing. Mark my words, son, you may fall in love with someone else, but it'll never be the same. That first love will always be the love of your life."

Luke closed his eyes. He'd never heard his father talk like this before. Not about love. Not from the heart. Maybe now was the time for honesty. "So, why did you screw it up by seeing another woman?"

Abe's eyes clouded over. "Because I was an idiot. Because I loved her first. And I never stopped."

Luke lifted his head. "What?"

"We were high school sweethearts. We were going to be married when I came back from Vietnam. But she stopped writing and was gone when I returned. I was angry and instead of finding out what happened, I went on a binge. I let my stupid pride get in the way. Your mother and Stella were best friends back then, so finally Lizzie told me why Stella moved away…which is her secret to keep. But by that time Stella had married. I ended up marrying your mother and when the Hancocks moved back here, we all became friends. Living so close, being together so much, especially when your mother was sick…we…leaned on each other." He closed his eyes. "We made a mistake. But that doesn't mean I didn't love your mother."

Luke bolted to his feet. "I—I don't want to hear this." He didn't want to hear about his dad cheating on his mother. He'd seen his dad with that woman when he was thirteen…when his mother was dying. The vision was like a monster emerging from a dark closet. The closet he'd locked decades ago.

"Maybe you don't want to hear it," Abe said. "But it's time you did."

To Luke, talking about his father's affair

seemed almost a sacrilege to his mother. "I don't. What you have to say doesn't matter. It doesn't matter because no matter how many reasons you had, mom died knowing you betrayed her—and nothing can change that."

Grim, Abe nodded. He started to get up, but then sank back in the chair. "Okay. But for what it's worth, what you think matters to me."

Luke scoffed. "Since when?"

"I don't know. Maybe it always mattered and I was too stubborn to let you know. But what's done is done and we can't change it. Right now I care more about what *you* think of yourself."

Luke looked at his dad. "What's that supposed to mean?"

Abe shifted in the chair, obviously uncomfortable. Hell, Luke felt antsy, too.

"I know it's hard for people to get over some things," Abe said. "But believe me, if the love is there, it can be done."

Luke clenched his teeth. He couldn't do this. Not if he was going to stay alert and protect Jules.

"Your mother forgave me, you know." Abe's voice cracked. "She wrote me a letter. But I never forgave myself. Because of that, I never forgave Stella. I've ruined what little happiness we might've had, and when I see you and Julianna making the same mistakes, it makes me mad as hell."

"Mom wrote a letter?" Luke's throat constricted.

He nodded. "I still have it if you want to read it."

Luke cleared his throat. "Not now, Pops. I've got other things to do."

CHAPTER FIFTEEN

JULIANNA COULDN'T FIGURE out why everyone was so quiet at breakfast. Neither Luke nor Abe said a word. In fact they hardly looked at each other.

Luke got up to put his plate in the dishwasher.

Still sitting at the table, she asked, "Everyone sleep well?"

She hadn't. She'd barely slept a wink after Luke left her room. She couldn't stop thinking about what he'd said. But now she had to put it out of her mind. She had a job to do and that was that.

"Not very well," Abe finally answered. "But then that's nothing new when your body's old and everything aches."

"You could take some medication for that. The doctor gave you a prescription."

"Makes no difference."

"Well, if it helps you move faster, that's

kind of important considering what we're doing here," Luke said.

Abe frowned. "Okay, okay. You made your point. I'll get the damned pills."

"Jules, I need you to look at something on the laptop. Rico sent it to me last night."

"And you're just telling me now?"

"That's right." The hard set of his jaw meant he wasn't going to discuss why he'd waited. She'd seen that look before.

"Okay. Let's go." They went into the den and Abe followed.

"Turn it on and go to the attachment Rico sent."

She did as he asked, then noticed there was more than one message and all had been opened. "Did you read my e-mail?"

"Yes. You went to bed and I didn't want to wait until morning to see if our psycho had sent another message."

She clenched her teeth. "You couldn't tell by the subject line or the names on the messages?" Her words came out sharp.

"No," he answered, seemingly unaffected by her irritation. As usual.

As angry as she was, she had to admit if she were in his position, she'd probably have done the same. She clicked on Rico's message then opened the attachment. A chart came up and she could see instantly what it was. "Wow. That's amazing. It's a star pattern." She looked at Luke. "What does it mean?"

"Don't know. I thought maybe you'd have some idea since you've researched some of the cases."

She sat in the chair and studied the screen. "Southern Cal is dead center. That's where Mark went to school."

"Mark?"

"Yes. My editor."

Luke gave her a strange look.

"He's a pussycat. Don't even think about it."

"Okay, but I guess he's the *M* in the other message."

She glanced at the e-mail. "Uh-huh. That's him."

She leaned back in the chair. "Does the star have to mean something?"

Luke rubbed the bridge of his nose. "Not necessarily, but in this case I can't believe it's just a coincidence. It's too perfect. What are all the things a star could indicate?"

"A Hollywood star. A celebrity," Julianna ventured.

"A constellation," Abe added. "Or a star on the Hollywood Walk of Fame."

"Maybe it's not the star that's important," Julianna said. "But the university in the middle. Maybe his next victim will be someone from there?"

"This guy likes children, not adults," Luke said.

"Maybe there's a day-care center at the university?"

Luke pondered the idea. Finally, he said, "Rico and Jordan are going to the university this morning. I'll call and tell them to check it out."

Abe pushed through to look closer at the screen. "Maybe you should check to see if any of the other victims or their families are connected to the university in some way?"

Luke turned to Abe and smiled. "Good thinking, Pops."

Abe beamed like he'd just won an award. Then, noticing that both Luke and Jules were looking at him, he sobered, apparently embarrassed. "I better go feed the horses," he said.

"And I better make a phone call." Luke pulled his cell from his pocket and he left the room.

Julianna glanced at the screen again, her mind searching for possible meanings. She and Luke had no connection to the university that she could think of. So that theory didn't hold up. The only luck she had was Mark. He'd gone to school there. But she hadn't known him when Michael...

Dammit. She couldn't go there. Taking Luke's cue, she told herself this was an intellectual problem, one where emotions only got in the way. She had to distance herself as Luke did. Think logically, not with her heart.

As her thoughts settled, she realized Luke's way of dealing with what he had to every day was pure self-protection. He had to be dispassionate or he couldn't do his job. How many times had he told her that? And how many times had she accused him of being cold? Uncaring?

Staring at the screen, a message popped up. You've got mail. Her heart skipped a beat. She closed Rico's attachment and clicked to retrieve her e-mail. As it popped up, a chill of fear jagged down her spine.

In the cicada's cry
No sign can foretell
How soon it must die.

No one travels
Along this way but I,
This winter evening.

In all the rains of day
there is one thing not hidden—
the ranch at Santa Fe.

"LET ME KNOW what you hear," Luke said, then hung up. He glanced at his watch. Just as he was thinking the guy who was coming to interview for the job should be here by now, there was a knock at the front door.

He strode to the entry, wondering where Jules had gone. She wasn't supposed to leave his sight except to go to the bathroom. "Hold on," he called out, casting about for a sign of Jules. Then he saw the door to the den was closed. She was writing again…or reading an e-mail from the guy who missed her and wanted her to come back. Probably some *GQ* executive type. The kind of guy she'd always wanted him to be.

He checked his thoughts, went to the door and pulled it open. A tall man dressed in a black hat and dark jeans stood there.

"I take it you're Mike Ryan," Luke said.

"And you'd be right," the man said and stuck out his hand.

He looked familiar, and then Luke realized it was the guy who'd asked Jules for directions at the gas station. "I think we've met before," he said, shaking hands.

Ryan frowned. "Have we? I haven't been in New Mexico for too long and don't know many people."

Luke craned his neck to see the man's car. Same car. "At the gas station outside Santa Fe about a week ago."

The man smiled, his expression searching, as if he might remember but wasn't sure. "Oh, yeah."

"C'mon in."

As the man walked inside, Luke took note that he was older than Luke, but not as old as Abe. He looked to be in okay physical condition. But something struck Luke as odd. He couldn't put his finger on it. Maybe it was the eyes. Flat gray eyes that scanned the room, examining, studying. Not unlike himself, Luke realized. But he was never as obvious. Maybe the guy had been in law enforcement in another life.

Ryan took off his hat revealing a full head of dark hair. Hair almost too dark to be natural, unless he was a Native American. But he'd said he wasn't from here and his name was definitely not native.

"Please sit down," Luke said, indicating

the couch. He took the leather chair across from the man.

"What is it about this job that interests you?" Luke asked.

"To be honest—" the man scratched his chin "—I liked that the job included room and board. Since I'm new here, it would save me from renting an apartment."

Not exactly what Luke wanted to hear. Minus one.

"I also like working on a ranch. It's what I've done all my life."

Luke gave him a mental point for a good answer, glancing at the man's hands. Rough, callused. Ranch hands. "And if you find the people you work for are sometimes hard to get along with? How would you handle that?"

"I've worked with a lot of bosses and ranch hands in my time, and found the best thing is to let them simmer. I never take it personal and I let most problems work out on their own."

Not proactive, but not reactive either. Luke neither added or subtracted points. "Did you bring a list of past employers?"

"Right here. It's my résumé."

Plus two. Luke felt a spurt of hope. He

hadn't had much of that when he set out to find someone to help Abe because many ranch hands were drifters. Maybe he'd lucked out this time.

After more questions, Luke asked Ryan if he wanted to ask anything.

"I think you explained it all pretty well," he said. "But I thought you said there were no women here."

Luke's attention piqued. "I did. Why do you ask?"

The man pointed behind Luke. Jules's purse was on the counter top. "Oh, she's just visiting."

He nodded.

When they finished, Luke suggested they go out to the barn. "My dad went out to feed the horses and it's taking him longer than it should. You'd have to keep an eye on him, but without his knowing it."

"I did the same with my own dad before he passed away."

Experience with old codgers. A plus.

"Pops," Luke called from the door as they entered the barn. "I have someone I want you to meet."

Abe poked his head up from Balboa's stall. "I'm busy, can't you see?"

"Take a break. I want you to meet Mike

Ryan. He might be interested in the job. That's if he can stand being around a cranky old man."

Abe practically flew out of the stall. "The only cranky one around here is you." He held out his hand. "Nice to meet you, Mr. Ryan."

Luke held back a smile. All he had to do was make his dad think they were on opposite sides and Abe was all over it.

Just then Luke noticed that Abe's wire was sitting on top of one of the hay bales. He quickly pointed Mike to the stalls, urging him forward with a hand on his shoulder. "This is Balboa, and the Appaloosa over here is Cheyenne."

"Nice stock."

Though he was looking at the horses, Ryan's eyes never stilled, making Luke's skin itch. But anyone he didn't know would make him uncomfortable right now. It wasn't as if hiring a ranch hand was all they had to think about.

"When would I start?" the man asked. He glanced at Luke. "If you decide to hire me."

The question took Luke off guard. He hadn't thought about a start date because he was so preoccupied with just finding someone. But obviously this was not a good time to bring anyone else onto the scene. "Two weeks," Luke said. "We have some things to tie up first."

"When will I know whether you're interested or not?"

It was a valid question. But Luke hadn't made up his mind yet. And he still had references to check out.

"You can start right now," Abe said.

Luke was both surprised and encouraged that his dad suddenly seemed agreeable to having someone working on the ranch. But he wasn't going to hire anyone without checking him out first. "It would be two weeks, Pops. If you recall, we have some other things to deal with right now."

Awareness dawned in Abe's expression. His gaze shot to his wire on the hay bale. Luke led Mike toward the door. "Let's say I give you a call by the end of the week to let you know."

Luke walked back to the house and just as Ryan started for his car, Jules appeared in the doorway. Her eyes went wide when she saw the man.

"Howdy, ma'am," he said and continued on to his vehicle.

After Ryan left, Luke walked over to Jules. "What's wrong? You look like you've seen a ghost."

"That man. What was he doing here? I've seen him somewhere before."

"You're right. He was at the gas station when we stopped on the way to see Abe at the hospital. And he was here interviewing for the job."

She seemed relieved, but not totally. "I don't know. He gave me the willies."

"Well, fortunately, you won't have to be working with him. Abe will." Luke went inside.

Jules followed him into the kitchen.

"Is Abe okay with that?"

"Yeah. He seemed to be. Maybe he's resigned to it. He knows he can't fight it forever."

"He's been in the barn for a long time. How come?"

"Don't know. We had a pretty heavy discussion last night. Maybe he's hiding until I'm gone."

She shifted from one foot to another. Rubbed her hands together.

Picking up on her nervousness, Luke said, "Something bothering you? Besides the fact that I looked at your messages."

He'd have been upset, too. But given their *plan,* he considered it all part of the job.

"It's not that. Come with me. I want you to see something."

ABE STUCK THE WIRE back in his ear. He'd seen doubt in Luke's eyes when he saw it on the hay bale. A look that said Luke thought he was losing it. Anger flared inside him thinking that his son considered him an old man, too sick and addled to manage the ranch by himself.

It wasn't true. Not all of it anyway. Maybe his body wasn't working as well as before, but his brain was still as sharp as ever. If he had to have someone help with the physical work, maybe that would be okay. But no one was going to tell him he couldn't think for himself.

The mirror might say one thing but Abe didn't feel any different inside than when he was twenty. He just knew more about life and its consequences now than he did then.

He hoped that someday Luke would realize that giving up love for pride was a huge mistake. Abe knew only too well that he'd forever pay the price if he didn't.

He'd wanted to explain, tell his son the whole story, but Luke wasn't interested. Maybe someday, when all this stuff with Julianna was over.

Abe's hands clenched. He got angry just thinking that someone wanted to hurt his daughter-in-law. Ex-daughter-in-law, he reminded himself. Fact was, he was glad Luke was there. If there was one thing Luke was good at, it was protecting people. He'd done it all his adult life, sometimes to his own detriment.

That his son was making the same mistakes he had, broke Abe's heart. If only Luke realized before it was too late. His own biggest regret was that he'd taken so long to realize the mistakes he'd made. And now he had to live with the mess he'd made.

A vision of Stella's face formed in Abe's mind. She was a beautiful woman. Even now. If years ago he hadn't been such an idiot… He sighed, suddenly feeling very old.

All those wasted years.

And now it was too late.

"IT DOESN'T MAKE SENSE," Luke said.

"It does to the person who wrote it. I looked up the original haiku and he's changed some of the words in this last part. I think he's giving me notice that he's going to strike, but I won't know when. A scare tactic."

"He could be bluffing."

"He mentioned the ranch in Santa Fe. I think he knows where I am, Luke."

"But isn't that the idea? Are you having second thoughts?"

Julianna paced the room while Luke wrote something on a pad of paper.

"I have to let Rico know."

"Has he gotten anything on the e-mail trace he was doing before?"

Luke shook his head. "He said it would take a while, and even then he may not get anything."

"So, that leaves us where?"

"With the same plan as before. We all continue doing what we're doing. One of us might get lucky."

"Any news about the grid?" she asked.

"Rico is getting a faculty list from the university for the time periods surrounding each crime. Jordan has some thoughts about narrowing in on staff involved in the writing programs. That haiku stuff only appeals to a certain kind of person."

Julianna stopped pacing and dropped into the chair next to Luke. She was emotionally drained. It was so hard to hold onto a hope that seemed more elusive by the moment.

She leaned over the table, resting her head on her arms. A second later, she felt

Luke's warm hand on her back. Her stomach clenched.

"Do you have any thoughts?" she mumbled.

He didn't say anything for a long time, just kept gently massaging her back and shoulders, and then finally he said, "I have lots of thoughts. And they all have to do with you. With us."

With us. Lord, she wanted nothing more than to lean into him, to feel his warmth and strength wrapped around her. She wanted him to hold her and make her feel safe again.

The dull ache of loneliness she'd fought for so long began to overwhelm her. Could they ever…was there even a thread of hope that they could maybe find each other again? Find the love they once had.

No matter how much she'd pushed those thoughts from her mind, no matter how many years she'd refused to acknowledge it, she was still in love with Luke.

She bolted upright. "Luke…we have to focus on what we need to do."

Just then her cell phone rang. Her heart leaped to her throat. She'd forgotten to shut the phone off after calling Mark. Luke glared at her, but nodded for her to answer anyway. Picking it up, she glanced at the number.

Mark. It was only Mark. Relief swamped her. She stood, answering at the same time. "Mark. I'm so glad to hear from you."

Luke got up and left the room.

"What's up?" she asked, hitching her hip on the corner of the desk.

"I need you here," he said. "This place isn't the same without you."

"I can't come back yet."

"Why not? We haven't heard anything more, so why not come home?"

Julianna couldn't tell him why she couldn't. She couldn't tell him anything. But…she had a thought. "Mark, when you were at SCU, did you know any professors interested in haiku?"

"Haiku? You mean the poetry?"

"Yes."

The line was silent for a while. "I'm not sure about haiku, but there was one prof who was big in the English and poetry department. Received all kinds of awards."

"What was his name?"

"Man, you're testing my memory here. That was ten years ago, and he probably isn't there anymore."

"It's important."

"Uh, let me think. And I've got another call. I'll get back to you in a few. Okay?"

"Sure."

As she hung up, Julianna walked to the window. What was she going to do about Luke? What *could* she do about Luke? She hadn't a clue what he wanted to talk about. *Us,* he'd said. He wanted to quit their plan. That had to be it. He didn't trust her because she'd walked out on him.

But hadn't he done the same by drowning himself in booze? And what good did it do to think about any of that now? They were done.

Pushing the thoughts away, she sat at the desk and pulled out her briefcase. She had research to do on the next story. Anything to forget the ridiculous thoughts that seemed to crowd her brain. *Us,* he'd said. She pulled up FindLaw.com and set to work on the Darnell case.

Before she knew it, it was dusk and time for her to feed the horses. Luke hadn't come back all afternoon, and she had to find him before she could go out to the barn.

She didn't have to look far. He'd already come looking for her.

"You ready?" he said as they stood in the hallway. He seemed distant.

"Where were you? I thought I wasn't supposed to be out of your sight?"

"I knew exactly where you were." He pointed to a corner of her room, but she couldn't see anything. "You've bugged my room?"

"Clever, aren't I? You can't even see the camera it's so small."

"You…you creep." She punched him in the arm, whirled around and started for the door, clicking on her wire as she hurried outside and toward the barn. The sun was dropping rapidly behind the mountains and a quick wind whipped her hair into her face. She felt weary and tired and wondered how much longer she could do this.

It had to end soon, she decided, as she opened the barn door. Luke and his team were reinvestigating the case. Wasn't that her goal in the beginning?

The pitchfork lay to the side of one of the hay bales, not where she'd left it. Was Abe getting forgetful again? One of the horses whinnied. A thrashing fluttering sounded at her side. She jerked around, heard a shrill squawk, wings flapped violently in her face.

She jumped back, her heart banging through her chest. She gasped for air. Geez. A chicken. How the hell had it gotten in here?

Her eyes darted. Nothing out of place. Just the stupid bird that was now shrieking and acting like she'd scared it instead of the other way around. She calmed herself, grabbed the pitchfork handle and went to soothe Balboa. "It's okay, boy. It's okay." Her words were as much for herself as the horse.

As rattled as she was, she knew Luke was watching her every move. With cameras inside and out, he could see everything. Oh, Lord. He was going to razz her like crazy about this later. She stuck her tongue out at the camera. Still, knowing he was there gave her a sense of comfort and security. She'd missed that. She hadn't realized how much.

After feeding both horses, she tapped the microphone, the signal that she was coming out. "I'm leaving now," she said.

Balboa whinnied.

She turned. "What's up, big guy?" She reached to brush his face, but he jerked away, skittish. She heard rustling behind her. The hair on the back of her neck prickled. She sensed she wasn't alone.

Oh, God! A scream formed in her throat, but in that split second, a hand clamped over her mouth from behind. Then an arm came around her neck like a tourniquet, pinching her windpipe…crushing her against a man's body.

She fought to get away. The viselike grip at her neck tightened. Her blood roared in her ears. She flailed helplessly at the mike. He ripped it off. She couldn't scream to let Luke know. She couldn't even groan.

But Luke would know. He was watching. She glanced at the camera. Oh, God. They were under the camera, not in front of it. Luke thought she was coming out. He was waiting for her. He'd know when she didn't come out. But would that be too late.

"Hi sweetheart," a gravelly voice hissed in her ear. "You still think I'm a crank?"

In a split-second decision, she went limp, remembering from somewhere that it would take an assailant off guard. But as she slid downward, he yanked her up by the neck, compressing her windpipe even more.

She stomped at his foot but felt only air.

"You want to fight, sweetheart?" he growled. "I like women who fight."

True horror set in. She'd set a trap…for herself. He squeezed harder. Stars flared in her eyes. But Luke would come. He had to. Unless…someone got to him first.

"You should have listened to me. Left things alone. It's your fault that I have to kill you."

Her head spun. The world blurred. His words muffled in her ears and now he was dragging her, dragging her. Where was he taking her? Balboa flashed in her peripheral vision. The gun. She'd hidden the gun behind a barrel two feet away. But she couldn't move and light and dark strobed before her eyes. Just as blackness overtook her, the grip loosened.

He thought she was unconscious. Or maybe that he'd strangled her. Somewhere in the foggy recesses of her brain, she knew not to move. He let her fall to the floor, thudding like a sack of flour. Hay matted against her face. The scent cleared her brain. She saw a glint of metal. The gun. If he thought she was passed out or dead she might have a chance. Somehow she had to alert Luke. If she didn't, he could get away and kill again. She wouldn't let that happen, even if it cost her her life.

Mustering her strength, she readied her legs and then giving it her all, she leaped forward like a frog, grabbed the cold handle of the .38, rolled over and pointed it in the face of the man hovering over her.

For one fraction of a second she saw fear in his hard eyes. "Move and you're dead," she growled, no question in her mind that she meant it. It was only when he grabbed for the gun that she recognized him.

"LUKE!" Abe shouted into his wire. "Julianna isn't answering."

"Did you see anyone?"

"No."

"I've got all the cameras working. Everything seems okay. She said she's coming out."

"That was sixty seconds ago. Where is she?"

"I heard her say something to Balboa. She's calming him down." Then Luke saw movement near the side of the barn. A horse rounded the corner. Stella Hancock.

"What the hell—" Abe spat out.

A gunshot rang out. Then another.

Luke saw Stella slide off her mount and run into the barn. He bolted out the door, gun in hand. "Cover me, Pops."

"Stella's inside," Abe hollered. "Don't let anything happen to her, Luke."

Luke reached the half-open door and froze. A man's voice.

"You can't shoot me, old woman. If you do, your friend here is dead."

His heart in his throat, Luke crept around the corner to the window and eased himself up. Jules was sprawled on the floor, a man standing over her with a gun, while Stella Hancock pointed her weapon at him. Jules wasn't dead or the man wouldn't be dealing with Stella. But she looked badly hurt.

Anger gnawed at Luke's insides. If anything happened to Jules… It was his fault. He never should've allowed her to do this…

It took everything in his power not to rush inside. If he did, the guy might panic and shoot. His hands shook as he readied his gun. He had to stay calm. Think. Dammit. He wasn't in any position to get off a shot, not without endangering Jules and Stella. But it was the only way.

He aimed dead on and pulled the trigger.

Almost simultaneously another shot rang out. The man crumpled. Luke raced for the door. He had to make sure the guy was down for good—and that Jules was okay.

As he tore inside, he saw Abe at the back of the barn, rifle in hand.

CHAPTER SIXTEEN

JULIANNA AWAKENED to bright lights and the dry scent of alcohol. The first thing she saw was a big vase of roses next to the bed…and then Luke's face came into focus.

"Hi," he said.

She smiled. "I'm alive? Or is this a dream?"

"You're alive."

"My head hurts."

"The doc says you'll have a sore leg and a headache for a little while."

She glanced down at her leg but the covers blocked her view. She reached for her head and felt bandages.

"It was a clean wound on the leg, the doc said. The head wound is minor, a graze. A week or two and you should be as good as new."

Luke smiled, but his eyes looked sad.

"Did we get the bad guy?"

Luke nodded. "He's behind bars as we speak. My dad had called the sheriff immediately after we heard the shots, and Yuma was there before the ambulance."

Julianna pushed up on her elbows and Luke came closer to help her, puffing up the pillow behind her head. "I got the gun," Julianna said. "But he overpowered me. I think it went off and hit my leg. I don't remember exactly."

"You're alive, that's all that counts."

She smiled. "A lot of good that gun training did, huh?" Her leg throbbed and her head hurt, but it didn't matter. The sicko was in jail.

Luke gently sat on the edge of the bed. "You had a narrow escape."

"What happened after Stella came in? It's all a blur in my head."

"We're still not clear on it either. But what we do know is that he was taking aim when Stella made an appearance. She surprised him enough so when he shot you, the bullet only grazed your head. I heard the first shot, but when I got there, I saw Stella had her gun on him. Just as I was taking aim, our bad guy went down."

"Who—?"

"Abe." Luke smiled proudly. "The old guy is still a crack shot. He'd come in from the back."

"Where is he now?"

"Out in the hall with Stella. You up for seeing them?"

"Absolutely."

"I'll send them in."

He stood, started to go, but she caught his sleeve. "The man. He was the one who came for the interview. I recognized him. He was right there in the house." The horror of it hit her.

"We're still getting the facts together, but we're pretty sure we have—" Luke's voice cracked "—the person who took Michael from us."

Seeing the pain in Luke's eyes was almost her undoing. But hearing that they might finally have justice for Michael was simply too much for her brain to process. She pressed her face into her hands, tears suddenly streaming. Luke put his arms around her, holding her tight, and then she felt his body shake.

They shared the bittersweet tears, their sadness mingling with the knowledge that finally there was closure for Michael. Their son was at peace with the angels and now, God willing, maybe they could find peace themselves.

After what seemed like an eon, Luke pulled

himself together, rubbed his eyes with his shirt-sleeve and brushed the tears from her cheeks with his fingertips. He stood, ready to leave.

"There's someone else here, too. Your friend Mark. He was instrumental in identi-fying the guy."

"Mark?"

"He said you asked him about a professor at the university. He got the name and when he couldn't get hold of you on the phone, he e-mailed it to you. Rico picked up on it and with some other e-mail data he'd received, they got a search warrant for the professor's house. While the psycho was at the ranch, they were collecting evidence from his place."

Choking on his words, Luke shoved a hand through his hair. She'd never seen him like this before. Not even when Michael had dis-appeared. He'd always kept his emotions buried.

"They found a knife with animal blood on it and figured it's probably the calf." He took a big breath and then went on. "So far they've collected enough evidence to put the guy on death row. His name is Anton Orion. Hence the star clue. Weird, I know."

She put a hand up to stop him saying more. She was familiar with all the cases from her research. She didn't want any more details, she didn't even want to know if they'd found anything that belonged to Michael. It was enough that their beautiful son would finally rest in peace.

She wasn't sure Luke could handle telling her either, and her heart ached at seeing him in so much pain. Between that and the wrenching emotion of knowing they'd finally found justice for their son, words simply wouldn't come.

Their eyes met in a mix of emotions. And then Luke turned and walked out the door.

THREE DAYS LATER, Luke paced across the patio as he waited for Julianna to arrive and get her things. She'd told him her friend Mark would give her a ride from the hospital because they had a lot to talk about.

Just as well. He'd had time to do some thinking. And had managed to find someone to stay with his father. Someone Stella knew, and Abe seemed okay with that.

"Pacing won't solve any problems, son."

Luke turned and saw Abe settling himself on a chair. "It's cold out here, Pops. Might not be a good idea for you since you've—"

"Maybe for you it's cold, but it isn't to me.

I've lived here all my life and I can handle a little chill."

Luke raised his hands. "Okay. Okay."

After a moment of silence Abe said, "Waiting for Julianna?"

"Yes. She's going back to San Francisco."

"You sure she wants to do that?"

He looked at his father. "That's what she said. Why wouldn't I be sure."

"Because people don't always say what they mean, that's why."

Yeah, Abe had told him that before. Was there something he knew that Luke didn't? "She's with her…friend from San Francisco."

"So?"

"So, that's what she wants."

"Is it what you want?"

Luke felt angry and mad and hopeless and torn between what he should want and what he really wanted. His emotions felt as if they'd been pulled inside out like an old shirt and tossed in the trash. Still pacing, he raked a hand through his hair. "Hell no. But what I want for me doesn't matter. I want her to be happy, even if that means she's with someone else."

"Well, that sounds noble as all get-out."

This was ridiculous. How could his father,

a man who never went anywhere, had hardly had a decent conversation with anyone in twenty years have any clue what he felt? "It's not noble. It's reality."

"So you're saying that you love Julianna, but instead of telling her, you'd rather see her with someone else?"

Talking to his dad was pointless. "That's not what I'm saying and you know it."

"Then maybe you should forget your high-falutin' pride and tell her."

"Pride?" Luke scoffed. "That's ridiculous. It's not about that."

"Okay. Whatever you say. My theory is that if we want something bad enough, we just have to bite the bullet and ask for it, even if the result might hurt like hell."

"And you live by those words?"

Abe's expression turned thoughtful. "No. I haven't for years. But I plan to. The other night made me realize I've wasted a lot of time. But I'm not going to squander what little I have left. Not if there's one iota of a chance I can do something about it."

Luke heard gravel crunch in the drive, saw a truck pull up. It was Stella's truck. He watched as the woman got out and then came around to the passenger side. She opened the door and his jaw dropped. Jules, holding a cane in one hand, turned to get out. Stella reached to help her.

Luke practically sprinted through the patio gate to the truck. "What's going on? Where's Mark?"

"If you let me come inside, I'll tell you."

Luke blanched. "Sorry. Here, let me help you."

Stella moved out of the way and just as Luke took Julianna's arm to help her out, Abe sidled up.

"Hello, Abraham," Stella said.

Once Jules was on her feet, Luke scooped her into his arms and carried her toward the house. He didn't want to hear what his father had to say to Stella. How could he feel good about a relationship between his father and the woman he'd had an affair with while Luke's mother was dying?

But as he thought it, the bitter emotion he'd carried for so long just wasn't there. It seemed unimportant now. He'd almost lost Jules, and the significance of that made everything else pale in comparison.

Was it wrong for his father to want to share the time he had left with someone he'd once loved? Still loved apparently. No, Luke realized. There was nothing wrong with that at all. And he'd give anything to do the same with Jules.

As they went inside, Julianna's cheek brushed against Luke's. He inhaled, breathing in—for possibly the last time—the scent he remembered so well. Remembered even in his sleep.

What he wouldn't give to erase all the heartache between them. He heard Stella and his father laughing in the background and, in that single moment, he realized he had to let go of the past. There was no going back. There was only the future.

Inside, he put Jules on her feet and before she had a chance to speak, he said, "Wouldn't it be better to stay a few more days to recoup?"

"Maybe."

"Abe would like it."

"And you?"

"What do you mean?"

She shrugged. "Nothing. Nothing at all." She looked down, then started for her room. "I think I'd like to rest right now, if you don't mind."

"Sure."

Watching her hobble down the hall and

close her door, Luke banged his palm on the table. Dammit. Why did everything have to be so hard? Why did loving someone have to hurt so much?

He went to the cabinets and searching for a glass, he found a bottle of Jack Daniels. His adrenaline surged. He picked it up, stared at the label. He felt a sudden urgent need. One drink. It wouldn't hurt. Everything else in his life was so screwed up, it would feel good to find oblivion for a little while.

He needed a drink. Badly. He could almost feel the smooth, yet biting liquid sliding down his throat. One drink. He gripped the bottle tighter and tighter until his hand started to shake. A vision of Julianna and Michael flashed through his head. A powerful vision that was all he needed to place the bottle back on the shelf.

Pride, his father said. Was that what was keeping him from telling Jules how he felt? He didn't think so.

But how would he know unless he told her?

SHE MUST'VE DRIFTED OFF, Julianna realized when she awoke two hours later. She'd been dreaming, not the anxious, fearful dreams she'd been having for the last month, but dreams of angels and exotic places. Of Michael and Luke and of playing on the beach together. For five years whenever she'd dreamed of them, she woke up in a sweat, anxious and tearful.

But this dream was soothing and wonderful. They'd been a family, the kind of family she'd always longed for.

If only it could be that way.

But it couldn't. Luke's job was still his main focus, and as much as she wanted things to be different, they never would. She knew it. Luke knew it. The only person who didn't know it was Abe.

Still, as she stretched out her arms and legs, she felt a sense of calm she hadn't experienced in a long time. It had been so long since she'd awakened smiling. Even before the threats, she'd been an anxious person. Or maybe driven was a more apt description.

She'd been relentless in her research, gathering information from families and other sources, writing article after article on the missing children, so relentless she didn't even have a life outside her stories. Luke was right, she was obsessed.

She could've died because of it. With the realization came the thought that she didn't want to live like that anymore. She'd been existing. Not living. But there was another reason. While keeping the stories in the public eye was important, she didn't feel the compelling need to write them that she had before. When Mark told her he wanted the series to end, that he wanted her to focus on something else for a while, other stories that were equally important, she'd felt a sense of relief.

But that feeling brought questions. Had she only been doing it for Michael? Had she convinced herself she had all these altruistic motives, when her goal had really been selfish? Had she been living a lie?

By the time she left the hospital, the thought that she was a fake began to eat at her. And if Mark didn't want her to write about missing children, what was she going to write about?

The ringing of her cell phone on the nightstand startled her. Then she remembered the man who'd been threatening her was in jail. She pushed to a sitting position. "Hello."

"Julianna Chevalair? This is Tom Black from NBC News."

Hearing a knock at the door, she said into the phone, "Excuse me," then, "Come in."

She'd had police at the hospital to intercept the media and hadn't anticipated them calling here. But of course they'd want all the information they could get.

As Luke entered the room, she handed him the phone. "It's NBC News. I have no idea how they got this number."

"This is Detective Luke Coltrane, LAPD. Can I help you?"

Julianna listened as Luke told the reporter that the police didn't want to compromise the case and they'd release more information when they could.

"Thanks," she said after Luke hung up. "I never know what to say in situations like that."

He came over to the bed. "No comment usually works."

She smiled then pointed to the bottom of the bed. "Sit down."

Instead, Luke pulled up a chair. "Don't want to bump your leg."

He looked serious, as if he had something disturbing to say. "The doc said it's fine."

A hollow silence filled the air.

"How's Abe?" Julianna finally said. "I heard him talking to Stella."

"They've gone riding. I think Abe has something important to say to her."

"She loves him, you know."

"I'm getting the drift."

"I know you don't like her, but it would be good for him to have someone. I mean someone he cares about—not a hired hand."

A petal from one of the roses in the vase fell off onto the bed. Luke picked it up, and holding it between two fingers, he studied the petal. "Nice flowers," he said.

"They are. Mark is a sweetheart. A little intense sometimes, but his heart is in the right place."

He pulled closer. "And where is that?"

She frowned. "Where is what?"

"His heart. Your heart. Are you in love with him?"

She stifled an incredulous croak. "With Mark? Whatever gave you that idea?"

When he didn't say anything and she saw the look in his eyes, she felt her throat close. She said softly, "Would it matter if I was?"

Luke stared into her eyes. "Yes. It matters because I can't imagine you with anyone but me." Still looking at her, he stood, shoved his hands in his front pockets. "It matters because I'm still in love with you, Jules."

Her heart raced. Words stuck on the back

of her tongue. She wanted to say she was still in love with him, too, but— *But what?*

"I never stopped loving you, and if there's any chance for us, I'd do just about anything to make it happen."

But—what would happen if every time she looked at Luke she thought of Michael and what they'd lost? It had been like that at the end. She couldn't deal with the guilt and the shame. What would happen when he was away every night and she was alone in that house?

When she didn't answer right away, he said, "I don't have any big epiphanies about what happened between us except that I let you down. When I couldn't find Michael, even using all my expertise, I felt so inadequate. I couldn't live with that and that's when the drinking got out of hand. I—I failed you. I failed Michael and our marriage."

She placed a hand over his lips. Tears welled in her eyes. Oh, God. Her heart ached for Luke. She'd been so caught up in her own pain she hadn't recognized the extent of his. He was the stoic cop. Always in control. How could she have not seen how much he hurt? No wonder they couldn't help each other. How could they when they couldn't help themselves?

She took his hand in hers and quelled the flood of tears about to burst.

"Then we both felt inadequate, Luke. You told me before that I wasn't to blame, you told me many times. But *I* knew I was and I couldn't live with that. Every time I looked at you I was reminded of it. Reminded of Michael. That's why I left."

His eyes searched hers. He steepled his fingers at his chin. She could almost see his mind clicking.

Finally he said, "Remember that night on the beach when you said you felt Michael in the wind, that it felt like his arms wrapping around you?"

She nodded.

"That's what I feel whenever I think about him now. I didn't at first. Like you, I railed at the injustice, I felt the sorrow so deep within me I thought I'd die from it. I wanted to forget and I found an easy way to do it. But one night when I reached for another drink, I saw Michael's face as clearly as if he were there, and something inside me came to life. I didn't take that drink and for a few days I kept remembering more and more. His smile, his laughter. And it felt good. I felt happy to have had him in my life, if even for a short time.

"I finally realized that I didn't need to forget. What I needed to do was remember Michael and to celebrate the time we had together."

Tears filled her eyes.

"Remembering our son and the love he brought to us is important. I never want to forget that, and I don't want to forget what we had either. We loved each other and just thinking about that is a lot better than having nothing. Yes, we had problems. And sometimes they seemed insurmountable. But that didn't make me love you any less. I cherish the love we had, Julianna. I always will."

Julianna reached for him. He'd revealed more in the past thirty seconds than he had in the whole time they'd been married. If she'd ever doubted his love for her, she couldn't now. Her heart broke for him and for her and all they once had. He was right. They'd had love. They'd had love and hope and a future and she'd thrown it away.

Like a bright sunrise lighting up her mind, she realized Luke was right. She didn't need to forget, she needed to remember. She needed to remember all that was wonderful between them. Including Michael. Everything else was an excuse. An excuse to run away just as she'd done when she'd left home to marry him.

God, it was all so clear now. Though she'd loved Luke with all her heart, she was the one who'd married for the wrong reasons. Not him.

Dangling her feet over the edge of the bed, she tried to stand, wobbling as she did. Luke caught her and they both landed in the chair, her on his lap.

He held her tight in his embrace, as if he might lose her again if he let go, and then he rested his forehead against her shoulder.

She pressed her lips against his head in a gentle kiss, and in doing so, she released a frail hope…

Drawing back to look at him she said, "Luke, when I left, it wasn't because of you or your drinking or anything else you did," she said, her voice hoarse with tears. "It had nothing to do with my feelings for you. I loved you then and I still do," she whispered. "With all my heart."

He pulled back. "And I you. I never stopped." His lips met hers. Softly, sweetly, lovingly, and in that moment, all the longing and the passions, all the emotions she'd denied herself for so long welled up inside. The pain and sorrow of the past faded in the wake of hope.

It had been so long since she'd felt hopeful.
So long since she'd even thought about more
than one day at a time.

Her future was with Luke. Their future was
together. It had always been. No, they
wouldn't ever get over the loss of their son.
But Michael had been the culmination of their
love, and he deserved that love to continue.

And when Luke kissed her again, her
heart swelled with love—and the promise
of tomorrow.

EPILOGUE

One year later

"VERY FEW LIVES are what we expect them to be," Abraham said to his daughter-in-law sitting beside him with her notebook and a tape recorder. "And I'm no orator. I doubt what I have to say will be of interest to anyone."

Julianna, pregnant with his son's child—his grandchild—looked radiant, just as his wife Lizzie had looked when she was carrying Luke. Abe had doubted he'd ever have another grandchild after Luke and Julianna lost Michael.

But now that a new life was growing, a life that was part of him as well, he didn't think about his own mortality as much. He supposed he should be at seventy-one, but knowing a part of him would continue on in this world made it easier to face that he wouldn't be around forever.

Not that he planned on going anywhere soon. Shoot, he'd just gotten married and had a whole second life to live with the woman he'd been in love with for more than sixty years. He'd been a fool to waste so much time. When Stella broke off with him, his damned pride wouldn't let him forgive her. Then Lizzie died and he'd been overcome with guilt and retreated into himself. Well, he'd lived with false pride and guilt long enough. He was still alive and he planned to enjoy every second he had left.

"Okay, Abe, before I start the recorder, I hope you don't leave anything out just because I'm your daughter-in-law or because you're afraid I'll be judgmental. I'm a journalist and we're not allowed to judge people. But if you don't want me to know something, I'm okay with that, too."

Abe pulled himself up in his favorite chair, the worn leather lounger now shaped to his body after so many years, the chair Lizzie had always threatened to burn years ago. "So, what's the point of keeping secrets? It wouldn't be my life."

She smiled. "I like that philosophy."

"Why are we doing this again?"

"For our family history. So your grand-daughter will know her heritage."

"It used to be people didn't know what the baby was going to be until they had it. I'm not sure it's a good thing to find out all these things before they happen."

"It was necessary because of my age, Pops. The tests show if there's anything wrong and can also tell if it's a boy or a girl. Modern medicine has come a long way."

He didn't like it. He didn't like a lot of things happening in this so-called modern world. But he had to live with it. He'd buried himself on the ranch for too long. Now he and Stella were going on a honeymoon to Hawaii. He'd never in a million years thought he'd see Hawaii again. But then he'd also thought he'd die in a Vietnam prison camp.

"So, are you going to write a story about me, or what?"

"Gee, I hadn't thought about what I'd do with it, Pops. I just wanted to record the in-formation befo—" She frowned. "Before I have the baby and I get too busy."

He placed a hand over hers. "You want the information before I kick the bucket. That's okay. It's good. But I'm not going to do that for a while, so we do have time."

"Okay. But I'm here now. And we probably won't be back until after the baby's born."

"Fine with me, but remember we're coming to Los Angeles when the child gets here. Stella wouldn't have it any other way."

"Me neither, Pops." She smiled sweetly. "So, where do you want to start?" Julianna asked. "Can you tell me about your childhood, your parents?"

"You want me to tell you everything?"

She smiled. "Yes, I do."

He shifted in the chair. He hadn't thought about his parents in a very long time. Not since he'd left home at sixteen. He'd put them out of his mind like he did most hurtful things, things he couldn't do anything about.

No point in thinking about all the nights he'd shivered with fear in the corner. Mostly he remembered that he'd just wanted it to be over, one way or another.

"It wasn't a noteworthy childhood, just a kid growing up on a poor ranch. A mother and father who didn't have much and who died too young." His father hadn't died soon enough for him. "I left home at sixteen."

"What about school?"

School. The thought conjured the singular

most important day in his life. The day he'd met Stella Nez. He was ten and it was her first day at the tiny two-room school. One room each for two grades. She was in the lower grade, and she'd just come from the reservation.

He'd thought her the most beautiful girl he'd ever seen. Her straight, shiny dark hair went all the way down her back, and her eyes weren't dark brown like most of the Navajo kids, they were a lighter color, like his pinto, Chakura, that his dad had won from some drunk during a card game.

He'd seen her standing alone on the edge of the playground when a couple of the bigger kids went over and started shoving her, calling her names like half-breed, saying she should go back to the reservation.

He'd gotten mad. He didn't like bullies, people who picked on others for no reason at all. People like his father.

That's when he strode over. He didn't say anything, but planted his feet apart and stood in front of her with his arms crossed. One of the boys spit on him, called him "Injun lover," as if that was the meanest thing they could say.

Hell, he'd heard a lot worse. The girls called him names, too, and one threw a rock as she was leaving, hitting him in the forehead. But he stood there.

He didn't know what to do or say then, so he sat on the grass and after a minute, she sat next to him but not too close. The sun was burning hot overhead and he started sweating. He remembered that because he didn't want her to see him sweat. Or smell him either.

They didn't say anything for the longest time and then finally she asked, "How'd you get that black eye?"

He shrugged. "Bumped into a door at night." He pulled his shirt tight at the neck and tugged his sleeves down to hide his other bruises. But he knew she'd seen them.

"Want an apple?" she said, reaching into her pocket, then held one out to him.

Her voice was soft and she had an accent, the kind the kids had who came from the reservation. Like she'd just learned English or something. He rubbed the apple on his sleeve and took a bite. It was the best apple he'd ever tasted.

"IT'S OKAY, Abe. We can do more later," Julianna said then shut off the recorder. Abe had told her about the two-room school, and meeting Stella for the first time, and then his mind seemed to go somewhere far away. She figured they'd done enough for the day.

"I'll be outside," he said, getting up to leave. "Stella will be back soon and we're going shopping for luggage and all that, then we have to look at plans for the new house."

Julianna smiled. "That will be fun." Abe and Stella had decided to build a new house on the property between their two places. It would be a place of their own, not one that he'd shared with Elizabeth or she'd shared with her husband. Abe wanted Luke to take over the ranch, but Luke was still undecided. He loved his job. She knew that. They had both made some concessions when they got married again, Luke in not working so many hours and she embracing the time they shared even if it was less than she wanted.

Still, she couldn't think of a better place to raise a child than here on the ranch. She felt a need to get away from the city altogether. A new beginning. She could do her job from almost anywhere, but she knew Luke would never leave the LAPD. So, they'd made another compromise. They'd keep the house in Venice and the ranch. How they'd divide up their time was the question.

Luke came inside. "Look what I found in the storeroom." He held up a baby rocker. "It was mine when I was a kid."

"It's adorable."

"There's more. A crib and an old high chair."

"Are they useable?"

"I don't see why not."

"I can't believe your father saved all that stuff."

Luke's eyes softened. "I can't either. I guess no matter how much we think we know about a person, we can never know it all."

She smiled wide. "Like you saying your dad fired the shot that saved me. I heard that's not the case."

He grinned. "But he doesn't know that. As far as I'm concerned, he saved us both."

She reached up to kiss him.

"So what do you think about the baby furniture?"

"I think it's a sign."

He gave a skeptical glance. "Now you're sounding like your mother again. A sign of what."

"That this should be our home."

Luke put the chair down. The doorbell rang. "That's the sheriff."

"Sheriff Yuma? What's he coming here for?"

She saw a glint in Luke's eyes. "He's got a job for me." He eyed her narrowly. "If I want it."

"Oh, my." She couldn't think of anything else to say. She wanted this to be their home so much, but only if Luke did, too.

The doorbell rang again. Luke started toward the door, but then he stopped and took an envelope from his pocket. "Here, hold this for me."

"What is it?"

"A letter from my mother. We'll read it together."

MILLS & BOON
Super ROMANCE

On sale 17th August 2007

A CHILD'S WISH
by Tara Taylor Quinn

Meredith Forster is sure her pupil, Kelsey, is hiding something. But Kelsey's father, Mark Shepherd, wants to dismiss her hunches – and the attraction he feels for Meredith…

A MAN OF DUTY
by Linda Warren

Texas Ranger Caleb McCain will do anything to help Josie Beckett regain her memory. But will he be able to let her go when she returns to her previous life?

MAN WITH A PAST
by Kay Stockham

After ten years in prison, Joe isn't welcome back in town – but newcomer Ashley Cade sees beyond his reputation. Could they have a second chance at happiness together?

LONE STAR DIARY
by Darlene Graham

A night of passion with Luke Driscoll has left Frankie McBride unexpectedly pregnant. After years of heartbreak, she can hardly believe she's having a baby, but as Frankie faces reality she must also face Luke…

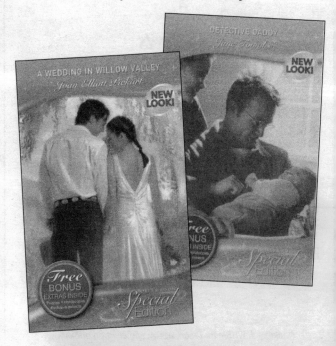

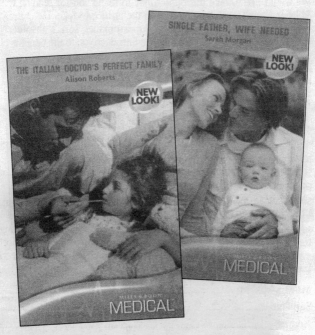

FREE

2 BOOKS AND A SURPRISE GIFT!

We would like to take this opportunity to thank you for reading this Mills & Boon® book by offering you the chance to take TWO more specially selected titles from the Superromance series absolutely FREE! We're also making this offer to introduce you to the benefits of the Mills & Boon® Reader Service™—

- ★ **FREE home delivery**
- ★ **FREE gifts and competitions**
- ★ **FREE monthly Newsletter**
- ★ **Books available before they're in the shops**
- ★ **Exclusive Reader Service offers**

Accepting these FREE books and gift places you under no obligation to buy; you may cancel at any time, even after receiving your free shipment. Simply complete your details below and return the entire page to the address below. You don't even need a stamp!

YES! Please send me 2 free Superromance books and a surprise gift. I understand that unless you hear from me, I will receive 4 superb new titles every month for just £3.69 each, postage and packing free. I am under no obligation to purchase any books and may cancel my subscription at any time. The free books and gift will be mine to keep in any case.

U7ZEE

Ms/Mrs/Miss/Mr...Initials ....

BLOCK CAPITALS PLEASE

Surname ....

Address ....

....

....Postcode ....

Send this whole page to:
The Reader Service, FREEPOST CN81, Croydon, CR9 3WZ